# DEATH
## ON THE
### SCOTLAND EXPRESS

# BOOKS BY FLISS CHESTER

# DEATH
## ON THE
## SCOTLAND EXPRESS

FLISS CHESTER

*bookouture*

Published by Bookouture in 2023

An imprint of Storyfire Ltd.
Carmelite House
50 Victoria Embankment
London EC4Y 0DZ

www.bookouture.com

ISBN: 978-1-83790-913-1
eBook ISBN: 978-1-83790-912-4

This book is a work of fiction. Whilst some characters and circumstances
portrayed by the author are based on real people and historical fact, references
to real people, events, establishments, organizations or locales are intended
only to provide a sense of authenticity and are used fictitiously. All other
characters and all incidents and dialogue are drawn from the author's
imagination and are not to be construed as real.

*For my brothers and sisters*

# PROLOGUE

Great veils of steam billowed past the window of the compartment in which the expensively dressed man stood. Beyond the white vapour lay the Highlands of Scotland, breathtakingly majestic, but he had no time to contemplate them, not when he could only think about *her*.

'Why is she here, dammit?' he muttered as he gripped the edge of the mahogany-veneered vanity unit, its width the only space he had alongside the bed, despite booking the biggest and best compartment on the sleeper train.

The steam cleared. Scotland, all green hills and densely wooded forests, continued to hurtle past. He noticed his reflection in the window, his new suit, his smart tiepin. The large gold signet ring on his little finger caught the light and he flexed the muscles in his hand, making it glint and reflect against the glass. He didn't wear a wedding ring.

*Why is she here?* The thought crowded his mind.

The carriages of the Scotland Express rattled on, and steam from the great locomotive once again obscured his view from the window. He didn't mind. It helped him find his own reflection again and he admired his fine moustache. Everything would be all right, he reassured himself. Everything was under control.

He looked down at his hands again and allowed his fingers to unclench. She would have to accept the fact their marriage was over. He looked back up. His own piercing blue eyes stared back at him.

As did those of another figure, who he saw in the window's reflection; a silhouette standing behind him, framed in the compartment's narrow door frame. Surprised, he turned around to face the intruder.

'What do you—' he started, but the blood ran cold in his veins and he watched in terror as the gun was levelled at his chest. Fear – not an emotion he was used to – pinned him to the spot. He opened his mouth but couldn't speak; the words clawed at his throat, desperate to get out, but they were as stuck in there as he was in this compartment.

The glossily veneered walls seemed to close in tighter, narrower, and he felt himself stumble as the train bounced over another set of points. The clatter of the giant steel wheels over the tracks masked the sound of the gun cocking.

He looked at his assailant. 'You...' The word formed on his lips, but still no sound came.

The train's whistle pierced the air, then, a heartbeat later, the deadly shot rang out.

Steam and smoke filled the air of Inverness station. The powerful locomotive of the Scotland Express gleamed in the sunlight that flooded through the iron-framed glass of the station's roof. Its sleek blackness and silver trim gave it the look of a black stallion in polished harnesses. Even the steam that blew off and then bowled around the great locomotive was like the breath of a war horse on a cold morning as it stamped its hooves, impatient for the off.

'Dotty, do hurry!' the Honourable Cressida Fawcett called to her friend, Lady Dorothy Chatterton, who was counting her pieces of luggage, as Dotty's brother, Alfred, beckoned another porter over to the pile of suitcases.

Cressida, who had already boarded, leaned out of the window of her sleeper compartment and allowed Ruby, her pug, to rest her paws on the lowered pane.

'Oh dear,' Cressida said to herself, as the porter did valiant battle with Dotty's cases, heaving each one onto the trolley.

Cressida let out a sigh, then cast her eyes along the platform. Inverness station was a grand Victorian construction made mostly of local stone with cast-iron struts that laced the glass ceiling. She took in the arches that lined the platform, the well-kept newspaper kiosks with their inhabitants shouting 'Press! Press!' and the great wide platforms edged by ornate ironwork columns. As much as the architecture interested her, what with her love for interior design and decoration, it was the people on the platform who really caught Cressida's attention.

'Look, Ruby, isn't that woman glamorous?' She pointed Ruby's snub nose in the direction of a lady who looked to be in her early twenties, and who was sashaying along the platform. Her red suede high-heeled shoes matched her handbag, while her shoulders were draped in a fox fur that elegantly hung down her back. Her black felt hat was placed at a jaunty angle, revealing bleached blonde waves on the other side of her head. She was doing an excellent job of navigating the platform as her black pencil skirt seriously limited her length of stride. As Ruby's excited snuffling was testament to, she had on the end of a lead a small, fluffy and perfectly white Pomeranian.

The elegant young woman was followed by a man in a pinstripe suit, a white fedora on his head and his overcoat placed loosely over his shoulders. He looked for all the world like one of those American mobsters that Cressida had seen in films, but older, and considerably more stocky and cantankerous. Several paces behind him was a tall and beak-nosed man in a brown tweed jacket, slacks, a checked shirt and a sensible V-neck jumper and tie. Despite the glamour of his companions, he was most certainly *not* dressed in the style of those American gangsters.

Cressida watched as the three of them consulted the porter, who had been following behind them and now pointed to the door of the carriage next to hers. With a crisp note of a very generous denomination slipped to the porter, who tipped his cap in thanks, the trio boarded the train.

She looked back at Dotty, who was now trying to hold as many books and magazines as she possibly could, without troubling the porter or her brother. Frustratingly for Dotty, the glossy fronts of *The Bystander* and *The Tatler* were causing her pile of novels to slip, not to mention the thumping great big *Bradshaw's Railway Guide* she'd insisted on buying.

'I should go and help, I suppose, Ruby,' Cressida said, and was about to move away from the window when another couple of passengers caught her eye. There was something familiar about these two, bickering as they were, staring at their tickets and checking the number of the locomotive against them. Cressida smiled to herself. Two such similar people, he a bit taller, she a bit softer around the edges, hair identical in colour – his was fashionably slicked to a quiff, while hers was cut in a neat bob. Both in sensible woollen suits and smart hats.

Cressida looked over to Dotty and Alfred, a devoted brother and sister who could also match that description. Though Dotty and Alfred shared the most beautiful conker-brown hair and eyes, while these newcomers were blonde and fair. She watched as the unfamiliar pair consulted their tickets one last time, decided they were in the right place and climbed aboard the train.

Turning from the window and making sure Ruby was comfortable on the neatly made-up bed in her compartment, Cressida left her snorting away happily in order to help Dotty out of her fix.

'But the *Bradshaw's* shouldn't go in a bag, Alf,' Dotty was protesting as Cressida approached.

'But you won't need it now, Dot.' Alfred shrugged. 'Here's the train, we know we're on the right platform, we don't need to change trains and the whistle is blowing again. Why do you need your timetable?'

'I like to look and see who we're passing in the night, Alf. And which train it might be. The ten-oh-five to Crewe perhaps or the five-fifty-three to Peterborough.'

Alfred blew an exasperated breath out through pursed lips.

'Fine. But let's let this fellow get most of your cases on board, can we? What did you buy in Inverness? Chunks of granite? I'm sure you only had one valise when we arrived!'

Dotty glowered at her brother and then said something about bulk discounts and how he wouldn't understand decent millinery if it, quite literally, hit him over the head.

'What ho, chaps!' Cressida interrupted their bickering. 'What's the hold-up?'

Alfred smiled at her. To most people, he was Lord Delafield, confusingly not Lord Chatterton – that was his father, the earl. Alfred was a viscount and the Delafield title was a secondary one to the Chatterton name, so he held it while his father was still alive. To Cressida, though, he was just Alfred. She looked at him as he stood there, baffled by his sister's luggage, and smiled at her handsome friend. She was well known among her chums, and their chums, and most importantly, her mother's chums, for having no truck with the idea of marriage. She valued her independence above all things and loved nothing more than her snazzy Bugatti sports car, her delightful pug and the freedom her generous allowance gave her to have as much fun as possible. Swoon, she did not, at the thought of marrying well. She had, on several occasions already, swerved out of the way at the vital moment when a bride's bouquet sailed past her head; yet recently she had been experiencing some hitherto unfelt feelings when it came to Alfred, Lord Delafield.

'Talk some sense into her, Cress, won't you?' Alfred pleaded, his eyebrows raised.

Cressida smiled at him. *Those eyes...* She shook herself out of her brief reverie and looked instead to his sister, her dear friend.

'Come on, Dot. Hand me the magazines... that's the ticket... No, actually, *that's* your ticket. Here we go...'

'Thank you, Cressy,' Dotty said, relief on her face as she

was left merely holding her books, her railway guide and her handbag.

'You're hot to trot, chum. And I've found your sleeping compartment, you're next door but one from me. And Alfred's on your other side. A Dotty sandwich, if you will.'

'Ooh sandwiches.' Dotty looked up at the large clock that hung suspended over the platform. 'It's almost half past four. Do you think we'll get tea?' Dotty asked, following Cressida across the platform to the shining, glossed door of the *wagon-lit* they were ticketed for.

'Tea? Now that's a thought. But we'll get nothing if we don't get on board. Come on, you.'


Once they were all aboard the Scotland Express, ready to head back to London, Cressida leaned out of her compartment's window for a final look at the impressive station. One of the porters on the platform edge secured the door and waved a flag to a colleague down the line, steam enveloping him like an eiderdown.

To her surprise, there was one last passenger still boarding, the exasperated porter now helping her up as she struggled with the step. The black netting veil that fell over this woman's face, widow-like, probably wasn't helping. Neither perhaps was her large dark coat, far too heavy and thick for the summer weather. Cressida could make out nothing of her features, yet watched as she furtively looked about her before disappearing into the carriage, allowing the porter to slam shut the door of the train behind her.

Another shrill whistle filled the air, and with a heave and a shudder, the great locomotive pulled out of Inverness station, the first few inches covered of their 570-mile journey south to London Euston.

Cressida closed the window, coughing as the smoke of the

engine curled across the platform. As she sat down on her neat, white bed sheets and absent-mindedly stroked the velvet-like fur between Ruby's ears, she took a moment to take in her surroundings. Rich, glossy veneered wood lined the walls and the back of the door. A simple yet stylish stainless-steel basin on an equally veneered vanity unit was positioned next to her bed, which doubled as somewhere for her to sit. She'd placed her valise on the floor, but noticed convenient netted racks above the bed for storing suitcases and hatboxes and suchlike. A mirrored cupboard for her toiletries was set into the wall close by the basin, but the dominating feature of the compartment was the large window, framed with red velvet curtains, that would give her the most wonderful view of the beautiful Highlands of Scotland as the train powered its way south. This, and the communal carriages of the Scotland Express, would be her home for the next fifteen hours.

She sighed. After what she'd been through recently, she hoped they'd be blissfully uneventful hours, too.

## 2

'Well, this is jolly, isn't it?' Dotty said as they finished their tea.

The three of them had found themselves a table together in the dining car and had tucked into some delicious finger sandwiches and a fine Madeira cake, all washed down with gallons of good strong tea. Dotty had lugged her *Bradshaw's Guide* with her to the table and had placed it on the seat next to her, ignoring the eye-roll from her brother. However, she was unable to consult it due to the fact that Ruby, suffering as she did from ridiculously short legs, had decided it made a rather useful booster seat.

They'd been trundling along through the rolling hills, and thickets dense with pine trees and silver birch, for about an hour. The train had just made its first stop at Aviemore, waiting a few minutes at the rural station. An elderly, well-to-do couple had boarded, but, otherwise, not much of any note had happened.

Cressida took in her surroundings. The dining carriage on the Scotland Express was very smart indeed, decorated as it was with more of the same glossy wood veneer as the sleeping compartments. Cream silk curtains, trimmed in a complementary shade, framed the windows, while etched glass partitions separated the dining tables from a natty little bar area at one end of the car. A sneaky peek under her teacup's saucer revealed that the tea set was made by Wedgwood, and it looked very stylish atop the starched white tablecloth. Cressida noticed this sort of thing. She was a keen interior decorator, and although she didn't need to work, she loved to keep herself busy helping her aristocratic friends choose curtains and cushions, patterns and papers.

She settled herself into the comfortable, upholstered armchair-like seat and took a sip of her Earl Grey tea, while the white-jacketed waiters held trays aloft as they elegantly moved up and down the aisle, bringing fresh pots of tea to waiting passengers. Alfred was just raising a hand to order another one, when the convivial atmosphere was interrupted by a thunderous voice.

'Damn you, woman. What are you doing here?'

Cressida, intrigued, craned her neck around to see what the commotion was about. Dotty followed suit, pushing her horn-rimmed glasses up the bridge of her nose as she peered around her friend to get a better look.

The man, who was the one whom Cressida had thought was dressed like an American mobster, had clearly been the one to speak so loudly, if the redness of his face and flaring of his nostrils was anything to go by. He and the very glamorous blonde, with the enviably shapely calves and beautiful red suede shoes, were sitting at a table for two, but it wasn't her that he had shouted at. In fact, she too was turned around in her chair and was glaring at the table over the aisle.

'What am I doing here?' A carriageful of eyes turned to look at the woman answering him back. 'Lewis Warriner, I am your wife!'

Cressida gasped, and turned to look, wide-eyed, at her friends. Dotty raised her eyebrows and even Alfred lowered his hand. Cressida, despite the good manners that had been drilled into her at birth, turned around again and watched as the mysterious woman unpinned her hat from her hair. She recognised it; the black felt, the netted veil... this was the woman who had slipped onto the train at the very last moment. The woman who had been head to toe in black.

*No wonder she'd disguised herself if her plan had been to surprise her husband in this way*, Cressida thought as she saw the woman rise from her seat and raise an accusatory finger at her cheating spouse. As she spoke again, her finger was pointing directly at the floridly red face of her husband.

'The question should be, should it not, who is she?' Her shaking finger moved to point at the glamorous blonde.

The blonde, with quite some gumption, made to stand up and it looked as though she was about to rebuke the lady dressed all in black, but the man in the pinstripe suit, Lewis Warriner, got there first.

'Business, Geraldine, this is *strictly* business.' His face was puce and white flecks of spittle had appeared at the corner of his lips. Cressida wrinkled her nose, and then looked again at the angry woman, who was still pointing at the blonde.

'*Business*? Business, is it? It must be very secretive if you *must* share a cabin all the way to London together.'

There were audible gasps from the other diners. They had all seen fit to put down their teacups and, at the most, nibble quietly on their cucumber sandwiches while this dramatic interlude played out. Cressida looked across the aisle to the table of two next to them. It was the pair she guessed might be a brother and sister, twins even. Like everyone else, they had set their teacups down, though the young man had a coconut macaroon hovering silently in front of his mouth. The young woman caught Cressida's eye and twitched a smile. This was entertainment indeed.

'You wouldn't understand, Geraldine.' The man in the

pinstripe suit pulled his napkin out from his collar and made to get up. The train at that moment shuddered over a connection in the track and he stumbled backwards, which only made him more angry. The glamorous blonde reached out an arm to steady him, but he swatted it away. 'It's been years since you had any notion of my business dealings. Years since you've been any use at all!'

'Oh, I understand all right, Lewis.' Geraldine had steadied herself by gripping onto the back of her chair. 'Once a cheater, always a cheater, is that right?' She spat the accusation at him and turned around, muttering, 'I should have known, I should have known.' Cressida could see tears spilling over the brims of her eyes and watched as she raised a black-gloved hand to wipe them away.

Much to Cressida's surprise, she felt Alfred leave the seat next to her and then he appeared in the aisle, and with a gentlemanly arm offered to escort the woman back to her compartment. Cressida saw her nod, and watched as Alfred gently led her past their table and through the bar area, out to the carriages that housed the sleeper compartments. Once they were out of sight, the passengers in the dining car all seemed to release their collective breath, and once more the sounds of clattering teacups and hushed conversations filled the air.

Cressida was no different and leaned in to speak to Dotty. 'Oh, your dear brother, what a lovely chap he is.' She said this, genuinely impressed by his chivalrous act. She was also deeply unnerved by the warm, fuzzy feeling it had created in her stomach, but she tried to ignore that.

'Yes,' Dotty agreed, though paused a moment as she straightened out her skirt and blouse. 'I've no idea where he's suddenly got such nice manners from. Spent his boyhood flicking slugs at me and John, and I doubt school did much more than drill some Ancient Greek into him.' Dotty looked across at her friend and arched an eyebrow. 'Maybe he's trying to impress someone?'

Cressida felt her face flush. She knew it was Dotty's wish that her best friend and her brother would marry. Not just marry, if Dotty had her way, but fall helplessly in love as she had done herself recently with a dashing young archaeologist. But Cressida had told her time and again her views on marriage and as Dotty received a frown from her best friend, she muttered, 'Yes, I know, I know. Your little car, Ruby, independence and all that.'

'Indeed. As much as I admire your brother...' Cressida struggled to think of the right words to say. She did, after all, admire Alfred very much, but she was saved from having to try to explain it all to the ever-wistful Dotty when another voice from behind them caused them both to put down their teacups and stare down the aisle once again.

'Miss de Souza? Is it really you, Miss de Souza?'

The glamorous blonde nodded to the bespectacled, tweed-jacketed man who was standing in front of her and Lewis's table. He was rummaging around in his jacket pockets while spluttering out more conversation.

'Would you mind signing my autograph book? I have it here somewhere. Always carry it with me when I go out, as you never know who you might meet and, boy, to meet you, Miss de Souza. Boy, oh boy. What luck to meet you here like this.'

'Is she famous?' Dotty whispered to Cressida, who turned around to face her friend. 'A film star maybe? I don't recognise her.'

'Nor do I,' Cressida agreed, then pressed her finger to her lips and turned around to listen in to the conversation a few tables down.

'Come on, young man,' said Lewis, who obviously wasn't having quite the romantic lunch he had planned and was losing patience. Luckily, the newcomer produced his red leather-bound autograph book and placed it in front of Miss de Souza.

She looked at him blankly until a further rummage through his pockets produced a pen.

'You'll need my name too... It's Edwards, Owen Edwards,' the young man said, passing the pen to her.

'Thank you, Mr Edwards,' she said in what sounded like an American accent, then signed his autograph book and passed it back to him.

'There, be off with you,' Lewis grunted, then pushed his chair back and stood up. He pointedly stretched out a hand to Miss de Souza, who graciously accepted it. He then led her down the aisle in the direction of the private compartments. Cressida was sure that almost every pair of eyes in the dining car was on them. Including those of Owen Edwards, who after a moment followed them along the carriage and out past the bar.

'Gosh,' Cressida said, once they were out of earshot.

Dotty nodded, then waved as Alfred appeared at the end of the dining car. He covered the distance back to their table in a few short steps, but moved aside before sitting down, to let the brother and sister from the table next to them get up and squeeze past him.

'Alfred, that was awfully gallant of you,' Cressida praised him, then raised an eyebrow. 'Did she say anything?'

Alfred sat down in the seat next to Cressida and puffed out his cheeks. 'No, nothing at all. Except to thank me, of course. Poor woman. What was he thinking, bringing his mistress on the train like that?'

'You think that's definitely the case?' Dotty asked, folding her napkin up and placing it on the table.

'What else could it be, Dot?' Cressida asked. 'It's fairly damning, the whole sharing a compartment thing. I wonder where that darling little dog of hers went, though?'

'And I wonder how Mrs Warriner knew they were sharing a compartment?' Dotty added.

'I saw her board,' Cressida said thoughtfully. 'Very much on her own. And almost too late, later than us even, as if she were waiting for the last possible moment.'

The three of them sat in contemplative silence as the tea service was cleared away and the unoccupied tables around them were re-laid for the dinner service. The train stopped at Kingussie for a few minutes, but no one boarded. Cressida smiled as Dotty fed Ruby slices of ham from the left-over sandwiches and she flicked through the pages of Dotty's glossy magazines as her mind whirred. She was just about to ask Alfred more about the stricken woman he'd accompanied back to her compartment when the train's whistle pierced the air around them.

Then, to their horror, a shot rang out. A gunshot.

Mere moments later, while they were all still wide-eyed and looking about them in disbelief, another, equally horrifying, sound was heard.

A woman's scream.

And both had come from the direction of the sleeper carriages.

The look of shock on Cressida's face mirrored that of Dotty, Alfred, and even Ruby. As one, along with almost everyone else left in the dining car, they scrambled up from their upholstered seats and joined the startled waiters in the bar area, craning their necks to peek down the dimly lit corridor. Their curiosity over the scream seemed to outweigh any fear of there being another, possibly deadly, shot.

'We should take a look? See if anyone needs help,' a stout man in too-tight tweed said, trying to sound confident, while backing away from the door. Cressida recognised him, and his wife standing behind him, as the couple who had boarded at Aviemore. He gestured to Alfred. 'You, young man, have a look, won't you?'

Alfred nodded.

'I'll go too,' Cressida said, holding Ruby tight to her chest. The small dog snuffled in agreement.

'And me,' added Dotty, though with a little more of a tremor to her voice. 'Andrews is on board, isn't he?'

'Yes, I believe so,' Cressida reassured her friend, and felt the relief of that realisation sweep over her too.

Detective Chief Inspector Andrews was a trusted and good man, a Scotland Yard detective who had connections to Cressida's own father. Andrews had been called to the Highlands only a few days ago to solve the murder of a castle's former laird; a mystery Cressida had helped him with, as she had on several other cases recently, much to his chagrin. And now, by a stroke of luck, he and his sergeant were on this same train on their way back to Scotland Yard in London.

Cressida, Alfred and Dotty had only managed to cram through the narrow connecting door to the first of the three sleeping cars, before the comforting sight of DCI Andrews greeted them.

'Miss Fawcett. Lady Dorothy, Lord Delafield.' He nodded to them, but his face remained stony and serious. Andrews was in his mid-forties with a neatly trimmed beard that was starting to grey a little at the edges. He looked at home in the three-piece tweed suit he so often wore, its formality suiting his military bearing, not lost since he left the army. He looked at the few passengers who had followed the three friends into the carriage. 'Please, ladies and gentlemen, return to the dining car, there's nothing to see here.'

'We heard a shot,' the older man's voice piped up from further down the corridor.

'Yes, and a scream,' his wife added.

Cressida raised her eyebrows at Andrews, and was impressed when he didn't relent one jot.

'Please, ladies and gents, file back down the corridor. This is police business.'

The passengers behind Cressida and her friends mumbled and chuntered as they returned to their tables. Cressida was about to turn around too, but her natural inquisitiveness made her stop. Andrews would know what had happened. And even though one couldn't expect him to open up to strangers, he might be convinced to at least tell her just a smidgen of what had just occurred.

She gave Dotty's arm a squeeze. 'I'll join you in a jiffy,' she whispered.

'Oh Cressy...' Dotty rolled her eyes. Cressida knew why. Dotty was wonderfully protective of her. Not just because they were such good friends, but because Dotty knew how tempting Cressida had recently found investigating crimes to be. But there was no time to reassure her that she would be perfectly safe under the guardianship of DCI Andrews, not when he was already walking away from her down the corridor towards where the gunshot – and the scream – had been heard.

'Andrews, coo-eee!' Cressida called out towards the retreating back of the policeman. This made him stop and turn, and then steady himself against the woodwork of the corridor as the train skipped over a connection on the tracks. Cressida wobbled too, but couldn't let go of Ruby, so leaned against a window to stabilise herself.

'I thought I told you to go back to the dining car, Miss Fawcett?'

'Surely you didn't mean me, Andrews? Quite right to send all the others back, though.' She looked at him seriously. In turn, he sighed with resignation.

'There's been a murder, Miss Fawcett.' He shook his head.

'Oh, Andrews, not another one?' Cressida sighed. It had barely been twenty-four hours since she had helped him gather evidence against a murderer at Ayrton Castle; an endeavour that had almost got her killed. Stumbling across another murder had definitely *not* been pencilled into her social diary for today. Still, her natural curiosity won out. 'Who is it, who's dead?'

DCI Andrews rubbed his beard with his hand. 'A certain Lewis Warriner. By all accounts, a bastion of local industry, quite the wealthy industrialist—'

'And a cheating husband to boot.' Cressida let Ruby down

as she'd been wriggling. The small dog toddled a couple of steps and then promptly flopped down, deciding that this was the time and place for a good tummy lick.

Cressida looked up to see an expression of bewilderment on Andrews' face.

'How on earth do you know that, Miss Fawcett?'

'Well, Andrews, I don't know where you've been, but in the dining car, we were all treated to quite the spectacle. Mr Warriner was confronted by his wife, caught in the act of enjoying a cream bun with another woman.'

'I see.' Andrews scratched his beard again. 'That's not necessarily—'

'I'll stop you there, Andrews, because yes it is. Mrs Warriner had apparently already discovered that Mr Warriner and Miss de Souza, I think her name is, were not only sharing a table, but a sleeping compartment!'

'I see,' Andrews said again, but this time with much more conviction. 'A case of a wronged woman then perhaps. "Hell hath no fury" and all that.'

'Perhaps. Alfred escorted Mrs Warriner back to her cabin after the set-to, and Mr Warriner and Miss de Souza left fairly promptly afterwards. Then, of course, after a little while, we heard the shot and, a moment or two later, the scream.'

'Which was Miss de Souza, who discovered the body on returning from the water closet.'

Cressida and DCI Andrews fell into silent thought for a moment.

'Well, poor chap. He didn't seem like the most gentlemanly person in the world, but to be shot! Blimey. Thanks for letting me in on it, Andrews.' Cressida turned and clicked her fingers at her pup, who was rocking from side to side with the motion of the train as she studiously licked her rump. 'Come on, Rubes, that's no way to show the nice policeman what a well-trained pooch you are. Andrews, I know you'll want me to keep my nose out of this, and I promise that I'll keep my trap shut from the rest of the passengers... but I'm afraid I can't not tell Dotty and Alfred.'

Andrews puffed out his cheeks and exhaled, then with a note of resignation in his voice, said, 'If you could try to keep it to just yourselves, that would be appreciated.'

Cressida beamed at him. 'That's the spirit. And you never know, Andrews, three aristocratic noses might end up being even better than one.'

'Miss Fawcett,' Andrews closed his eyes briefly, summoning some sort of inner strength. He'd tried many times to warn her about getting involved with police business. 'Kirby and I have this in hand. Please don't interfere in our investigation.' He gave her a pleading look and turned back to the compartment, which Cressida, with a shiver running down her spine, realised must be the last resting place of Lewis Warriner.

## 5

'Cressy, there you are. What did Andrews say? Where's Kirby?'
Dotty spilled out her words as she reached for Cressida's hand
as she got to their table. Alfred had been sitting down opposite
his sister, but he got up as Cressida approached and gestured for
her to have a seat.

'The worst news, I'm afraid.' Cressida sat herself down,
letting Ruby down to snuffle around the floor of the carriage for
any titbits left from high tea. She dropped her voice to a whisper. 'That chap we saw arguing with his wife, the one who'd
just been caught with his mistress. It was him. Shot dead.'

'Cripes,' Dotty exclaimed, then pushed her glasses back up
the bridge of her nose.

'Dead?' Alfred asked. 'Are you sure?'

'As the proverbial dodo, I'm afraid.' Cressida paused. 'And
you know what this means, of course?'

'That we're really starting to have the most terrible luck?'
Dotty asked with a sigh.

'Well, yes that. Although, at least it's something interesting
to put in your letters to the dashing George over in Egypt, Dot.
I'd wager our dead bodies are starting to become much more

interesting than his mummified ones out there in the Valley of the Kings.' Cressida looked out of the window, gathering her thoughts, and felt a prickle go up her arms as the realisation properly came to her. 'What I meant, though, was that no one could possibly have got off this train since that shot rang out. We must be steaming along at fifty or sixty miles per hour since we left Kingussie. There's not a chance an assailant could jump off without risking serious injury.'

'You're saying whoever did it, is still here on the train?' Alfred asked.

'Exactly that. Andrews made no allusions to it being a self-inflicted wound. He said it was murder. Someone on this train just shot Lewis Warriner in cold blood. Someone here is a murderer.'

'Oh, Cressy.' Dotty blanched at the suggestion. 'Another murderer in our midst... But tell me, Andrews hasn't asked you to help, has he?' A look of concern clouded Dotty's brow. 'It's just, last time you looked into a murder, you were almost killed.'

'And we can't have that.' Alfred joined his sister in looking frightfully concerned. And they had cause to, as Cressida was prone to sticking her nose into mysteries – and recently she'd paid a high price for her curiosity. She reached up and rubbed the still egg-sized lump that had stopped her from wearing her favourite cloche hat to the station earlier.

She sighed. 'No. He didn't ask me to investigate.'

'Good.' Dotty sat back with a look of satisfaction on her face, having avoided the usual fight with her headstrong friend.

'Even though I suggested that three aristocratic noses would be even better than one,' Cressida teased as Dotty let her mouth open into a gawp and Alfred chuckled. Cressida looked at her darling friends. *Of course* she wanted to investigate, but she was still getting headaches from the coshing she'd received in that dank tunnel back at the castle. Perhaps letting Andrews do the legwork and seeing what he came up with would be the best plan. Still, it didn't stop her from wondering just a little about the case before them. 'I suppose his first port of call will be searching this train fore and aft for the gun,' she mused.

'Assuming it wasn't tossed,' Alfred said. 'It might be too calamitous for someone to jump from the train, but a gun could have easily been thrown from the window.'

Dotty frowned at her brother, and it made Cressida smile.

'Now who's investigating, Alfred?' Cressida leaned over and nudged him.

His cheeks flushed and she grinned even more.

Still, Alfred had a point.

'I'm sure he'll want to come and talk to you actually, Alf,' Cressida said, remembering Alfred's gallantry in escorting Mrs Warriner to her compartment.

'I'm not sure I can tell him much, but he's welcome to ask,' Alfred replied.

'What did happen? Moment by moment?' Cressida pushed.

'Cressy...' Dotty furrowed her brow.

'Dot, I'm only quizzing your brother. Possibly the safest witness interview one could have.'

'Safest and least interesting, I'm afraid,' Alfred said, before his sister could launch any more objections. 'Mrs Warriner didn't say a word while we walked back to her compartment, which, by the way, is between both of yours, second carriage along from here.' Cressida nodded thoughtfully and Alfred continued. 'I said something about "Ah well then, here you are" or something and she opened her compartment's door and went inside. Then I came straight back here.'

'And she shut the door behind her?' Cressida asked. 'A proper click shut?'

'I think so. To be honest, Cress, I didn't really notice. Mind on other things.'

'Probably things such as sandwiches and how many might be left,' Dotty teased, then gasped as the train clattered over another junction and let out an almighty whistle. 'I think it only does that when we're nearing stations or crossings or things. We're not stopping, are we?' Dotty asked, her eyes wide again.

'You're the one who insisted on bringing your *Bradshaw's*,' Alfred reminded her. 'Have a look.'

'Oh yes, hang on a tick.' Dotty leaned over and picked up her weighty, red-bound travel guide, now that it wasn't being used as a booster seat for Ruby.

As she looked, Cressida stared out of the window. Ruby had jumped up onto an empty chair the other side of the aisle and was watching the majestic mountains of the Highlands go by as well. Cressida let her mind wander, though her thoughts came back to one thing... *There's a murderer on the train with us and if the train stops the murderer could get off. Maybe I should help Andrews... help him find out who it is before that can happen.*

She looked back to where Dotty was riffling through the pages, until she stopped and started running her finger down the finely printed rail timetable.

'It says here we pass Dalwhinnie and Blair Atholl, then Pitlochry and Perth—'

'But we don't stop at those stations?' Cressida interrupted, aware that much was resting on Dotty's answer.

'Not that I can make out. These things are so dashed hard to decipher.'

'If anyone can, you can, chum,' Cressida reassured her and Dotty kept looking, flicking back to the front index for a key.

'Well, there's no arrival and departure time like we had for Aviemore. I think perhaps the guide just shows us the times we pass the stations.'

'This is why I always usually drive.' Cressida sat back in her chair, her arms folded across her chest. 'No silly timetables to hem one in. The open road and a full tank of petroleum, that's what I love.'

'Hear, hear,' Alfred agreed. 'But look, this is serious, Dot. Where do we actually stop?'

Dotty frowned at the guide again, and then tapped the page with her finger. 'These symbols here mean the train *could* stop if given "timeous notice".' She took her finger off the page and used it to push her glasses up her nose again. 'I rather like that phrase – "timeous notice".'

'What does it mean, though?' Cressida asked, still perplexed.

'That the train won't stop until Edinburgh unless someone has telegrammed ahead in advance to request it,' Dotty said, more sure of herself now. 'And we reach Edinburgh at precisely sixteen minutes past ten tonight.'

Alfred pulled his watch out of his waistcoat pocket and consulted it. 'And it's just gone half past six now.'

Cressida sighed. It might have been better if they *had* stopped, allowing the murderer to flee and for them to enjoy their journey in peace. She looked out of the window again at the majestic Highland scenery, so open and vast, yet they were confined to these eight carriages with whoever had hated another person so much that they had pointed a gun at them and pulled the trigger.

As the familiar shiver prickled across her back, she realised that, bump on the head or not, she really *did* want to know who had murdered Lewis Warriner, and why. And with the Scotland Express thundering down the track south towards Edinburgh, she only had a few hours to get to the bottom of it.

## 6

After the initial shock of the gunshot, the passengers of the Scotland Express had started to settle again in the dining car. Instructed by Andrews to carry on as normal, the white-jacketed waiters had cleared away the final remains of the tea service and were brushing down the tables with comb-like crumbers. Cressida had picked up Ruby from her lookout post by the window as the table next to them was needed for the train's two-legged passengers instead. That it was the brother and sister who she remembered leaving the dining car just before the gun was fired piqued her interest.

*What caused them to follow Lewis Warriner out of the dining car, moments before he was murdered?* Cressida wondered. She could feel another headache coming on and was happy to gently run her fingers over the velvet soft ears of her pug, and just listen as Dotty and Alfred chatted. It seemed that they had a relatively good working knowledge of most of the other passengers and Cressida was in part both entertained and delighted by their running commentary.

'Who's that then?' She'd started off one of their conversations, subtly as possible pointing to an older couple at the rear of the carriage, and Dotty and Alfred had obliged.

'That's the Fernley-Hoggs,' Dotty said with confidence. 'Boarded at Aviemore. Recently retired bank manager and his wife. They've toured the Highlands in a rented motor car, if you can believe such a service exists, and are returning to Buckinghamshire.'

'How do you know that, Dot?' Cressida asked, intrigued.

'While you were with Andrews, we all got quite chummy. Trench spirit and all that, I suppose. Mr Fernley-Hogg said it was a darn shame that the train had to take us all the way into Euston, as they'd only have to double back on themselves and get a train back up to Chalfont St Giles. Apparently this one doesn't stop—' She picked up her *Bradshaw's* again, 'Yes, he's right, no stops for us all the way to London once we've been through Edinburgh.'

'They don't like stopping these sleeper trains in the small hours,' Alfred said matter-of-factly. 'Gets in the way of the mail train.'

Cressida nodded thoughtfully.

Dotty was the one who replied to her brother. 'And it would probably give one an awful night's sleep, slowing down and speeding up for every station from Edinburgh to Euston. Anyway, back to our fellow passengers.' She tried to nonchalantly nod in the direction of the bar area, but ended up dropping her *Bradshaw's* with a clatter on the table. Tutting to herself, she gave up and just explained it out loud instead. 'That chap sitting on that bar stool, I haven't seen him before.'

Cressida followed her gaze. *Dotty's right*, she thought. *She hasn't seen him. But I have...* 'He boarded with Miss de Souza and Lewis Warriner. The now-dead Lewis Warriner,' she whispered to her friends.

'He appeared when we all came back in here, but whether it was from the sleeping carriages or the other end of the dining car that leads through to the lounge car, I didn't see,' Dotty remarked.

'So, he wasn't in here when the shot was fired?' Cressida asked, trying to remember.

Dotty confirmed what she was thinking. 'No, I don't think so. I don't remember seeing him at any of the tables at the far end of the carriage—'

'And he wasn't sitting there at the bar either. I was facing that direction through tea,' Cressida interrupted her friend, who didn't seem to mind.

'Sounds like he could be one for the old suspect list, Cress,' said Alfred, reaching into his pocket and then pulling out his pipe.

Dotty wrinkled her nose at him and then turned back to face her friend. 'Well, whether he was here or not, I'm afraid I don't yet know his name. He hasn't left that spot since he showed up in here. But, over there, though, that's Lord Hartnell.'

'Where?' Cressida craned her neck to where Dotty was pointing, this time without bothering to try to use her *Bradshaw's* to complicate matters, but she couldn't see another man sitting close to the Fernley-Hoggs. 'I can only see that young woman, travelling with that small boy. Oh, nose-picking. Charming. The boy, of course, not the woman.'

Dotty stifled a laugh, so Alfred continued. 'That is Lord Hartnell. Aged nine, I believe.'

'Gosh. Still, Alfred, I can imagine you were a similar young rogue at the same age.'

'Rogue is right,' Dotty agreed, pushing her wayward glasses back up the bridge of her nose. 'About you, Alfred, *and* that little pickle over there. He came past and tried to steal the sugar lumps right off our table, under our noses even. Cheeky devil.'

Cressida, despite the horror of what had happened to Mr

Warriner, couldn't help but find Dotty only too amusing. 'Oh Dot. Please carry on, I have to hear more.'

'Well, you can guess the rest really. The young woman with Lord Hartnell is his nanny, I believe. She hasn't said much, but then looking after a small boy like that would probably drive me to elective mutism too.'

Cressida let out a laugh, then clamped her hand to her mouth, remembering that a man had just died and laughing, even at Dotty, was terribly *infra dig*.

Dotty saved her friend's blushes by carrying on in a lowered voice, 'And we haven't seen Miss de Souza or Mrs Warriner since the gunshot, but that Owen Edwards chap is over there. He seems nice enough, though a little in shock after meeting Miss de Souza. Hasn't said a sensible thing since getting her autograph.'

'He's another one who wasn't here in the dining car with us when the shot was fired,' Alfred said, then concentrated on packing some tobacco into his pipe as his sister glared at him.

'Honestly, Alfred. We're not meant to be investigating,' tutted Dotty. 'And if you're going to smoke that thing, I wish you'd take yourself off to the engine room or something.'

'Leave you two here while there's a murderer on the loose? By jiggers, I don't think so!'

'You had a point though, Alfred.' Cressida pulled Ruby up closer to her chin as she thought about it. 'He left just after Mr Warriner and Miss de Souza did, didn't he? And I don't recall seeing him come back into the dining car before we heard the shot. This dining car is splendid, really rather beautifully done, but it's not the most spacious, and I do think we would have noticed him squeeze back past us.'

'Absolutely, I had far too good a view of that small boy's nose-picking. Mr Edwards wasn't there to shield me from it,' Dotty agreed. Then she paused, and a flicker of fear passed across her face. She looked at her older brother. 'And Alfred's right about not leaving us either. Perhaps we should all stay together until DCI Andrews has found the culprit. For safety's sake?' The slight tremor was back in her voice and her chestnut brown eyes were wide behind her spectacles.

Cressida, despite her usual hot-headedness and enthusiasm for helping her favourite policeman, nodded and reached out for Dotty's hand. She gave it a squeeze. 'We'll all be quite safe, Dotty, I promise.'

As she squeezed her friend's hand a second time, Cressida really hoped she was right. However, the entrance of a now familiar face into the dining carriage – and, in particular, the frown wrought across that pale face – gave her cause to worry. Perhaps they weren't all so safe after all...

## 7

Cressida pulled her hand away from Dotty's and looked up at Sergeant Kirby. The lightly freckled face and ginger hair of DCI Andrews' second in command were now quite familiar to her, but she was sure she hadn't seen him look this vexed before. As for the other man standing next to him, a man in overalls with slicked-back hair and blackened tips to his fingernails, well, she'd never seen him before in her life. She held Ruby tight to her as the policeman cleared his throat and announced his presence to the carriage.

'Ladies and gents, um, lords and honourables, please remain in your positions a moment or two longer and, furthermore, don't attempt to perambulate. Myself and Mr Sawyer here, the train engineer, will perform a thorough, though hopefully brief, search of this carriage for item or items as yet undisclosed to you the public but of high importance and paramountcy to us, the police.'

Kirby gave a bow and Alfred leaned into Cressida, his unlit pipe clenched between his teeth.

'You know, I don't think I've heard Kirby speak more than two words together since I first met him back at Chatterton

Court and now here he is, giving us a hearty rendition of the entire thesaurus.'

Cressida elbowed Alfred in the ribs. But his light-heartedness had broken the tension – even Dotty had giggled – and Cressida realised with some relief that poor Kirby's expression of vexation had most likely arisen from having to talk to a carriageful of tweed-clad passengers; not because he and Andrews had discovered any other gruesome finds.

Kirby and Mr Sawyer commenced their search of the dining car, but even to Cressida's untrained eye, she could see that this wasn't a terribly thorough one. In fact, it seemed Ruby was more exhaustive on her hunt for cake crumbs, having been released from Cressida's lap. And at least she had a good view at ankle height for anything hidden under tables.

'Kirby!' Cressida whispered over to the policeman while Mr Sawyer was describing the workings of the locomotive to Lord Hartnell, who had taken his finger out of his nose for the occasion.

'Yes, Miss Fawcett. Hello Miss Fawcett.' Kirby stopped making a show of prodding the panelling above the empty table next to them and gave her his attention.

'Hello, Kirby. Darn mess we've all got ourselves into again, don't you think? How's Andrews doing? And do you really think the gun is in here. With us?'

'Gun, miss? I didn't say anything about a gun, miss.'

Cressida raised an enquiring eyebrow at him.

'Well, yes, miss. And yes, miss, very well, I think. And then no, miss.' Kirby counted the answers to Cressida's questions off on his fingers.

'So why the pretence of the search?' Cressida was joined by two pairs of chestnut eyes, courtesy of the Chatterton siblings, and one pair of very dark frog-like ones from Ruby, who had scrambled back up onto Cressida's lap, as she looked inquisitively at the young policeman.

'Well, miss,' Kirby said, pulling at the knees of his trousers as he crouched down so that he could lower his voice to speak to the three of them. 'As it happens, miss, we have already found the murder weapon.'

'Jeepers,' Dotty whispered, though her eyes were wide with shock.

'Not thrown out of the train then,' Alfred mused, his back teeth still clenched around his as yet unlit pipe.

'No, my lord, and in a very interesting place too.'

'Go on, Kirby, spill the beans. It's only us,' Cressida coaxed, and to her delight, with but a glance to the left and then the right, and a quick 'ahem', he whispered the answer.

'The gun, that being an old service revolver, and reeking of powder so it was, which implies to us, the professionals, that it was just recently fired, was just where the chief inspector thought it would be.'

'Where?' Dotty asked, but Cressida had a feeling she knew the answer already. The hairs on her forearms prickled and she hugged Ruby a little tighter.

'In a manner conventional for the common criminal, it was stashed under a mattress in one of the compartments, Lady Dorothy. The bed in question, in the compartment in question, belonged to Mrs Warriner.'

'No!' gasped Dotty, risking her glasses falling into her water glass.

'The wronged wife. Knew it.' Alfred nodded.

'The chief inspector is preparing to interview her now, my lord.' Kirby then tapped his finger against his nose and lowered his voice into an even more conspiratorial whisper. 'The inspector had the notion that Mr Sawyer and myself could keep everyone in here, occupied as it were, and therefore not alarmed or in a perambulatory state—'

'You mean he doesn't want us walking around while he's

busy cracking the case?' Alfred said, taking his pipe out of his mouth and jabbing it vaguely in Kirby's direction.

'That is correct, my lord. The...' He struggled for the word, squinting into the distance as he thought, 'Vignette in Warriner's compartment is quite...'

'Grisly, I should imagine.' Cressida finished the sentence for him.

'Quite,' Kirby said, standing up and looking about to check that no one else had heard his revelation. It helped that Cressida – and her chums – had assisted DCI Andrews in investigating murders on three different occasions now. Kirby obviously saw them as police-by-proxy, despite their lack of uniform or, indeed, any formal training in anything other than etiquette, conversational French and riding side saddle.

'Mrs Warriner,' Cressida said to herself. 'The wronged wife, indeed. And apparently the murderess.'

Kirby nodded a goodbye to the friends and Cressida turned to look out of the window. As the fields and hedgerows raced past, her mind ran similarly quickly over what she'd just learned. She *should* feel relieved that the murderer had been apprehended so quickly. Stuck as they all were on this galloping train, the thought of a killer being on the loose among them and throughout the night made her feel claustrophobic at best, terrified at worst.

But, like paint applied over fresh plaster, she had a feeling this charge wouldn't stick. Something wasn't quite adding up, something about all this was just too *easy*.

And Cressida didn't like it one bit.

## 8

*Was a not-so-secret affair enough to drive Mrs Warriner to murder her husband?* Cressida thought to herself. *If indeed it really was her?* 'Divorce surely would be a far less drastic action...' She found herself saying the last bit out loud while tapping a finger on the table. She realised after a moment or two that Dotty and Alfred were staring at her.

'Are you feeling quite well, Cressy? You look rather dazed,' Dotty said, concerned.

'Hmm. No, not tip-top actually, Dot. I feel all in all rather done in after our most recent adventure,' Cressida replied, rubbing the back of her head. Then an idea occurred to her, helped by the fact that she knew that her own compartment was next to that of Mrs Warriner. Mrs Warriner, who was about to be interviewed by Andrews. And suddenly she felt a trifle better, though she kept that to herself. 'You know what, chum, the old noggin hurts a bit. That cosh to the back of the head I had and all that. Not helped by all that sugar in those cakes and all this excitement. Do you both mind if I go and have a lie-down? Retreat to my compartment for a little bit.'

'We just said we'd stick together, Cressy.' Dotty's eyes had widened, and she looked uneasy. 'In case the murderer strikes again.'

'Murderer's with the chief, sis,' Alfred countered, jabbing his pipe in Dotty's direction. 'Are you sure you're all right though, Cress? Would you like an arm?'

'You are all chivalry, Alfred, but no thank you.' Cressida smiled at him. Despite some unfamiliar feelings she'd been having towards Alfred recently, she, and he, had to remember that she was an independent woman; she prided herself on that. She didn't need a man to help her down corridors, especially ones as narrow as these. And, in any case, time was of the essence if she were to get back to her compartment before Andrews finished questioning Mrs Warriner. One slim socialite could squeeze down the corridor next to the compartments much more speedily alone than if she were accompanied by a man.

Clutching Ruby to her, Cressida rose from the table.

'Well, if you're sure?' Dotty asked, reaching up and giving Ruby a last stroke as Cressida stood there, steadying herself as the train clattered over a set of points. 'We'll come and get you in time for drinkies.'

'Oh, rather. No knock to the head could keep me from a martini, Dot,' Cressida said, giving her friends a little wave as Dotty put the *Bradshaw's* down in favour of one of the magazines she'd brought with her.

Cressida swayed past the dining tables and eyed the beak-nosed man sitting at the bar as she passed by, earmarking him for a chat later. But the clock was ticking on this particular mission.

She hastened her step and was in the first of the wood-veneered corridors that ran alongside the sleeping compartments when she felt a sharp tug on her wide-legged woollen trousers. She turned round and for a moment thought she must have been imagining things, as there was no one to be seen.

Then she lowered her gaze and saw the freckled face and untidy ginger hair of Lord Hartnell.

'What ho,' the young lord said, addressing Cressida with the confidence his birthright had gifted him. 'Is it true that you know the detective who's on board with us?'

'I do, that's right,' Cressida replied, wondering if the hand that had tugged on her trousers had been the same one that was home to the finger she'd spied up Lord Hartnell's nose earlier. 'How did you know that?'

'Mr Sawyer, the engineer. He told us the detective was a fine man and had friends in high places, and then nodded at you.'

'Oh.' Cressida was slightly taken aback. *High places, indeed...* She rolled her eyes.

'Has he found the gun, miss?'

'I wouldn't know,' Cressida said, crossing her fingers under Ruby's tummy.

'Is it true the man who got shot was some gangster? A Glasgow mobster and all that. Blam! Blam!' Lord Hartnell shot Cressida with his forefingers and she instinctively pulled away. She didn't know many children in her day-to-day life. If they were all like this specimen, she was rather pleased of the fact. He seemed excitable, possibly because of the amount of sugar his nanny must have thoughtlessly allowed him during tea, and was still mock-shooting her when Cressida tried to disabuse him of the notion.

'I don't think he was a gangster... I'm sorry, we haven't been introduced? I'm Cressida Fawcett, Hon.'

'Monty Beaumont. Viscount Hartnell.' He stopped shooting her and stuck out a sticky-looking hand, which Cressida took with some trepidation and shook lightly. As they released, she resisted the urge to wipe her hand on her own trousers and instead slipped it back under Ruby, who she also introduced.

'And this is Ruby, my pug. But back to Mr Warriner, I don't

think he was a gangster. But I think he might have been one of those gentlemen—'

'Nanny says he's definitely not a gentleman,' Monty said, the voice of his governess discernible in the judgement.

'Well, quite. But we mustn't think poorly of the dead.'

'He's dead?' The formerly rambunctious young viscount suddenly paled.

'Oh dear. Yes. Well...' Cressida didn't quite know what to do. She hoped that wasn't his lower lip wobbling, in fact she was sure it wasn't. Usually, when Dotty got upset, Cressida handed over the warm and comforting canine treasure that was Ruby, but she didn't think the poor pup deserved being petted by a snotty-nosed viscount. No matter how shocked he might have just been from discovering he was on a train with a dead body – and therefore a murderer. As it turned out, some Ruby-shaped comforting wasn't needed at all, if the very small viscount's change in expression was anything to go by.

'Cor,' the young lad finally said, grinning up at Cressida. 'That's the most exciting thing that's ever, *ever* happened to me. Wait until I tell—'

'Oh, Lord Hartnell. I don't think you should tell anyone else in the dining car. Our secret, yes?' Cressida had crouched down to the small boy's level. He stared at her. 'For now, anyway.'

'All right. But only because you know the policeman. And I like your dog. But I'm going to tell everyone at school about this next term. It'll be wizard!' At that, the child ran off, finger firmly up his nose again, back in the direction of the dining car.

Cressida muttered something under her breath about certain age groups being seen and not heard, then turned back to her mission.

She hoped the diminutive lord hadn't held her up too much with his theories of Glasgow gangsters, though it did strike her as quite some coincidence that Lewis Warriner had appeared to be emulating that dastardly Al Capone chap she'd recently read about and seen pictures of in the newspapers, what with his white fedora and pinstripe suit. *Odd*, she thought, *for a wealthy, middle-aged, Scottish businessman.*

With that thought in mind, she reached her compartment. The door next to hers, the one she knew belonged to the compartment of Mrs Geraldine Warriner, was closed. She opened her own as quietly as possible and hoped she wasn't too late to eavesdrop on whatever was being said next door.

*The aristocratic nose is one thing,* she thought to herself, *but it's time for these noble old ears to have a go too...*

## 9

It had been at her esteemed boarding school that Cressida had first found out that a glass, held against the wall, with its base to one's own ear, was a most useful tool for helping to listen through walls. She credited her friend Minty O'Hare with the discovery, as she had had the bed at the end of the dormitory, closest to Matron's own bedroom and was on lookout – or listen-out – most nights.

But it was Cressida who was now sitting cross-legged on her bed, her head cocked to one side and leaning on a glass that was firmly clamped to the wall.

'I'm not investigating,' she told Ruby, who was sitting opposite her, snuffling away in her usual style. 'Just keeping an ear to the ground. Or, in this case, the wall.'

Cressida tried to tune out the noise of the train and listened hard. And her efforts were not in vain. She'd obviously missed quite a bit of the interview, but she tuned in just as Andrews was grilling Mrs Warriner about her reasons for being on board. Through the wall, she heard the following:

'Do you mean to tell me you came aboard this train with no prior knowledge of your husband already being on board?' That was Andrews, and Cressida could imagine him perched on one end of the neatly made-up bed, leaning forward, his elbows on his knees as perhaps Mrs Warriner sat at the other end, nearest the window.

'No, I knew he'd be on board.' Mrs Warriner's voice was softer than the inspector's, but she must have been closer to the wall, so Cressida could still make out what she was saying.

'A premeditated attack, then?'

'No.' She paused. 'I mean, I don't know. But not by me at any rate. You see, I didn't know he would be... accompanied.'

'I see. But you knew your husband was coming aboard, just not with whom. And he didn't know you were going to join him?'

'That's right. But I didn't come on board to *join* him. Not necessarily. Though, of course, I assumed...'

There was a pause, then Andrews spoke again. 'Did you discuss your travel plans with him at all?'

'No. We hadn't been speaking much lately. He was working away a lot of the time – business meetings down in Glasgow, I believe, though I had access to his diary, of course.'

There was another pause and Cressida could imagine Andrews giving out one of his sighs and scratching his beard. Then he spoke again. 'Mrs Warriner, I'm finding it hard to believe, having found the murder weapon here in your compartment, that you didn't come on board, knowing that your husband would be on this train with his mistress, so that you could confront him and then kill him.'

'Oh no, Chief Inspector, I wouldn't, I wouldn't. I didn't.' It sounded like Mrs Warriner had begun to weep. 'Neither of those things. I didn't come to confront him, or kill him. Please, Chief Inspector, you must believe me.'

'And how long have you been married, Mrs Warriner?' It sounded like Andrews was changing tack.

Cressida adjusted her sitting position and tuned back in.

'Almost fifteen years.'

'Children?' Andrews asked.

There was a pause. Then Mrs Warriner continued. 'No. Sadly not,' she sighed. 'I knew Lewis would be on this train, because, as his former secretary myself, I'm adept at keeping the diary. But I didn't know he would be travelling with that woman. I don't book his travel for him, his current secretary does that. And he knew nothing about me being aboard as I... well, I booked rather late in the day.'

'Because you suspected him of having an affair?'

'No, no. Nothing like that, Inspector. You see, I received this.' There was another pause.

Cressida wished there was even the smallest spyhole she could peek through to see what was being shown to the chief inspector. She ran her hand across the smooth mahogany veneer in the vainest of hopes that some crack would reveal itself, but, alas, no. All she could do was keep her ear clamped to the glass, which, in turn, was clamped to the wall.

Finally, Andrews spoke again. 'I see. This is all very peculiar.'

'Yes, it is, isn't it. A very strange thing to receive, but you can see my predicament. And the booking of the train was no matter. As I said, I used to be a secretary – his secretary – before we married so that hardly worried me. "What's the harm?" I thought to myself.' Mrs Warriner sounded like she was giving a hollow sort of laugh, but it was hard to make out over the noise of the tracks.

'The fact remains, Mrs Warriner, that you have the motive, the means and the opportunity for committing this crime. Not to mention, we have a witness who says they saw you in the vicinity of Mr Warriner's compartment just after they heard the shot.'

There was a long pause.

'I was.'

'And what were you doing out in the corridor at that time?'

'I heard the shot, so I came out to see what had happened. But that gun isn't mine, Inspector, you have to believe me. I've never seen it before and I wouldn't even know how to use it. And wouldn't you think I might have discarded it out of the window at the first opportunity rather than hide it under my mattress? I'm not a simpleton.'

'People in traumatic and stressful situations do all sorts of foolish things, Mrs Warriner. Including, perhaps, killing their husband when faced with the shock of finding out that he's having an affair.'

There was silence for a few moments and Cressida thought about what Mrs Warriner had just said. *Why on earth would she have hidden the gun under her own mattress?* As Cressida churned over the thought in her head, Mrs Warriner spoke again.

'I didn't kill him, Inspector. I loved him. I've never seen that woman before and I didn't know he'd be on this train with her. Oh Lewis.'

There was a pause as she sobbed.

Andrews spoke again. 'You were seen in the corridor outside your husband's room just after he was murdered. You have no alibi for the time of the murder, Lord Delafield having left you here in this room by your own admission at least fifteen minutes before the shot was heard. And the murder weapon, pending bullet analysis, of course, was found here, under your mattress. I'm afraid, Mrs Warriner, I'm left with no alternative but to arrest you in the name of the law, for the murder of your husband, Mr Lewis Warriner. Anything you say...'

Cressida pulled her ear away from the glass as Andrews finished reading Mrs Warriner her rights. 'Well, Ruby. That was interesting. What was that thing that she revealed to Andrews? A voucher? An invitation? Something made her come aboard this train.'

'And I bet she wished she hadn't.'

Cressida jumped at the voice and looked up from talking to Ruby. 'Oh Dot. You nearly gave me a heart attack.'

Dotty just folded her arms across her chest and glared at her friend.

'What is it, Dot?' Cressida felt a flush across her cheeks. She was in the soup for something, that was for sure.

Finally, Dot relented and uncrossed her arms and held out a small white packet for Cressida. 'Here. Little Lord Hartnell's governess, or nanny, or whatever she is, had some headache powders spare. Seems to me like rather a nervous woman. I thought you might want one, as I imagined you here, lying still, a cold flannel placed across your aching brow. But no, there you are, right as blooming rain, Cressy. And I know what you're doing.'

'Sorry, Dot.' Cressida reached out and took the headache powder from her friend anyway. She did have a bit of a sore head after all. 'I just couldn't help having a little listen in.'

'Listening in is one thing, Cressy.' Dotty came and sat down next to her on her bunk. Her tone softened. 'But it sounds like you were investigating again. And it's not like Andrews isn't already here and already on the case.' She pushed her glasses up the bridge of her nose, her face covered in concern for her friend.

'I know. And he's just arrested his prime suspect. But the thing is, Dotty. I think he might have got the wrong person.'

'Why?'

'Well, something lured Mrs Warriner onto this train, else she wouldn't have been aboard, so there's that. And she claims not to know how to even shoot a gun.'

'Stands to reason she'd say that, when caught red-handed with the weapon.'

'Yes, but as Alfred pointed out earlier, why not just ditch

the gun out the window? And, also, she told Andrews that she loved him.'

'She loves Andrews?' Dotty looked perplexed.

'No, silly. Her husband. Lewis.' Cressida sighed and sat back against the wall, stretching her legs out. 'But then Andrews did sum it all up rather neatly when he arrested her. She was in the right place and the right time, with no other alibi, and the murder weapon was found under her mattress.'

'That all seems to add up to me,' Dotty replied, instinctively reaching out and pulling a very willing Ruby onto her lap. 'Also, did you notice she had gloves on during that fracas with her husband? Maybe she was all prepared for not leaving fingerprints.'

'Maybe,' Cressida nodded, impressed at Dotty's observation. 'Maybe she did and she's just a very good liar. But what if she's not, Dotty? What if she's an innocent, as she says she is? What if whatever it is that she showed Andrews can prove that she had no idea that Warriner had a mistress with him. What then?'

'I don't know. What then?' Dotty asked warily.

Cressida took a deep breath and then exhaled as she put her thoughts together. 'I suppose it means that if Mrs Warriner didn't kill her husband, then someone else on this train did.'

## 10

A knock on the compartment door made them both jump and Cressida shushed Ruby as she yapped in reply to the sharp rat-a-tat-tat.

'Come in,' Cressida called, a tremble to her voice. Dotty still looked somewhat panicked at who might be knocking, but stood aside so that the narrow door to the compact sleeping compartment could open.

'Hot drop?' The gentle Scottish accent of the uniformed tea lady allowed both Cressida and Dotty to breathe again. The middle-aged woman was greeted with more enthusiasm than perhaps she was expecting. That Cressida and Dotty's smiles were that of relief that she wasn't a gun-toting murderer, she didn't realise and met the beaming faces of the two young women, and small dog, with one of her own. 'Well, isn't it lovely to see two such bonny lassies smiling away at me. Anything for you? Something sweet for the shock? I know it's too late for tea, but sometimes a hot, sweet drink is just what we need. Biscuit? I've got shortbread.'

'Better not,' Dotty said ruefully. 'I think I had a surfeit of sandwiches and enough sweet treats over tea, so much so that this waistline has become rather tight.' She sucked in her tummy as she declined the kind tea lady's offers.

'Ach, no lassie. You look bonny as I've ever seen.'

'Gosh, thank you.' Dotty beamed even more.

'Quite right,' Cressida agreed, thinking twice before declining something from the tea trolley herself. She even went as far as placing a finger on Ruby's ever-hopeful nose. 'Thank you, Mrs...?'

'Drysdale, lassie, I'm Margaret Drysdale. Thank you for asking.' She bowed her head and Cressida wondered if she'd embarrassed the woman as she swept a few stray hairs under her starched white cap. The thing was, Cressida hated the anonymity of serving staff; how those in the upper classes would dismiss them without ever learning their names.

'And I'm Cressida and this is Dotty,' Cressida completed the introductions. 'Thanks ever so for thinking of us like this. I must admit after everything that's just happened, I wouldn't blame anyone for needing something for the shock.'

'Oh, aye. It's a terrible thing, that it is,' Margaret agreed. 'To think it happened just down the way there. And that wife of his already arrested for it, so I hear. Found him and the mistress together and took aim,' she shuddered. 'Terrible thing, it is.'

'The shooting aside, how anyone can find the right compartment on this train is beyond me,' Dotty said. 'I got confused trying to find this one a few minutes ago. They all look the same! And I was sure there was a sort of lounge car, wasn't there? I thought I'd walk through it on my way to these sleeper carriages, but I didn't.'

'That's the other side of the dining car from here, Dot,' Cressida explained.

Mrs Drysdale chipped in and added, 'Aye, and that's where you'll mostly find me, the near end of it is where there's the main urn and little tea area.'

'So, you see, Dot, it goes engine and coal truck and all that, then the lounge car—'

'Sorry to correct you, dear,' Mrs Drysdale raised a finger. 'But there's a luggage car in between the coal and the lounge. And before that even somewhere for the driver and his mate, and the other staff, to lay their heads. Then it's the lounge car, the dining car, with that nice bar bit at the end, where that scamp Bernard makes those naughty cocktails.' She shivered as if remembering the last time she had one too many and Cressida warmed to her even more. The tea lady recovered herself, then continued. 'Then there's these three sleeper cars each with a water closet at either end, another luggage car, and that's your lot.'

'Thank you, Mrs Drysdale,' Dotty said. 'The train does seem to have everything one could want on board. Well, except a library, of course. And a piano.'

'You do play beautifully, Dot,' Cressida praised her friend. 'One day, we must go on the Orient Express. That train has a baby grand in the bar car, apparently.'

'Gosh, really? How utterly wonderful.' Dotty bit her lip and Cressida could only imagine what romantic fantasies she was concocting as her eyes glazed over.

Cressida shook her head, thoughts of eastern adventures replaced with the more pressing matter of the here and now. She was still convinced that Geraldine Warriner wasn't the killer. But she didn't want to go around spreading that rumour, or the panic that it might create. But still, here was the train's tea lady. If the servants in country houses were anything to go by, she would know a lot more of the goings-on aboard this train than most of the upper-class passengers.

'Mrs Warriner arrested then, eh?' Cressida raised an eyebrow at Mrs Drysdale. 'How do you know?' *I only know from listening in on Andrews' interview with her*, Cressida thought, *and that was mere moments ago.*

Mrs Drysdale, far from being affronted or taking any offence at Cressida's remark, merely bent over the tea trolley in a conspiratorial way and lowered her voice to reply. 'I just passed that handsome policeman in the corridor. Quite a squeeze it was getting him past my trolley, but I asked him outright what had happened.'

'And he told you?' Cressida asked, wondering why, if so, he was always so reticent in filling her in on the investigations they'd done together.

'Ach, no lassie. But as soon as he'd passed me, he met that young sergeant of his and told him the news.'

'Ah.' Cressida sat back. That made more sense. And just went to show that even DCI Andrews could forget at times the presence of staff and how their ears were as functioning as anyone else's.

Mrs Drysdale carried on. 'And, of course, I listened in as I recognised the name. Warriner. Well, I ken his name from many years ago now.'

'How's that?' Cressida was intrigued. Dotty leaned against the wall and Ruby shuffled around, settling herself in for the story.

'Well, it's my brother who had the beef with him at the time, of course. Got himself fired, didn't he? Hughie was only trying to do right by that young man, but Warriner blamed him for the losses.'

'You've lost me there, Mrs Drysdale. Hughie's your brother, is that right?'

'Aye.'

'And he was fired by Mr Warriner for losing something, but it wasn't his fault?'

'Aye, well, "losing" might be a stretch too far for the word. He hired a young man. Straight back from the Western Front, he was. Had nothing to his name, of course, but had a slightness to his fingers, shall we say.'

'Oh, I see. So, as our American friends might say, the buck stopped with your brother for the misdemeanours?'

'Aye, that's right, lassie. Hughie was devastated. Loved his job at Warriner Industries, so he did. He was there back in the early days when Mrs Warriner and her bairns were always visiting and saying their hellos to the workers. Felt like a real family business then.' She shuffled some of the cups around on the top of her tea trolley, arranging them as she did her thoughts. 'Didn't last long, though, mind. Still, Hughie and me, we're both on the trains now, and that's that.'

'Bairns? Did you say Mrs Warriner had children?'

'Aye, that's right. Two wee little ones she had back then.'

'But Mrs Warriner doesn't have children. She...' Cressida stopped herself from telling Mrs Drysdale that she'd been listening in on the widow's police interview. Cursing herself for approaching the subject so gauchely, she had no choice but to change it. 'Did you work at Warriner Industries too, Mrs Drysdale?'

'No, not I. I was in service at one of those big granite houses outside Inverness, but what with all the death duties and the war and all those young men lost, well, it wasn't the same as it was. And then Mr Drysdale passed away, so I thought, "Margaret, get yourself on the trains like Hughie," and here I am.'

'Condolences for your husband, Mrs Drysdale,' Dotty said, taking her glasses off and cleaning them with her handkerchief.

'Aye, aye, thank you, lassie. Now, did I mention I had something stronger under here? Anyone for a Scotch?'

## 11

With whiskies declined in favour of the martinis to come, Mrs Drysdale had continued her way along the corridor. Cressida and Dotty had barely had time to debrief one another on what the tea lady had told them when another sharp knock on the door startled them.

'Heavens!' Dotty exclaimed, her hand at her chest. 'I wish I wasn't this jumpy.'

'Come in!' Cressida called again and was surprised when this time Dotty had to make way for the burlier figure of DCI Andrews.

'Evening, ladies.' He bowed his head. Cressida thought she saw his eye flicker over to the glass that was lying on her pillow.

'Good evening, Andrews,' she greeted him. 'I would offer you a seat, but we're a bit like sardines in here already, I'm afraid.'

'Very posh sardines,' Dotty said, admiring the chrome and brass fittings around the basin unit upon which she was still perched.

'No need, no need,' Andrews dismissed the offer with a

wave of his hand. 'I just thought you'd like to know that I've arrested Mrs Warriner for the murder of her husband.'

'Oh yes?' Cressida asked, innocently enough, though this time she clocked Andrews giving the glass on her pillow a much more lingering stare. 'And why's that?'

Andrews drew his eyes back from the glass-cum-listening device and, with a resigned look on his face, simply answered, 'You tell me, Miss Fawcett. Let me guess, you heard every word of it?'

Cressida chewed her lip. She hadn't banked on Andrews being quite such an astute detective, or at least not turning his perceptive eye onto her. She was almost sure, though, that Andrews wouldn't be cross with her. It wasn't like she was hiding behind a decorative screen in the actual room that he was interviewing suspects in, like she had done once before. Plus, he himself had been carelessly talking in earshot of the train staff, though she decided to keep that nugget of information to herself. The last thing she needed was him becoming tighter lipped around people she could possibly glean information from.

She arched an eyebrow and replied, 'Well, almost. I got caught talking to the diminutive Lord Hartnell, so I missed the first bit. But I did hear the bit where she showed you something. That was annoying. I could have done with a peephole for that.' Cressida got lost in her thoughts, then looked up again at Andrews. 'So yes, I heard some of it. Sorry.'

DCI Andrews sighed. He was a good man and an excellent policeman, who would usually have no truck with members of the public doing such a thing, but he was inordinately fond of Cressida. It was thanks, in part, to the close friendship he'd formed, despite the difference in their rank and classes, with her father in the Boer War. And even Andrews at times had to grudgingly admit that Cressida was more than just a little help with his investigations. She did seem to notice things...

'Well? What do you think then, miss?' he asked.

Dotty looked at Cressida expectantly too.

'She seems adamant that the gun wasn't hers.'

'Yet Kirby found it in her compartment.'

'Under the mattress, yes.' Cressida looked askance as she recalled overhearing the interview. 'Bit of a silly place to stash it, don't you think? As Alfred remarked at the time when Kirby told us—'

'Kirby told you? I see.' Andrews rolled his eyes.

'He did, yes. Seems you're not the only policeman around here with a soft spot for us amateur detectives.' Cressida thought she heard Dotty stifling a giggle, but carried on, pulling her legs up and crossing them under her. Ruby climbed into her lap. 'And a good thing it was too, as it got us all thinking. Why *wouldn't* the murderer have just lobbed the gun out of a window? There are so many streams and fields we're swooshing past, it would have been near impossible to find. And if it was Mrs Warriner, and she didn't think to throw it out of the window, why stash it in her own compartment?'

'Necessity? Speed? We heard the gun go off, then there was only a short spell before Miss de Souza entered the compartment she was due to share with Mr Warriner and screamed.'

'I noticed that Mrs Warriner was wearing black evening gloves,' Dotty added, rather excitedly, then brought herself up short as she saw Cressida grinning at her. Crossing her arms, she added, 'I'm not investigating, Cressy. Just telling DCI Andrews here what I saw.'

'Thank you, Lady Dorothy, that's well noted.' Andrews took his notebook out from the inside pocket of his tweed jacket, flicked over a page and wrote it down.

'And did Mrs Warriner have an alibi? I missed that bit, unfortunately,' Cressida asked as soon as he was finished.

'She had no alibi. She claimed she was walking off her upset up and down the corridor, hoping to find a lounge car of some sort. A stiff drink as far away from her husband and his mistress as possible. But, of course, the lounge car is the other side of the dining car, and it's only sleeping compartments and a luggage car down train from here.'

Dotty nodded knowingly at this now.

'And no one saw her?' Cressida asked, gently pulling at Ruby's ears, much to the small dog's evident satisfaction.

'No.' Andrews flicked back a page or two of his notebook. 'She said she passed no one. Hard not to notice when you do in that corridor out there. I believe most passengers were in the dining car, and she said she didn't make it very far along the corridor before she heard the shot and scream. We then saw her in the corridor soon after we found her husband. Miss de Souza, who had screamed in alarm, said she'd seen Mrs Warriner in the corridor just after the shot had been fired.'

'Ah. So she was the witness,' Cressida said thoughtfully. Then, after a pause, she carried on. 'But Mrs Warriner might have been in the corridor for the reason she told you, not necessarily because she'd just killed her husband and was hot-footing it away. Also, you know what else that tells us?'

Andrews sighed again. But it was Dotty, who had been concentrating hard and suddenly looked as if a bulb in her brain had lit up.

'Oh, I know. Mrs Warriner may not have an alibi, but she also said she *wasn't* in her compartment.'

'Exactly.' Cressida gave her friend a little clap. 'Andrews, this means that not only was she not in her compartment stashing the weapon away under her mattress—'

'But,' Andrews continued Cressida's train of thought, 'someone else could have stashed the gun there before we saw her in the corridor.'

Cressida nodded. 'There you go, Andrews. She might not be your murderer after all.'

## 12

'Let's keep an open mind, shall we?' DCI Andrews looked back at Cressida and over to Dotty. 'For now, all I can go on, the only concrete proof we have, is that a gun was found under the accused's mattress, she had a motive, a means, an opportunity...'

'I understand, Andrews. But as you say, let's keep these minds of ours as open as the bar at the Savoy at nine o'clock on a Saturday night.' Cressida uncrossed her legs and thought it safe now to place her glass back on the bedside unit.

'Woolly?' Dotty asked, looking at the glass, and Cressida nodded.

Andrews looked perplexed.

'Minty O'Hare, school lacrosse captain and inventor of the glass-to-the-wall earpiece for spying on a snoring Matron. Mohair, you see, from M. O'Hare. Hence Woolly,' Cressida explained, and Andrews shook his head in disbelief. 'But enough of her and her inventive ways. Andrews, tell me what was it that Mrs Warriner showed you? She seemed to think it put her in the clear.'

'It was a letter. Here.' Andrews reached into his jacket pocket and, using a handkerchief, pulled out an envelope. He handed it to Cressida, who took it, handkerchief and all, and held it out in front of her. Andrews cautioned her. 'Do keep that handkerchief around it, Miss Fawcett. Kirby will dust it for prints, and it might show us something that could keep Mrs Warriner from the noose. Adding any of our fingerprints to it now could harm her case. If she is innocent, of course.'

Cressida saw Dotty raise her hand to her throat. Andrews' mention of the hangman's noose had made her feel uneasy too. And even more determined to keep her fingerprints off the letter.

'I can do better than that, Andrews,' she said, carefully laying the letter and its protective hanky on her bed. 'Dot, be a chum and pass me my valise, will you?'

'This one?' Dotty reached up to the luggage rack and at Cressida's insistence pulled down a smart brown leather bag.

Cressida took the bag from Dotty and had a good rummage. 'Mama shudders at the thought of me travelling without a lady's maid, so, as a compromise, I agree to wear – aha, these, when I dress.' Cressida pulled out a pair of clean, white cotton gloves.

'Oh, hosiery gloves. Of course,' Dotty said, understanding completely, while Andrews not only blushed but looked darned perplexed, once again, by it all too.

'Hosiery gloves?'

'Yes, simply marvellous things for not laddering one's stockings,' Cressida said, pulling on the soft, white gloves. 'And also excellent for handling a delicate letter without getting my grubby fingerprints on it.'

Cressida pulled the letter out of the envelope, pausing first to look at the address on the front and the postmark pressed into the stamp, then read it out loud.

*Dear Mrs Warriner,*

*Book passage on the Scotland Express to Euston tomorrow evening. This is the same train that your husband, Lewis Warriner, will be on. Disguise yourself and make no fuss as you board and you will discover something to your advantage.*

*Yours in most sincerity,*

*A friend*

'How sinister.' Dotty shivered when Cressida had finished.

'Yes. Though only perhaps as we know what happened.' Cressida read the letter to herself again and turned it over to look at the back of it. '*Make no fuss as you board.* What a strange thing to say. Not to mention the rest of it. I wonder why Mrs Warriner took it so seriously?'

'I suppose everyone likes to find out something to their advantage, don't they?' Andrews suggested. 'I couldn't see much relevance to the postmark or the address.'

'Inverness. Meaning it was sent locally,' Cressida noted. 'Otherwise, all typed by what looks like a fairly standard typewriter, not that I'm an expert in such things.'

'And have you noticed something else?' Andrews asked, looking pleased with himself.

Cressida held the letter up again. 'Yes, that smear. What is it?' She placed the letter down and let Andrews pick up his handkerchief and then take back the note.

'Some sort of grease, I thought. Oil or lubricant perhaps.'

'Looks like someone else around here has an eye for details,' Dotty said conspiratorially. She knew better than to wink at Cressida, something her friend abhorred as winking usually occurred after midnight and by someone with lascivious intentions, so she wriggled her eyebrows instead. This made her spectacles slide down the bridge of her nose, so she pushed them back up as Andrews huffed out a sort of laugh.

'Well, I'm not saying I have Miss Fawcett's eye for all these little things, but even I couldn't miss that,' he acknowledged.

'Shame there's no obvious fingerprint on it,' Cressida remarked, handing back the envelope too, and then taking her hosiery gloves off. 'Still, that's a very interesting letter and it does chime with what Mrs W was saying. If I heard correctly, of course, she says she had no knowledge of her husband being accompanied on board. She knew he'd be on the train—'

'As did the author of that letter,' added Dotty.

'Yes, as did they. But we don't know that the letter writer knew that Mr Warriner would be with his... well, his close friend, Miss de Souza.'

'I would say that's a reasonable assumption, though,' Andrews insisted. 'Something to your advantage? Disguise yourself? If this letter isn't just some ruse dreamt up by Mrs Warriner herself as a sort of alibi, then it's possible the writer intended for her to come across her husband in that way, confront him and then...' Andrews paused.

'Exactly. Then what? Could someone really have expected her to kill him? It's quite a leap, isn't it?'

'Maybe the letter writer thought if Mrs Warriner caught Mr Warriner *in flagrante*, as it were, she might do rather well financially out of a divorce? Hence the "to your advantage" bit,' Dotty suggested.

'She insisted she loved her husband. I don't think her mind was on divorce.' Andrews squinted in thought.

'Then she definitely didn't plan on murdering him. Oh, I don't know, perhaps we're overthinking it,' Cressida said as Andrews slipped the piece of evidence back into his jacket pocket. 'Maybe all it intended was to have her in situ. Tantalising enough to lure her on board so that when Mr Warriner was murdered, she, the betrayed wife, would be the prime suspect. QED, she's not your murderer.'

DCI Andrews exhaled a long breath. 'Miss Fawcett, I am

trying to keep an open mind, but you really can't jump to conclusions like that.'

Cressida raised an eyebrow at him. 'All right then, Andrews, how about this for a plan. There's two scenarios here. Either Mrs Warriner did do it, and that's fine as you have her locked up, or she didn't, and we still have the real murderer on board. Dotty, the train won't stop will it, not for a while?'

'No, we're direct to Edinburgh now, I believe. If I've read my *Bradshaw's* correctly.'

'Good. Andrews, can I implore you to contact the police at Edinburgh? I don't know how, Kirby might have to hurl a bag with the message in it out of the window at Pitlochry for the telegraph man to wire. But ask them to guard the platform. They mustn't let anyone off the train. Not Mrs Warriner, not anyone. Not even the body of Mr Warriner. That way, the murderer will think that the train is on lockdown until London, with Mrs Warriner on board until she can be taken to Scotland Yard and charged. Who knows, if the real murderer isn't Mrs W, he or she might let their guard down.'

Cressida glanced up at Dotty, who merely rolled her eyes.

'We can use the time from now until we pull into Euston to find out everything we can about what happened, even if it's just proving you right, Andrews.' Cressida puffed out her cheeks as she checked her smart sapphire-jewelled wristwatch, then continued. 'Cripes, less than twelve hours. If this note is just a ruse by Mrs Warriner to throw us off the scent, then we've lost nothing. She's still in custody at the end of the line. This way, though, the other suspects are none the wiser, and we can confirm who killed Mr Warriner. And who among us all now, on this train, is a murderer.'

## 13

DCI Andrews had begrudgingly agreed with Cressida that the plan was a sound one and he left in order to work out how to send the request down the line to Edinburgh.

Dotty was less pleased with the plan – and the thought that a murderer was still on the loose – and left to go and fill in Alfred. Cressida could detect a slight flounce to her exit, and it made her smile to herself. Dotty was always insistent that she shouldn't get herself into trouble, but it had been Dotty herself who had helped her so much recently as she'd run her own little investigations alongside the official ones of DCI Andrews.

'She'll come round, Rubes. She always does.' Cressida, now with her room to herself, was able to stretch out her legs. But, finding that she did feel much invigorated by the investigation, she decided a lie-down was no longer needed, not even a pretend one. So, she stood up, straightened her silk blouse and made sure it was neatly tucked into her wide-legged woollen trousers. She slipped her smart cashmere cardigan over her shoulders like a cape and spritzed on some cologne. Smacking her lips together to even out a quick reapplication of fashionably red lipstick, she felt shipshape again and ready to leave her compartment. Looking round to see Ruby fast asleep on the bed, she decided that might be the best place for her, so blew her a kiss and left the small bedroom, closing the door behind her.

Although her intention had been to go and join Dotty and Alfred, Cressida was distracted by the sound of sobbing. It was nearby and as Cressida edged closer to the door of the compartment next to hers – Mrs Warriner's sleeper, no less – the sobs grew in intensity.

Cautiously, Cressida knocked on the door. The crying stopped. Cressida looked down. Andrews had left the key in the lock, so Cressida carefully turned it and then tried the handle.

'Mrs Warriner?' She peered around the door and looked in. The compartment was a mirror image of her own, with a small dressing area next to the comfortable single bed.

Mrs Warriner, still dressed in black, was sitting on the bed, her hands on her lap. She raised her head up to look at Cressida. It was clear she'd been crying for a while and Cressida praised the efficacy of Minty O'Hare's Glass Receiver, as she'd taken to thinking of it, for really helping to overhear the conversation in here earlier. She hadn't heard *these* sobs at all from her compartment without it.

'Yes?' the weeping woman asked, and Cressida realised that, of course, poor Mrs Warriner would have no reason to know who she was, despite Cressida now knowing so much about her.

'Mrs Warriner, I'm Cressida Fawcett. Hon. Your neighbour here on the train. I heard you crying and, of course, I've heard about the death of your husband.'

'It wasn't me. I didn't shoot him,' Mrs Warriner blurted out.

'I believe you,' Cressida said, entering the compartment and closing the door behind her with a crisp click. She hoped no one would come by and check the lock while she was inside. 'I couldn't help but overhear that policeman chap say something about a letter that lured you on board.'

Mrs Warriner was too exhausted to question *how* Cressida had overheard this and spoke freely about it. 'Yes. Yes, that's right. He has it as evidence now. Proof that I didn't come on board this train to kill Lewis. And to think, I was going to throw it away with the eggshells at the breakfast table. But, you see, I was intrigued.'

'Did you really think there would be something to your advantage on board?'

Mrs Warriner shrugged. 'No, not really, but I knew there was something the matter with Lewis.' She started weeping again and Cressida went over to her and sat down next to her on the narrow but beautifully turned-down bed.

'My condolences,' Cressida said, wishing Ruby wasn't snoring to herself the other side of the wall. She was always a useful tool for consoling people.

'You're the first person to offer them. Thank you. I suppose that's what happens when everyone thinks you killed your husband. They don't think you deserve sympathy.'

'I don't think you killed him, for what it's worth. I think you've been set up. But I think this compartment and you being in here is possibly the safest place for you while we try to work out what's going on.'

'The policeman thinks I did it,' Mrs Warriner sniffed.

Cressida was about to assure her that she was on the case too, but she remembered one of the tenets of her own plan. Secrecy was of the essence.

Mrs Warriner continued talking, wiping a tear from her eye and blowing her nose as she went. 'Just my luck. To be on board the same train that Lewis has been murdered on... and for a Scotland Yard detective to be on board at the same time.'

*This is what I suggested to Andrews just now,* Cressida thought to herself as she gently rubbed the weeping widow's back. *That letter must have been a cunning ruse to get Mrs W on board as a scapegoat.*

'We shall have to do what we can to persuade DCI Andrews that you didn't do it,' Cressida said, hoping it sounded soothing and reassuring.

'I hoped that letter would. Oh, Miss Fawcett, I knew something was up. I hoped it was Lewis planning a surprise for me, that was my truest wish. Fifteen years we've been together. I thought it might be an anniversary surprise. After the upsets we've been through...'

'Upsets?' Cressida asked softly.

Mrs Warriner wiped her eyes. 'Aye.'

Cressida waited for more of an explanation, but none seemed to come. Despite her curiosity, she had enough sense to realise that the poor woman, who had just lost her husband and been arrested for his murder, might not be in the mood to be pressed on the matter, so she asked again about the note she'd received instead. 'You thought he'd sent the letter?'

'Yes. But then he had been so distant recently.'

'Distant? You mean his mind was elsewhere?'

'And his eyes and his... Well, I started to think he might have tired of me.'

Cressida looked at Mrs Warriner. Not counting the smudged make-up around her eyes and her red nose from crying, she was a very beautiful woman, with long, auburn hair and pretty hazel eyes. She couldn't have been more than forty at most, perhaps twenty years Lewis Warriner's junior, still with youth on her side and a lovely figure to boot. Not to mention all the smartest clothes that her husband's wealth and charge accounts could afford her.

'Why would he tire of you?' Cressida hoped it wasn't impertinent, but if a man 'went off' someone as beautiful as Mrs Warriner, then there was no hope for any of them.

'I think I'm a disappointment to him, and he's done it before. Divorce and cheating, I mean. I'm not his first wife, you see,' Mrs Warriner sniffed.

'Oh, I see,' Cressida said. Something tugged at her memory, but her train of thought was interrupted as the sobbing woman continued.

'I suppose, though, that I'm his first widow.' Mrs Warriner started crying again.

Cressida slipped her arm around her shoulders. 'There, there, Mrs Warriner.'

'Please, call me Geraldine. I hate all this Mrs this and Lady that,' Geraldine said, and Cressida could detect not just the formality of titles easing between them, but something about Geraldine's voice changing too. A stronger Scottish accent was emerging through the received pronunciation. 'Lewis wanted a knighthood, you know? Wanted to be Sir Lewis Warriner. Believed if he donated to the right political party and created enough jobs, it would be in the bag. And me, Lady Warriner. Could you imagine it?'

Cressida smiled at her. As a member of the aristocracy herself, and best friends with a Lady, she knew all about the lure of titles. 'You weren't at all tickled by that, then?'

'Lady Warriner? What would that get me that our money didn't already? No, I just loved Lewis for his mind, his gumption, his ambition. When I used to see him walk into the boardroom and take control, my knees would give way, I tell you.' She hiccupped a laugh. 'He was lord and master of Warriner Industries and that was enough for me. Enough for anyone surely?' She looked up at Cressida, her eyes full of unanswered questions.

'You spoke of board meetings. Is that how you met, at Warriner Industries?' Cressida knew this was the case; she'd overheard it through the wall, but she needed Geraldine to tell her all about it.

'Yes. I was his secretary.' Geraldine gripped the handkerchief in her lap. 'And I know what that sounds like. Little work strumpet that drew him away from his wife. But he loved me.

And I loved him. I dropped everything for him.' She buried her head in her handkerchief. Cressida looked at her and saw the monogram on the corner of the large linen square: LCW.

'I believe you, Geraldine, I really do. And I don't think you killed him. But if you're being set up, then who would do this to him? To you?'

Geraldine sniffed and looked up at Cressida. Tears still stained her cheeks, and her eyes were red from crying. *I've been fooled by a weeping widow before, though*, Cressida thought, subconsciously touching the back of her head and feeling the bump.

'Lewis had his detractors, of course. He was a man of business and not necessarily one of scruples. That woman he was with, don't you recognise her?'

Cressida shook her head. 'No, but someone else on the train did. He was a definite fan.'

Geraldine tutted. 'I'm not surprised. Calls herself a film star, but she's barely been in front of the camera. She's a singer, a showgirl. She's on the stage at the Firebird Club in Glasgow every weekend. Dances till all her clothes drop off, if you know what I mean. I've seen the playbills stuffed into the pockets of Lewis's suits. And you don't get from *that* to being in films, however bad they are, without some powerful friends.'

'Like your husband?'

'Yes. Though I don't think he was her only benefactor. I mean, the mob.'

'The mob?' Cressida asked, a note of incredulity in her voice. Of course, she'd noticed the glamorous clothes and American-style suit that Warriner and Miss de Souza had been wearing and had compared them herself to the mobsters she'd seen in the newspapers. Even young Lord Hartnell had mentioned something, though heavens knows how he would have known the real story about Lewis Warriner. Could Lewis Warriner really be in cahoots with Glasgow gangsters?

Geraldine blew her nose and then explained some more. 'Oh, I'm sure they're not so bad as all those gangs in Chicago, but yes. There's a Glasgow underworld and Lewis was dabbling. I thought it was a midlife crisis, a wealthy man like him suddenly changing the way he dressed and how he acted. You couldn't have got him out of his three-piece tweed suit when he was rubbing shoulders with the landed gentry at home in Inverness, but nowadays it was all pinstripes and fedoras.' Geraldine dabbed her handkerchief to her eyes and wiped her nose again. 'But I suppose it was because he wanted to fit in with that scene. Impress girls like that Miss de Souza, with her bleached hair and big—'

'Prospects. I see.' Cressida patted her on the shoulder. 'A real change of character for him, then?'

Geraldine looked up at her. 'Yes. But then, also no. He was an ambitious man, like I said, powerful and go-getting, which was part of his attraction, but that meant he was a chameleon of sorts. Acting like a Glasgow gangster wasn't like him, but embracing something new was. When he met me, he rid himself of everything to do with his first wife. Almost everything, anyway.'

'But what drew him to Glasgow in the first place?' Cressida asked.

Geraldine sighed. 'Business, I suppose. I did hear something about a new motor dealership opening up that he wanted a slice of. A way to expand Warriner Industries from just automotive parts to the actual cars themselves. Then, like I said, I started to find those playbills from the Firebird Club. Though I'm not proud of myself, I did go through his pockets once or twice after he'd got home from trips to Glasgow and found receipts for dinners and hotel bills. That's why I think he was tiring of me... I used to be the new thing. He divorced Myra, his first wife, when he decided he wanted me.'

'Had you been having an affair for long, before he divorced her?'

'Oh, no. Not an affair. Not as such. You see, I was involved with someone else at the time. Lewis and I had a kiss and a cuddle, but I never let him... not like that tart on this train with their shared compartment. I never allowed him that, not until I was Mrs Warriner.'

'Like Anne Boleyn,' Cressida mused, remembering the tragic story of Henry VIII's second wife.

Geraldine looked at her, tears still brimming in her eyes. 'Yes,' she whispered. 'Though I hope I won't lose my head once we get to London.'

## 14

With a heartfelt apology for both the death of her husband, and for mentioning one of England's most tragic queens, Cressida left Geraldine, closing the door to the compartment behind her. She relocked the door with the key Andrews had conveniently left in the lock. She took the few steps back to her own compartment and carefully opened the door, only to be met by the dark globe-like eyes and frog-like expression of her favourite little pup.

'I had a feeling your nap might not last long, Rubes. Come on then, let's find Dotty and Alf. It's eightish, so definitely drinkies time. I should imagine there might be a cheesy biscuit or two I could snaffle for you.'

With a happy snort, Ruby toddled out of the compartment and followed Cressida along the narrow, wood-lined corridor that ran alongside the sleeping compartments. Cressida paused and ran a finger over it appreciatively. The workmanship of the fine veneer was really very good indeed. They passed Dotty and Alfred's compartments, marked by neatly written cards in the brass plates of the doors. The doors all looked so alike, each one hiding a compartment the mirror image of its pair. It got Cressida thinking.

'What if Mr Warriner wasn't the intended victim at all? And the murderer got confused and shot the wrong person?'

Ruby grunted and as Cressida looked down at her, she sat herself down and then rolled onto one side, sticking one of her hind legs up as she studied her hairy tummy.

'Looks like you disagree? You're right of course, Rubes. Those name plates are really quite a sensible size and hard to mis-read.'

Cressida bent down and scooped up her pup. She rocked side to side as the train clattered over a crossing, and navigated the doorway between the two *wagons-lits*. A shiver passed across her spine as she walked past the door to Warriner's sleeping compartment and noted that both his and Miss de Souza's names were slipped into the name-card holders on the door. Cressida held her breath as a thought occurred to her. *No one would see me if I just for a moment or two snuck inside...*

Her hand was on the handle of the door when the sound of a sharp *click-clunk* slightly further along the carriage caught her attention. She pulled back from the dead man's door and looked about her. There was no one there. Then she heard what sounded like voices.

'Mr Warriner, RIP, will have to wait, Rubes. I can't not go and see what's going on down the corridor,' Cressida whispered to her pug as she edged her way as quietly as possible down the carriage.

It was when she was outside the very last compartment in the carriage, the one closest to the dining car, that she once again heard voices. Without a trusty glass to press against the door, it was hard to determine who was talking, but raised voices there definitely were, and it sounded like a man and a woman.

After a quick glance each way up the corridor, Cressida leaned in as close as she could to the door of the compartment.

'I thought you were just going to rough him up a bit?' the female voice said.

'I didn't even touch him!' the male voice counteracted.

'You didn't need to, the bullet did the job for you.'

'You know that's not what I meant.'

'What should we do now?' The woman's voice sounded scared, the angry tone gone.

'Nothing. Play dumb. It's all we can do. I'll work on Plan B. Someone else in the company might think differently. The new owner, whoever that will be.'

'And if that doesn't work?'

The voices became more muffled, and Cressida pulled back from the door. Much to her frustration, there was no handy name card in the holder. *That would have been too easy*, she thought to herself as she once again pressed her ear to the door of the supposedly unoccupied compartment. The voices were clearer again.

'Well, he's dead now. And his wife's copping for it.'

'Not a bad thing. She's partly to blame for all this. I'm sure we can use that to our advantage.'

'I hope so. I hope so indeed.'

Cressida heard footsteps from within, so quickly peeled her ear away. What had she just heard? A confession? No... not quite. But something close to one; whoever was speaking in that cabin had intended Warriner harm. And the woman had believed the man to be capable of murder.

Cressida was so absorbed in her deductions, she wasn't braced for the jerk as the train clattered over an uneven connection. She gasped as she knocked hard against the glass window and then jumped as a loud toot sounded from the steam engine. Unsteady on her feet, she wobbled as the train took a curve in the tracks and then she fell backwards, desperately trying to keep Ruby safe in her arms. All at once, darkness overwhelmed the carriage as the train entered a tunnel.

Cressida grasped Ruby tight with one hand, and with the other reached out desperately for something to hold onto. *Anything will do – a door handle, a curtain, a window frame*, she thought to herself as she groped around in the pitch black. Her fingers closed around what felt like thick paper, then it was ripped from her grasp. Clasping once again, she then found something cloth-like to hold. This was no lined silk curtain, though, it was thin and cotton. And, most importantly, it had the warm solidity of flesh behind it.

Cressida's blood ran cold as she realised that in the dark of the tunnel she had reached out and grabbed an unknown person in the corridor.

A person who could possibly be the murderer she was looking for.

## 15

Cressida pulled back her hand and moments later daylight flooded the corridor again. She blinked, acclimatising to the light, and got her bearings.

She was still outside the unnamed compartment in which she'd overheard the two voices discussing Warriner's death. But in front of her there was only one man, Owen Edwards, the fan of Miss de Souza, who was scrabbling around on the floor, picking up newspaper cuttings and articles that were strewn out of a manilla folder and across the narrow corridor's wooden floor.

'Oh, I'm so sorry.' Cressida stepped back as Owen swore under his breath.

'Damn it.' He hurriedly tried to shove as many of the pieces of newspaper back into the folder as possible.

'Let me help.' Cressida knelt down next to him, hoping the scowl on his face had more to do with the confusion of the situation rather than the fact that she had obviously, if unwittingly, just dashed this same folder from his hands. Cressida, not helped by Ruby being in her arms, tried to slide a few pieces towards him.

Her eye was drawn to the name Warriner as it appeared in various sub-headlines and within the text, plus she recognised the ruddy-cheeked face of Mr Warriner in one photograph printed alongside some column inches. A woman she didn't recognise appeared in one article, though Owen was picking up all the clippings so quickly, she barely had time to glance at any of the articles for more than a brief moment.

A typed letter was revealed as he swept newspaper articles over it and into the folder and once more Owen cursed as he grabbed it. Cressida noticed the name of one of Scotland's most notable newspapers on the letterhead as he filed it away.

Acting on pure instinct, and questionable morals, Cressida subtly flicked one of the stranded clippings towards her rather than Mr Edwards, and while he was occupied pushing as many of the articles back into the file as he could, she pulled it quickly under Ruby's tummy and hid it there.

'There. Have you got everything?' Cressida asked, straightening up and soothing a gruntling Ruby.

'I think so, miss, thank you.' Owen's disposition had changed and he seemed much more like the wide-eyed fan who had been so astonished and delighted to meet Miss de Souza earlier. The scowl, at least, was gone.

'My fault, I'm afraid. That tunnel rather threw me, and, of course, I couldn't let this precious load go.' Cressida tilted her head down to indicate Ruby, who snorted in appreciation.

'Oh no, miss. Could have happened to anyone. I shouldn't have been going so quick down the corridor, like. My mother, God rest her soul, used to tell me off for running down corridors. "Son," she'd say, "you'll cause someone an injury running like that!"'

Cressida smiled at him, thinking perhaps that the excitement of meeting Miss de Souza was still making him somewhat of a chatterbox. Then she remembered what Geraldine Warriner had just said about the showgirl and dancer, and her influential friends. *Could this young chap know anything about the seedy Glasgow underworld?*

'Jolly good luck to meet Miss de Souza on this train, wasn't it? I assume you're a bit of a fan of hers?'

Owen gulped in his excitement to speak about the pretty film star. 'Wasn't it.' He patted his pocket, which must have contained the autograph book. 'What a stroke of luck.'

'How did you first come across Miss de Souza?' Cressida asked, wondering if he was a denizen of the Glasgow nightclubs himself.

A frown glanced across Owen's face before he beamed at Cressida. 'Silver screen last May. Wow, what a performance she put in as Boudicca.'

'Oh yes, that film about ancient Britons. I saw that. Was that her? Hard to recognise her out of a beaver skin.' Cressida kept looking at Owen. 'Have you seen her dance live before? In Glasgow perhaps?'

'I... I, well, yes I have. And boy, was it a humdinger of a show.' He laughed nervously. 'Quite eye-opening, if you catch my drift, miss.'

'Yes, so I've heard. Quite a few characters in and around those places.' She lowered her voice to a conspiratorial whisper. 'I hear Mr Warriner was a frequent visitor.'

'I wouldn't know, miss, I wasn't aware of him.'

Cressida looked meaningfully at the folder of newspaper clippings.

'Oh this?' Owen looked at the file as if seeing it for the first time. 'It's not mine actually. I found it on the table in the dining car and thought one of the ladies might have left it behind.'

'Whose is it?' Cressida asked.

Owen looked flummoxed. 'Err, I don't know, but someone who was interested in that gentleman, I suppose.'

'A lady though? Why would you think it's a lady's?' Cressida could sense something not quite adding up about Owen's story.

'That wife of his, the one they've arrested. I thought it might be hers, to be honest, as it looks like maybe someone keeping tabs on her husband. And blam! Haha. There you go! Cheating husband dealt with.' He nodded towards the folder. 'Jealous of the lovely Miss de Souza, don't you think?'

'I don't know, Mr Edwards.'

Cressida and Owen looked at each other, the silence now growing more awkward. He moved to one side, just as Cressida did the same, blocking each other's way. This happened again and then Cressida spoke, pressing herself against the windows of the corridor.

'Best get that folder to DCI Andrews or Sergeant Kirby, don't you think? If it is Mrs Warriner's, it will need finger-printing and whatnot.' Cressida looked at the folder and Owen nodded.

'Yes, miss. Next mission.' He saluted and finally squeezed past her.

Cressida watched as Owen walked down the corridor, his loping gait helping him stay balanced with the rhythm of the train. Once he was out of sight, she retrieved the snaffled piece of newspaper clipping that she'd been concealing under Ruby. As she flattened it out, she wondered: could someone so in awe of Miss de Souza have a vendetta against the man she was having an affair with? Owen Edwards was quick to suggest that Geraldine had been betrayed by her husband, and maybe, when she found out he was having an affair, she did feel that way. But Owen had been a fan of Miss de Souza's since May... his jeal-ousy had been simmering for a whole lot longer. The train let out a blast of steam as the thought occurred to her. Had his jeal-ousy finally reached boiling point?

Cressida shook her head and looked down at the cutting. It was just a few inches taken from a side column of what looked like a daily newspaper. There was no indication as to which one, but the font and spacing didn't look like the broadsheets that she tended to read. Cressida assumed it was a local Scottish newspaper, and then read the headline and story:

### De Marco's Cars – To Be Trusted?

*Glasgow resident and long-term nightclub owner Alessandro 'Al' De Marco plans to open five new car showrooms in the Glasgow metropolitan area. De Marco is known to Glasgow residents as the co-owner of the renowned Firebird Club, a night spot with the dubious honour of holding the record for raids by the Glasgow police force.*

*Local resident, and neighbour to one of the proposed new showrooms, Enid MacArthur told us, 'No good can come of a man like that operating in the neighbourhood. He's a wrong'un.'*

*Sources tell us that De Marco will be operating a garage and mechanics service as well as selling cars, with rumours that wealthy Inverness industrialist Lewis Warriner is backing De Marco's venture and lending his credence to it. The council will convene on Monday 3 August regarding the planning applications.*

Cressida folded the newspaper column back up and slipped it into her pocket. It seemed Lewis Warriner was definitely getting himself involved with the Glasgow mob. But why? He had enough money, surely, without turning to risky investments with dodgy second-hand car dealers?

Cressida bit the inside of her lip as she carried Ruby towards the dining car. Miss de Souza... Was she the mob's bait, to hook Mr Warriner into making such a risky investment? And could he have paid for it with his life?

## 16

Cressida's thoughts were buzzing as she entered the dining car.

The carriage was separated into three distinct sections: the bar area, the dining space itself and a service and preparation area. The bar, at the end closest to the sleeping cars, drew Cressida's eye for more than one reason.

Designed to be one of the first of the communal areas one would see upon boarding, it had the same luxurious feel as the rest of the train. The deep mahogany bar and shelves were fitted with brass railings along their edges so bottles and glasses didn't go flying on rougher parts of the track. Etched mirror glass decorated the back and it had almost any liqueur and spirit one could want. Complete with several velvet-upholstered bar stools, it was, for all intents and purposes, like a miniature, mobile version of some of Cressida's favourite London bars.

It had obviously attracted someone else too. The tall, beak-nosed man in a plain tweed jacket was sitting on one of the stools, nursing a tumbler of what looked like whisky. He was staring down into his liquor and Cressida recognised him as being the one and only 'entourage' of Mr Warriner and Miss de Souza. She'd seen him board the train behind them and remembered thinking at the time that he looked nothing like a gangster, unlike the other two. But he was definitely part of their booking and that in itself made him interesting to her.

A barman in a smart white, cropped jacket walked past her and, seeing her looking at the man at the bar, mistook that for her own desire for a drink. 'Can I help you, miss? Something for the motion of the train?' he asked, a crisp white tea towel folded over his arm. He wasn't entirely mistaken.

'Yes, why not. Thank you. A gin rickey, if you can. I've had more whisky these last few days than I think I've had over the course of my entire life,' Cressida chatted away as she placed Ruby on one of the window-facing armchairs and then innocently parked her derriere on a bar stool. 'And I've been to several Caledonian balls and have an uncle with a distillery!'

The barman smiled at Cressida and mixed her cocktail for her.

She hadn't meant to stop and talk to the hunched-over man yet, but the barman had given her a wonderful opportunity. And while trains weren't the natural home for horses, she certainly wasn't going to look this gift one in the mouth. Surely even Dotty or DCI Andrews couldn't misconstrue this as investigating?

Although, if they did, they wouldn't be wrong. But Cressida lived by her family motto, which ran along the lines of fortune favouring the brave, though she knew her great-grandfather had added something slightly disparaging against the French in there after the Battle of Waterloo. In any case, she spun around on her stool to face him.

'What ho. Terrible business this, isn't it. Ghastly situation for everyone, I should imagine.'

The beak-nosed man looked up from his tumbler of liquor and sighed.

'I'm Cressida Fawcett by the way.' Cressida stuck her hand out to the beleaguered-looking man.

He took her hand and shook it. 'Clarence Derby.'

'Mr Derby,' Cressida repeated the name, cementing it into her memory. 'Oh, and that's Ruby, my pernicious if precious houndlette. Do ignore her. Although I fear the arm of that chair is finding it harder to do so.'

Clarence Derby smiled, which had been Cressida's intention. It was so much easier to quiz someone once the ice had been broken, she always thought. And speaking of broken ice, the barman passed her cocktail over and she took a sip.

'Delicious, thank you. So, Mr Derby, forgive me for asking, but I assume you knew Mr Warriner? I believe I saw you board the train together.'

'Yes. I'm his... well, I *was*, his private secretary.' Derby took a sip of his whisky, then went back to slowly turning the glass tumbler between his hands.

'Much like Mrs Warriner, before she married him?' Cressida asked, innocently enough. This made Mr Derby frown, however.

'No, not the same thing at all. She was a typist, that's all. I handle, and have done for years, all of his personal administration.'

'I see. I'm sorry. And what a hellish thing to have happened to him. You'll be up to your eyes in paperwork now, I should imagine.'

Derby nodded. 'His affairs will take some untangling, of that I can be certain.'

'Affairs, multiple?' Cressida picked her glass up, then put it down again. 'Gosh, poor Mrs Warriner.'

'I meant business affairs, Miss Fawcett.' He shot her a look, then laughed in a hollow sort of way. 'But you're not wrong. There were affairs aplenty too. The current Mrs Warriner being one of them.'

Cressida knew this, of course. Mrs Warriner had admitted to it. But Cressida couldn't let on that she'd been chatting to the prime suspect, locked in her compartment. So she merely opened her eyes wide as she sipped, hoping this would encourage Mr Derby to elucidate.

'Now she's implicated, of course,' he did continue, still staring into his glass, 'it makes tying up his business dealings all that harder.'

'Why's that?'

'Well, from what I remember of his Will and the company shares, she's his main heir. She stands to inherit the greatest proportion of his wealth, his shares in Warriner Industries, his personal art collection, the cars, the furs, the diamonds...' Derby waved a hand in the air, the limit of Warriner's wealth seemingly endless. Then he brought his hand back to the bar, back to his drink, and he looked Cressida squarely in the eye. 'But if she's convicted of his murder, she can't inherit a thing.'

'Because the law says so? Is that a legal thing?' Cressida asked, and was surprised when Mr Derby laughed at her, in that hollow way again.

'No. Well, yes, there are laws precluding the person who murders you benefitting from your death, but she'd be unable to enjoy any of the trappings of his wealth for the simpler reason that she'd no doubt be sentenced to hang if she's convicted.'

As Dotty had done earlier, Cressida instinctively brought her hand up to her throat and shuddered. This brought it all much more into focus for her, and taking a bigger slug of her gin, realised that if she, or Andrews, couldn't prove that Mrs Warriner hadn't killed her husband, the consequences would be fatal.

'Mr Derby, do you think she did it? Do you really?'

He shrugged, though he took a moment to think. 'No, I don't believe she would. I don't know what she'd stand to gain from it. That's where you look, isn't it? Who stands to gain. *Cherchez l'argent* and all that.'

'Follow the money. Yes, I believe so. And you think she was better off with him alive?'

'Unless he divorced her. Just for someone younger,' Derby said, twisting his tumbler again, slowly, between his forefingers.

'Miss de Souza.' Cressida bit the inside of her lip. 'Do you think he was going to?'

Derby shrugged his shoulders again. 'He has form, as they say in the racing world. I hadn't seen any paperwork, but Mr Warriner was a capricious soul. He divorced his first wife, Myra, when he fell for Geraldine. From what I hear, she never got over it. I don't think Warriner ever realised quite what he'd done to them.'

'Them?' Cressida asked, then a jolt rattled through the carriages and almost knocked them off their stools. It seemed to rouse Derby from his contemplative state and he got up.

'I think your dog wants you,' he said, pointing to where Ruby was now standing on one of the banquette seats, whining out the window, then occasionally turning round and panting at them.

'No doubt spotting squirrels in the pine trees. The sad thing is, even if we weren't travelling so fast, or indeed if she wasn't trapped behind that glass window, she still wouldn't have a snowball's chance in the Sahara of catching one of them.'

Clarence Derby smiled at Cressida again, then paid the barman and lurched away from the bar. He hadn't answered her last question – who was he referring to as 'them'?

Although that question was left frustratingly murky, something else was becoming abundantly clear to her. Lewis Warriner had been a powerful man, with potentially dangerous new friends and a personality that lent itself to hurting people in his ambitious wake.

Perhaps it was another of those people, not his betrayed wife, who had shot him in cold blood?

## 17

'What ho, Cress.' Alfred's voice interrupted Cressida's thoughts and she looked up at him. 'I see you've started – or maybe continued – without us,' he said, pointing to her gin rickey on the bar.

'Oh, this. Yes' – she turned to the barman with a winning smile – 'it is delicious.' She sipped it, then lowered her voice, 'But I really wanted to speak to the chap who was sitting here. A Mr Derby, private secretary to Mr Warriner himself.'

'Poor chap. He must be at sixes and sevens,' Dotty said, hoicking herself up onto one of the bar stools. Being just that bit shorter than Cressida made her ascent of the velvet-topped stool slightly less elegant, but she looked pleased as punch once she was perched on it. She pushed her glasses up the bridge of her nose and then gestured to the barman for another cocktail. 'Alf, do you fancy one too?'

Alfred pulled a smart silver pocket watch out of his waistcoat, looked at the time and nodded. 'After all the goings-on, dinner is delayed apparently. Why not?'

'Two then please,' Dotty asked and then turned back to Cressida. 'So, what did he say?'

'Not a huge amount. But I'm even more convinced that Mrs Warriner *isn't* the culprit.'

After going through the various things, including diamonds, which Mrs Warriner stood to gain if she didn't kill her husband, Cressida filled her friends in on what the newly widowed wife of the industrialist had told her, much to Dotty's gasps and Alfred's slight shakes of the head. Once she'd told them about the conversation she'd overheard and Owen's dropped file, which was reportedly not his at all, and the newspaper article that was now in her pocket, Alfred actually found it necessary to lay a hand on Cressida's shoulder, a look of concern on his face.

'Cressy, old thing, DCI Andrews is here on the train. Investigating Mr Warriner's untimely demise is his bag. If you put yourself in danger again, I...' He took a deep breath, but it was Dotty who interrupted him.

'It's too late for that chat, Alf, I'm afraid. I tried. And now Cressy – and me too this time, rather shockingly – are already elbows deep in the mire of this mystery.'

'You too, Dot?' Alfred asked, then looked at Cressida again. He shook his head, slightly bewildered at these two headstrong women and gratefully, if silently, accepted the cocktail from the barman.

Cressida smiled at Alfred. She wondered how strong the gin rickey was, and if it had been wise to have one while her head still ached from its knock a couple of days ago, as she couldn't fathom otherwise why her knees suddenly felt like flummery. She shook the thought off and looked at her watch.

'Hmm,' she bit her lip in thought.

Alfred took his own watch out of his waistcoat pocket again and looked at the time. 'It's getting on for eight thirty, Cress. What are you thinking?'

'That we reach Edinburgh at around quarter past ten. Is that right, Dot?'

'Yes,' agreed Dotty. 'Though I left my *Bradshaw's* over by the table.'

'I should imagine you've memorised it all by now, chum.' Cressida raised an eyebrow at her friend.

'Well, yes. Sixteen minutes past actually,' Dotty said, looking a cross between sheepish and proud.

'Oh Dot, you are a wonder. And the good thing is this means I definitely have time to go and speak to Miss de Souza. I mean, don't you think she's the link in all of this? The mistress of the murdered man, a singer in the nightclub that's mentioned in that newspaper article. The very person who first screamed and alerted us all to the body—'

'Isn't that why she wouldn't be the murderer, though?' Dotty asked, her voice low. 'If she hadn't screamed, none of us would have known he was dead until London. She could have left at Edinburgh and disappeared into the night with us none the wiser a murder had even been committed?'

'We heard the gunshot though, Dotty, remember?' Cressida reminded her. 'It wasn't just the scream. She could have screamed to cover the fact she was the one closest to the body when the shot went off.'

'Cripes. I hadn't thought of that.' Dotty shivered and absent-mindedly pushed her glasses back up her nose.

'Surely Andrews has been talking to her,' Alfred insisted. 'And, as I said, investigating this murder really is his bag, old thing. I don't want you to go careering off and get yourself hurt again.' Alfred's frown told Cressida his words were serious.

Cressida was about to put his mind at rest and reassure him that her investigating had been as safe to her person as a pastel colour palette was to a drawing room, when DCI Andrews himself appeared, walking down the length of the dining car.

'Ah, Andrews,' Alfred said, welcoming him into their little group by the bar. 'Drink? And please come and help me convince Cressida here, and Dot,' he shot a look at his sister, 'that they really shouldn't be investigating.'

Andrews looked pained. 'They really shouldn't.' He sighed. 'Miss Fawcett, what have I repeatedly said about—'

'Sticking my noble old nose into things. I know, Andrews. And I'm sorry. And I'm sure you and Kirby have it all sewn up, but—'

'Kirby at this very moment is talking to the driver.' Andrews took his turn to interrupt. 'I don't know whether messages have been hurled out of windows, but initial thoughts are that they'll have to stop the train at Edinburgh to take on more coal. Not to mention the evening papers and whatnot.'

'Which, if our murderer isn't under lock and key, could give them a chance to escape,' Cressida mused. 'Andrews, have you spoken to Miss de Souza since she first alerted us all to Warriner's death?'

Cressida wondered if she heard the faintest guttural growl from DCI Andrews, who then retorted with, 'Miss Fawcett, I can't tell you the things discussed in confidential interviews.'

'Unless you're listening in already,' Dotty whispered and Andrews sighed again.

'Fine. Yes, Kirby made sure Miss de Souza was comfortable a little while after we moved her to the far compartment in the last carriage. Only a few doors down from mine and Kirby's cabins. As far away from the crime scene as possible.'

'Because you think she might be involved?' Dotty asked, open-eyed.

'No, Lady Dorothy. Because the young woman looked distraught. Traumatised, you might say. As you can imagine, if you'd found someone you knew dead.'

'Someone you knew awfully well,' Cressida added, and Andrews glared at her, then went on explaining.

'Miss de Souza took a powder, I think. Something to help her rest.'

'I see. And she hasn't said much else?' Cressida asked.

'Nothing since she told me that she returned from the water closet to the compartment, having only left Warriner in there for a short while on his own. She found him dead on the floor and screamed.'

'And when did she see Mrs Warriner? Was it before or afterwards?'

Andrews reached into his pocket and pulled out his notebook. He flicked to the correct page and read aloud. 'Witness says she caught sight of Mrs Warriner after she had screamed and run from the compartment into the corridor.'

'Oh yes, you said,' Cressida tapped a finger against her temple.

'But it means Mrs Warriner was close by,' Dotty all but whispered.

'Yes, but by the sounds of it, alerted by the shot and the scream herself,' Cressida added. 'Thank you, Andrews. And, in return, let me tell you about how rummy it all got when I spoke to Warriner's private secretary.'

'Oh yes?' Andrews looked interested, as did Dotty, and even Alfred, despite himself.

'He said Mrs W stands to lose everything if she's convicted of Mr W's murder. And not just legally and financially. In that sort of noose-round-the-neck-way too. So why would she risk all that when she was in love with him, and being married to him afforded her all of life's luxuries.'

'Because she caught him cheating?' Alfred posed.

'I felt pretty swizzled when I found out Basil had been cheating on me,' Dotty said, remembering her former fiancé.

'But you didn't shoot him. You did what most broken-hearted ladies do and took to your bed with a comforting pile of dogs on top of you,' Cressida countered.

'And hit Mother's supply of laudanum pretty hard,' Alfred chipped in, earning himself an elbow in the ribs from his sister.

Cressida ignored them and turned back to Andrews. 'And how likely is it that Geraldine would come aboard with a loaded gun? We've just been up to a shooting party in the Highlands and even *we* don't have guns on us.'

'I know, I know,' sighed Andrews. 'But until we have proof otherwise, Mrs Warriner is our suspect. We'll monitor the platform at Edinburgh like hounds.' At this word, Ruby looked up at Andrews and he gave her a pat on the head. 'And see if anyone tries to make a break for it. Then we're non-stop to London. Still, this only gives us eleven hours.'

The four of them looked gravely at each other, the sombre atmosphere only punctuated by Ruby yapping in excitement as Sergeant Kirby entered the bar.

Cressida looked across at him as he approached, flattening his wayward red hair with the palm of his hand. He was not a man used to being in public without his helmet, but Cressida was pleased for his sake that he had decided to stop wearing it as he investigated the narrow corridors, low ceilings and tight compartments of the sleeper train.

'News from the engine, Kirby?' Andrews asked.

'Assuming I can speak plainly in front of company, sir?' Kirby asked, and Andrews nodded. 'Not much, to be honest. Neither the driver' – Kirby pulled his notebook out of his pocket and flicked it open – 'that's Mr Donaldson, nor the engineer, a Mr Sawyer, had left the locomotive itself during the time we heard the gunshot.'

'I see. Both alibiing each other out, I assume.'

'Yes, sir. Though Mr Donaldson didn't seem too upset about Mr Warriner's death.'

'Oh yes?' Andrews asked, putting into words exactly what Cressida, Dotty and Alfred were thinking. 'He's the one who's adamant we stop in Edinburgh, too?'

'Yes sir, for more coal, sir. Otherwise, we'd peter out just south of Newcastle apparently, sir. Anyway,' Kirby looked at his notebook again, 'Sawyer stood there and held his cap in his hand, said all the right things about what a shame it was and what a pity for the family. But Donaldson just shrugged.'

'Did you enquire more, Kirby?' Cressida asked, not waiting for Andrews to lead the conversation.

Kirby glanced at Andrews, who nodded, and he answered her. 'I did, miss, and he said he used to work for Warriner Industries and was pleased he was out of it, miss.'

'Gosh, did he now,' Cressida said and, thinking of the greasy oil stain on the letter, took another sip of her cocktail. 'That is interesting.'

While Kirby moved around to have a more confidential discussion with DCI Andrews about where to go from here with the investigation, Cressida thought to herself. And that thought was how exactly could *she*, a passenger, get herself to that engine room, and how could *she*, a smart young lady, get the driver of this entire train to pause his work for a few minutes to talk to her.

## 18

With her mind leaping to all sorts of conclusions regarding the train driver who seemed to have no love for the now-dead Lewis Warriner, Cressida took action.

A quick movement, a slip of the wrist over the highly polished bar and the remains of her gin rickey smashed to the ground. Poor Ruby had taken a soaking, and was now sitting on the bar stool next to Cressida looking perturbed with a slice of lime balanced on her head.

'Oh, dash and darn it!' Cressida exclaimed, looking, she hoped, to the world to be in shock and disbelief at her spilt drink, smashed glass and unimpressed dog. 'How unforgivably clumsy of me.'

'Please, m'lady, do mind, m'lady.' The helpful barman had ushered the others out of the way and was already at work cleaning up the shards of crystal that had covered the wooden floorboards. 'Ladies and gents, excuse me while I... Yes, thank you all.'

'Dear Rubes is soaked, the poor pup. I better find a cloth... the chaps up the other end of the dining car will have napkins, or perhaps I'll find something useful in the water closet closer to the lounge car.' And under this auspice, soggy pooch in her arms, Cressida waved a brief goodbye to her friends and headed through the dining car, towards the engine.

Under her breath, she thanked Ruby for her helpful stoicism. 'I like to think you anticipated my every move, Rubes. You positioned yourself perfectly for that lime. What a clever pup you are.'

She swiped a napkin from one of the white-clothed tables and carefully dabbed at the non-plussed Ruby as she made her way along the aisle of the train. Her first obstacle, that of escaping her friends and the policemen, had been achieved. Now to get into the engine.

Cressida slipped out of the dining car, and with Ruby still in her arms, navigated the jolting and jerking connection between the dining car and the lounge car.

The lounge car itself was elegantly set up, with upholstered chairs and two-seater settees, placed in small groups or facing towards the windows so that passengers could make the most of the stunning scenery, during daylight hours at least. Summers in Scotland, though short, did have the most wonderful long, late evenings, with the sun setting so much later than it did in the south of England. Still, even with that, it was clear from the orange glow in the sky that time was moving on and evening approached. And every inch the sun dropped towards the horizon was a reminder to Cressida that time was running out to catch this killer.

She nodded a hello to the Fernley-Hoggs, who were enjoying a drink in two comfortable-looking armchairs, and walked past, hoping they wouldn't think it was odd that she was walking through to the luggage car.

Another juddering connection between carriages later and Cressida was in a very different part of the train. Gone were the glossy veneers and comfortable upholstery, the brass finishings and crystal glassware. Instead, she found herself in a bare wooden cargo car, stacked floor to ceiling with rustic shelving. Ropes and nets hung from the roof, used to secure the luggage and travelling cases of the passengers, not to mention the necessities for life on board the train: bundles of linen, packing cases of dry goods, crates of wines and spirits, bundles of newspapers. Cressida was about to edge one of the newspapers out of its string tie when Ruby started yapping and snorting in quite an irate fashion.

'What is it, Rubes?' Cressida asked, letting the struggling pup down so she could carry out her own little canine investigation.

Ruby paused and stared back up at her mistress, blinked, then toddled over to a pile of luggage. Cressida followed her and quickly saw what had got her own darling pup so worked up.

There was the snowball-like ball of fluff Pomeranian, patiently sitting in a carry case, which was perched on top of other pieces of luggage.

'Oh, you poor little thing, trapped in there the whole journey.' Cressida slipped her fingers in through the bars of the carry case and gave the small dog a reassuring tickle. 'I would never do that to you, Rubes. Can you imagine? All those hours stuck in a little box. I hope Miss de Souza recovers enough to come and let the poor thing out every now and again.'

Cressida drew back from the carry case, aware that time was running out for her own mission to find and quiz the train driver. But she noticed Ruby had half hidden herself between two pieces of luggage, with only her curly little tail waggling out in the open.

'What are you up to, Rubes, come on you.' Cressida tried to pull her out, but Ruby pushed further in and then disappeared from view altogether. 'Oh Ruby.' Cressida knelt down and peered into the gap where Ruby had disappeared. Suddenly, two frog-like eyes met hers and Ruby appeared again, with a luggage tag in her mouth.

Cressida tutted and picked her up.

'What have you got there, Rubes? Honestly, the conductor will make me put you in one of those cases if you go around nibbling people's luggage!' Cressida pulled the tag out of her little dog's mouth. 'Smith, Glasgow.' She read. 'How odd. We haven't come across a Smith yet, have we?'

Cressida gave the luggage tag a quick wipe and slipped it into her pocket, whispering something about 'safekeeping' to her dog.

'Now, come on you. We have a train driver to talk to. A train driver who Kirby himself said sounded mightily unhappy with the late Lewis Warriner. A train driver who might not just be happy he's dead, but have been the one to kill him.'

## 19

Unlike throughout the rest of the train, the link between the luggage car and engine was much more utilitarian and needed a good tug once the catch was off to open it. Doing this obviously caught the attention of the man who happened to be just the other side of the door and he looked up at Cressida as she all but stumbled through the clackety connection.

Cressida straightened herself and took in the scene in front of her. She wasn't in the engine itself, nor in the coal car, but a room the size of a garden tool shed, that looked like one too, with large heavy implements strapped to the walls, shovels and stokers, crowbars and hammers and all that. There were also a couple of bunks, two chairs and a table and on the table a round, brown teapot and two old and chipped mugs. Cressida remembered Mrs Drysdale mentioning a place for the crew to lay their heads. This must be it.

The overalls-clad man spoke to Cressida, 'Evening, missy, can I help you?'

'Good evening. Mr Donaldson, is it?'

'Aye.' The train driver folded up a timetable he'd been looking at and placed it in his pocket. 'And who wants to know?'

'Cressida Fawcett.' She stuck her hand out to him, then instantly regretted it as her beautifully clean palm was pressed hard in the grease-covered grip of the burly old Scotsman. She tried not to look at how dirty it was as she returned it to its place under Ruby's belly. But she did catch sight of it, of course, and she recalled once more the small patch of grease on the letter that Mrs Warriner had received. But why would an engine driver have anything in common with the wife of a wealthy industrialist?

*If they both worked at Warriner Industries of course...*

'Mr Donaldson, I've been sent on a bit of an errand,' Cressida lied, secretly crossing her now grubby fingers underneath Ruby as she did so. 'Sergeant Kirby is busy interviewing Mr Derby, but asked me to confirm with you the dates between which you worked at Warriner Industries.'

Donaldson looked askance at Cressida and she wondered if he believed a word she was saying. It seemed not.

'Why would a policeman be sending a fine lady like you to ask something like that?' He pulled a cloth off a hook on the wall of the carriage and wiped it around his fingers.

Cressida, wishing he'd done that before he shook her hand, thought on her feet. 'I'm a writer, actually. Commissioned by the chief of police to write up a report about the goings-on during investigations. Jolly lucky to be aboard just as something like this happens.'

'Not sure Warriner thinks it's so lucky.' Donaldson chuckled, throwing the cloth onto the table next to the two well-used and chipped mugs and brown teapot. His reaction shocked Cressida; was this the cold-heartedness of a killer she was witnessing?

'That's true,' she replied, once again thinking quickly and working out how to reply. 'How crass of me. I'm sorry. But, of course, most passengers don't know that he's died. Only you up here in the locomotive and those who witnessed anything.'

Cressida kept her fingers crossed, knowing full well that her friends, the people she overheard talking and nine-year-old Lord Hartnell, all knew about Warriner's death now, too. 'So I hope that proves to you that I'm an insider on the case and all that.'

Donaldson shrugged and crossed his arms.

'Did you know him well?' Cressida persisted.

'Fine then,' Donaldson sighed. 'In 1910 I joined the business. Stayed for eleven years 'til 1921. As I told the sergeant.' He said the last few words with a certain emphasis.

'I see. What the sergeant, and of course Detective Chief Inspector Andrews, a close personal friend of mine, want to know, is why you left. What happened?'

'What happened? Lewis Warriner is what happened!' The engine driver staggered back as the locomotive shuddered and Cressida momentarily wondered who was up in the cab. As they steadied themselves, Donaldson continued, 'I was an engineer in his motorcar factory. Designing the crankshafts and submitting plans for a whole new suspension system.'

'That sounds very technical.' Cressida thought of her own Bugatti, and the clever chaps who designed its suspension, without which there would be a much bumpier ride, especially at the speeds she liked to achieve. 'And essential too.'

'Aye, you'd have thought. And I was a good worker, led the team, built the department up and brought in more good workers, especially latterly young men back from France.'

Cressida nodded thoughtfully. So many young men had returned from the terrible wasteland of northern France either injured in body or mind. And many of them had found it hard to integrate back into work and jobs. 'You were doing a worthy thing, Mr Donaldson, I'm sure of it.'

'Aye, well Warriner didn't agree, not when one of the young'uns was caught with some valuable parts in his bag.'

'Ah, I see.' Cressida held Ruby tightly. 'The poor young man.'

She listened as Donaldson told her about the other young men he'd helped reintegrate back into society, and how sad it was when they weren't given a second chance. Something felt very familiar about what he was saying. She carried on listening as Donaldson poured a cup of very dark tea for himself.

'These lads had given everything for King and country, and what had the country given them back, eh? A second chance? Not on Warriner's watch. I did what I could to shield them from that beady-eyed, beak-nosed private secretary of his—'

'Mr Derby?' Cressida quizzed, recognising his description.

'Aye, Clarence.' Donaldson pulled a face as he said Derby's first name in a faux-posh voice. 'Always checking up on us, watching the purchase orders like a hawk. That's how it happened. Bert was caught red-handed and—'

'And the buck stopped with you.' Cressida smiled to herself, not because of his story but because it had all started to make sense. 'You're Hughie, aren't you? Mrs Drysdale's brother?'

Donaldson looked at Cressida, held her gaze while he gulped down his tea from the chipped mug. When he finished, he smacked his lips together then spoke again. 'Aye. That's me. Has she been yapping?'

'Your sister is charm itself,' Cressida replied, protective of Mrs Drysdale's honour.

Donaldson chuckled. 'Aye, that she is. She got it all, none left for me.'

'Au contraire, Mr Donaldson, you're being exceptionally helpful,' Cressida praised him, hoping it would soften him up for the harder questions. Questions that, depending on how he answered, could make him her number one suspect. She looked at Mr Donaldson and carried on, 'I should imagine you didn't have a great liking for Mr Warriner after that?'

Donaldson stared at her, a glint in his eye that made the

hairs on the back of her neck stand on end. 'Do you think I killed him? Revenge for firing me?'

'N-no,' Cressida stuttered, glancing around her at all the heavy wrenches, sharp screwdrivers and various other vicious and hefty-looking tools that were secured to the walls but easily reachable by the burly locomotive driver. She remembered another of the tenets of her and Andrews' plan – tell everyone that Mrs Warriner was arrested and the prime suspect. 'How could I when Andrews has arrested the murderer. Well, murderess. Mrs Warriner most likely killed her husband.'

Donaldson shrugged. 'I did'na think she'd have it in her. Nice young thing. I remember her when she were back in the typing pool. But the first Mrs Warriner – now, she'd have had reason.' He shook his head. 'But I'm glad I'm no suspect. Excepting for talking to you now, Bruce, he's my engineer, has been with me every minute since we left Inverness. Late.' He looked at Cressida accusingly and she blanched, remembering how much Dotty had dithered on the platform.

'I see you have the perfect alibi. Though you do admit to not liking Mr Warriner. To hating him, would you say?' Cressida pushed just that little bit harder.

'Aye, but you won't pin this murder on me, missy. There is someone else on this train, someone with a face like a hawk, and eyes like one too, who worked at Warriner Industries who hated him even more, if you ask me.'

Cressida furrowed her brow, but it was clear to whom Donaldson was referring. And it wasn't Mrs Warriner. She looked the grease-smeared train driver straight in the eye and confirmed her thoughts with one name.

'Mr Derby?'

## 20

'Aye, Mr Clarence Derby.' Donaldson kicked the bottom of the wall with his steel-capped boot. 'You see, I can model a drive shaft out of a piece of iron and design you a functioning combustion engine, but all those numbers in rows in ledgers and all that—' He swiped his hand across the air. 'I'm no accountant.'

'Who is, quite frankly,' Cressida agreed.

'Aye, well Derby is. All part of the private secretary position. He's no typist or coffee maker, but he kept tabs on all the purchasing and spending across the departments. He was the one who went to Warriner saying my lads had been pilfering and I'd been letting it happen, but that's by the by. He's a nasty, shrewish man, but it's not me he hated.'

'He hated Warriner?' Cressida pressed.

'Even more than I did.'

'But he was working for Warriner. Forensically examining the accounts to find out if one of your lads was stealing from the company. That doesn't sound like someone who hated his boss?'

Donaldson sucked his teeth as he formed his reply. 'Did you

know Mrs Warriner worked underneath him in the typing pool of secretaries?'

'No, I didn't. I knew she was one of the under-secretaries, but I didn't realise she worked with Derby. What's that got to do with Mr Derby hating Mr Warriner?'

'Aye well, Derby assumed that she'd put a good word in for him once she was in Warriner's bed?'

'And she didn't?'

'Apparently not. And Derby wasn't happy, I can tell ye that.' Donaldson staggered as the train rounded a corner. Cressida really hoped someone, perhaps this Bruce chap, was competent enough to drive the train while the driver was here, talking to her. She kept hold of Ruby, but was grateful that she was in her sensible shoes. And hadn't finished that gin rickey.

'Why would he expect Mrs Warriner to put in a good word for him with Mr Warriner? He was already Mr Warriner's private secretary. Isn't that rather important?'

'If you want to be a private secretary all your life. Not if you see yourself as deserving more. A place on the board. Company secretary. Shares in the business.'

'And Derby was worthy of that? Experience and competence and all that?' Cressida didn't know much about business, but she had the distinct impression that people had to be awfully clever and very good at all sorts of things to be promoted to board level. Or own the company in the first place. Or be the son of the owner or some such.

'He certainly thought so. Derby believed he was doing all the work. Even back then. Heaven knows how he's kept a lid on it for the last four years. Do you know what that does to a man, missy? Knowing that in all truth you run the company, you pay the bills, you manage the employees and the suppliers, while your boss, the one raking in the money, swans off to Glasgow nightclubs and spends all his money on showgirls.'

'How do you know that?'

'There's always talk of it. Headlines and that.'

Cressida nodded. 'You think Mr Derby had had enough of being downtrodden and doing all the hard work while Warriner earned all the money?'

'Aye. And more than that. I heard rumours that Derby had had enough. Gamekeeper turned poacher and had to start lifting from the company coffers himself.'

'Derby was stealing from Warriner? Gosh.'

'Word on the factory floor was that he had his finger in the pot when Warriner was busy chasing skirt. Any time Warriner came close to suspecting something, he'd offer up another of my boys as a scapegoat.'

Cressida raised her eyebrows. This was an entirely new dimension to Clarence Derby. A light-fingered, cunning employee, who had expected the lowly, but obviously pretty, typist beneath him to help elevate him once she'd caught the eye of the boss. 'So, do you think Mr Derby hated Mrs Warriner as well as Mr Warriner?'

'Aye, possibly. I certainly caught him giving her the filthiest looks in the canteen. If I were you, missy, I'd go and tell your policeman friend to look into Mr Clarence Derby. He'll be the one winding up the Warriner paperwork. And burning the documents he wants no one to find as he does it.'

'Hiding the evidence,' Cressida murmured.

'Aye, evidence that might suggest he had reason to kill Lewis Warriner, especially if Warriner had just caught him with his fingers in the till, so to speak.'

'You're needed n'cab, Mr Donaldson!' The call came from the far end of the carriage, interrupting Donaldson.

Cressida saw a young lad poke his head around the door, the wind tousling his strawberry-blond locks. It brought it home to her how the engineers and drivers fought not only the great locomotive itself but the elements too, as they flew down the line towards the south.

Interruption or not, Cressida had gleaned plenty of information from the train driver. She bid him and the young lad goodbye and slipped out of the rough-and-ready crewmen's car and back through the luggage car, pondering all the while. *Donaldson hated Warriner, and he could have easily put that greasy mark on a letter to Geraldine summoning her on board as his patsy…* She shook her head. *No, he has the best of all alibis, having been no further down the train than the crewman's car all journey.*

She paused to give a tickle to the fluffy white Pomeranian and let Ruby down so the two small dogs could give each other a friendly sniff. Her mind wandered, thinking about how well Ruby got on with the Chatterton spaniels and if Ruby might like a four-legged friend. But then remembered how hard it was to get just one dog to sit still in the passenger seat of her natty sports car, let alone two. Giving the other dog a final scruffle, she was about to leave when a flash of colour caught her eye. Cressida reached up to one of the netted luggage holds suspended from the ceiling.

'How strange,' Cressida murmured, pulling a bright red high-heeled shoe from the net. 'These are Miss de Souza's, I'm sure of it.' She stood on tiptoes again and reached up for the other, then held the pair out in front of her, half wondering why on earth they were in the luggage car, and half admiring them for their fabulousness.

Ruby butted against her ankle and Cressida looked down at her pup.

'Oh, of course, you're right, Rubes. This is all Miss de Souza's luggage. Including that poor pup of hers. But why would she have taken these shoes off and have them stashed here?'

Cressida turned the shoes around, twisting them and peering at them from all angles. There was no trace of blood, so they hadn't been discarded in disgust.

'Can you imagine coming across the body of your lover, Ruby, and then, to add insult to injury, getting his blood all over your new suede shoes?' Cressida shivered at the thought. Then she noticed something: a balled-up piece of paper lodged in the toe of one of them. She looked in the other one, but there was nothing there. 'That's odd too,' she told Ruby. 'One would usually ball paper up in both shoes to keep their shape or help dry them if it had been wet out, but not just one.'

Cressida clenched the empty shoe under one armpit, and then fished the balled-up paper out of the toe of the other. She unfolded it and gasped.

## 21

Cressida held the piece of paper in her hand. She now had both of the red high-heeled shoes clenched under an armpit and used both hands to stretch out the crumpled paper. This was no piece of newspaper, used to help keep a shoe's shape. It was a handwritten note. And it was a strange one at that.

*The handbags are just the start of it. You know what comes next unless you do what I ask.*

'What does this mean?' Cressida looked down at Ruby, who looked up at her, then returned to silently communing with the Pomeranian by staring at it.

The train suddenly rocked from side to side and plunged into darkness and Cressida gasped again, steadying herself by reaching out for one of the piles of luggage.

She felt disorientated in the darkness and had an unnerving flashback to the cold, damp and utterly dark secret tunnel she'd been attacked in at Ayrton Castle barely a couple of days ago. Her head still ached thanks to it.

It was possibly only a few moments, though it felt longer to

Cressida, before daylight flooded back in from the narrow windows and roof light of the wooden luggage carriage. She let out the breath she hadn't realised she'd been holding. Hurriedly putting the shoes back up in the storage net, as she didn't want to linger in the dingy luggage car any longer, she folded the piece of paper up more neatly and pushed it into her pocket. She knew what she'd found was interesting, but she had no idea what it meant.

'Handbags, Ruby? A note about handbags found in shoes. It's all very odd.'

Cressida crossed through the connection to the lounge car, and tried as nonchalantly as possible to wave once again to the Fernley-Hoggs, who looked baffled to see a fellow upper-class passenger come from that direction.

When she finally headed into the dining car, she waved with more excitement at a cross-looking Dotty and Alfred, who were sitting once more at one of the tables laid for four people.

'Where have you been?' Dotty looked exasperated. 'You only went to dry off Ruby and you've been gone an age. Where were you?'

'Can't you guess, Dot?' Cressida said as she plonked Ruby down next to her friend and sat herself next to Alfred. Dotty reached down and petted Ruby, who responded with a rasping lick of her tongue, then looked longingly at the puffy cheese gougères on the table.

'Well, unless we have you to thank for these canapés, I'm going to venture it wasn't the kitchen,' Dotty said, her voice softened.

'You're right, Dot. I can do no more than boil an egg.'

'And judging by the state of your hand, Cressy, I'd jolly well hope you didn't have your fingers anywhere near my small eats.' Alfred nodded down to where Cressida was resting her hands on the table and she looked too at the grease on her fingers.

'Ah. Yes.' She picked up a napkin, dipped it in a water glass and set about wiping her fingers.

'So?' Dotty asked expectantly. 'After that charade with your drink earlier, you scarpered off in that direction,' she pointed towards the engine. 'Don't tell me... You found out something interesting?'

Cressida put the napkin down and tried her best not to look too self-satisfied. She couldn't hide it, though, and with more than a little twinkle in her eye told her friends about her adventure through the luggage car and the poor caged Pomeranian. 'Ruby spotted her first of course,' she continued. 'Then she spotted a rather neat little hiding place behind the rest of the pile of luggage there, and appeared from her nook with this in her mouth.' She pulled the luggage tag out of her pocket. 'It's probably nothing. No one on the train is called Smith, are they?'

Dotty and Alfred shook their heads.

'Left over from a previous journey?' Alfred ventured, picking it up and turning it over. 'Fell off a case or something and wasn't spotted?'

'Most likely, but it was in the pile of cases that belonged to Warriner and Miss de Souza. And speaking of Miss de Souza, I noticed her bright red shoes stashed up in the overhead luggage nets. And I found a crumpled note in one of them. Here.' She pulled the note out of her pocket too. 'What do you make of that?'

Dotty peered at the note through her spectacles and then passed it to Alfred, who read it and then shook his head.

'Someone who likes handbags and wants more?' Dotty ventured.

'The "unless" bit is rather sinister, though,' added Alfred, and Cressida nodded.

'I agree. I have no clue as to what it means, though.'

'Except that it might be a clue,' whispered Dotty. 'Even though we can't decipher it yet.'

The three of them paused, lost in their own thoughts. Then Cressida filled them in about her conversation with Donaldson.

'He made a good point, of course, about his alibi. Though I think he disliked Warriner even more than he was letting on. He kept pointing the finger at Mr Derby, said he'd been stealing from Warriner Industries and was furious with Warriner for not promoting him. But then he also said that Derby and Mrs Warriner had had a falling out.'

'Is there a chance that he might have been framing her?' Alfred asked.

'I wonder. She did point out that it was a very strange coincidence that she was on the same train as a loaded gun and her cheating husband. I think she very much feels like she's been set up.'

'But by Mr Derby? Why?'

'According to Donaldson, Derby rather hoped that Geraldine would put in a word for him once she had the ear of the boss. But she didn't. Or at least, if she did, Warriner wasn't listening. Donaldson said Derby was cross as two sticks about it.'

'Cross enough to frame a poor woman for killing her husband?' Dotty asked, leaning forward, her elbows on the table.

Cressida reached over and picked up a gougère from the plate on the table. 'Maybe, Dot,' she said between mouthfuls. 'Or cross enough to kill the boss himself.'

## 22

A waiter came over and handed the three friends a menu for their evening meal.

'I feel like we've barely moved since tea,' Dotty said, nevertheless pushing her glasses up her nose so that she could have a good look at the menu.

'Speak for yourself, Dot,' Alfred disagreed. 'Since jam last touched scone, we've had a murder, several police interviews, a rogue Cressida going off to the engine, and in my case at least, two cheeky snifters. That barman is a real find. Anyway, I've never been more ready for my supper.'

'Well, now you put it like that...' Dotty frowned and focused on the menu again.

Cressida looked too. She had to admit that her adventures up and down the train had made her rather peckish and keen to see what was on offer.

'Oh, how delicious, mulligatawny soup,' Dotty announced. 'I adore Indian cuisine.'

'Did you say Indian?' The lady's voice came from the table next to them and Cressida turned around to see who it was. As did Dotty, who introduced herself.

'Yes. Are you devotees too? I'm Dorothy Chatterton by the way, and this is my brother Alfred and my friend Cressida.'

'Louise Irving,' the lady with fair hair said. 'And this is my brother Callum. And yes, we adore Indian food.'

Cressida shook hands with them over the aisle and was pleased at her correct assumption that they were siblings.

'What brings you on the sleeper train?' Dotty made conversation over the aisle, while feeding Ruby one of the cheese gougères from the table.

Louise Irving answered her. 'Callum and I have been visiting family in the Highlands.' Her voice had a trace of a Scottish accent. 'Lossiemouth and Elgin mostly, but also a bit of time in Inverness—'

'Yes, we don't get over much,' Callum Irving interrupted, in the way Alfred usually did to Dotty. 'We live in India. Tea planters, you see.'

'Oh, how interesting.' Dotty pushed her glasses up the bridge of her nose. 'I love tea. Cressy, you prefer Indian tea, don't you? Over Chinese, I mean.'

'I do, yes,' Cressida said. 'I have a rather wonderful blend that a dear friend gave me the recipe for. Assam mostly, I think. I'm afraid I simply take the receipt to the nice man at Fortnum & Mason and he makes it up for me.'

'How smashing. I think some of our leaves end up in Fortnum's blends. We've lived there all our lives. India, I mean, not Fortnum's,' Louise giggled. 'Papa was a tea planter too, and his father before him. We have family over here, of course, and miss them all terribly, but we love it up in the hills near Ooty. Have you been to India?'

'Me?' Cressida asked, accepting a glass of champagne from the waiter as he carefully weaved between them with his silver tray. 'Gosh, no. What an adventure that would be. I've only been as far as the silk shelf at Liberty of London to my shame. I'd love to travel.'

'Would you, Cressy?' Dotty asked. 'I don't think I'd like it one bit. All that going outside and having to go on excursions.' She looked at Louise Irving apologetically. 'Not that I doubt for one moment that India isn't marvellous once you get there, but the journey must be exhausting. Give me an atlas and a decent book about the place any day.'

Cressida chuckled and, by way of an explanation to Louise, clarified Dotty's assertion. 'My darling chum here is the ultimate armchair traveller. She's been as far as Siberia and Samarkand, Vladivostok and Verbier, but all from the safety of her library.'

'And can you blame me, Cressy?' Dotty retorted. 'Going anywhere and doing anything outside seems to keep getting us in all sorts of hot water.'

Their conversation was interrupted by Alfred, who had leaned over in order to better speak to Callum Irving. 'Heard it's a tough old business. Hard times for the importers, what with the war and all that.'

Callum nodded. 'Yes, international trade has been tough. At least in the war all you had to do was dodge the U-boats. Now it's all stock markets and investments and convincing Scotland's elite that what they're missing in their portfolios is a nice tea plantation. And, sadly, for those of us brought up into the trade, there's nothing else we can really do. No jobs to fall back on here in Blighty. No Plan B.'

Alfred continued to talk to Callum about the import trade and Cressida smiled and nodded occasionally as Dotty and Louise debated the merits of Indian silks over Manchester cotton for dresses.

The thing was, all the time they'd been making such lovely chit-chat something had been nagging at Cressida's mind. But it was then, just at the end, that she'd realised. When Callum Irving had mentioned their livelihoods, she knew what had been making the hairs along her arms prickle.

The voices. Both of them.

She recognised them.

These were the two people she'd overheard in the supposedly empty sleeper compartment earlier. These were the two conspirators discussing 'roughing up' Warriner. A sister, it seemed, who had so little faith in her brother, she had to question if he had murdered Warriner. And now that he was dead, they were onto their 'Plan B'.

The realisation that Callum and Louise Irving were the two voices she'd eavesdropped on chilled Cressida to the core. These two perfectly pleasant people, talking with Dotty and Alfred and ordering champagne aperitifs had, only a little while ago, been talking of murder.

*But why?* What could these two possibly have against Mr Warriner?

And then Cressida remembered something else, and it made her rather clumsily spill some of her champagne from its elegant coupe.

Dotty looked at her and raised an eyebrow. Cressida shook her head, just slightly, and Dotty, pausing for no more than a few heartbeats, carried on talking about silks and cashmere with Louise Irving. Alfred either hadn't noticed or knew better than to ask Cressida what was wrong. Ruby, however, was staring at her mistress, her large brown eyes interrogating Cressida to the extent that she nearly blurted out what she was thinking across the table. Luckily, for social norms and the benefit of the investigation, she didn't.

She had, however, realised something. The Irvings had left the dining car just after Mrs Warriner had been escorted away from her cheating husband. In fact, Cressida could clearly remember that it was on Alfred's return that he had had to move to one side of the aisle to allow them to leave.

*Whatever it was that made them argue in that empty compartment could be their motive,* Cressida thought to herself.

*And we have no idea who brought the gun on, so that might be their means. And with them leaving the dining car moments before the fatal gunshot was heard... well, that's their opportunity.*

Cressida stared starkly at Ruby, who blinked back at her. The Irvings could have done it. They could have killed Lewis Warriner.

*They* could be the murderers.

## 23

Cressida shakily picked up her coupe glass and, trying not to spill any again, she took a sip of the champagne. Her mind was still racing, but she was doing her best to conceal it and act naturally.

*But Callum insisted he hadn't killed Warriner*, she thought to herself. If his hushed and rushed conversation with his sister was to be trusted.

However, they had planned to do something nefarious to the now-dead man, which meant they also had a motive. And Louise had cause to question her brother – even she wasn't convinced that he hadn't gone too far.

'Isn't it terrible about this husband-murderer we have on board,' Cressida said, during a pause in the conversation.

'She did it then?' Callum Irving said rather brusquely, brushing away the waiter who was topping up their glasses.

'As far as we know, yes,' Cressida said. 'Did you know Mr Warriner at all?'

'Us?' Callum asked, obviously prickling. 'No, why do you ask?'

'Yes, a bit,' his sister said at the same time and received a filthy look from her brother because of it. She closed her eyes and his glare turned back to Cressida and her friends, where it melted into a friendly smile again.

'We knew him slightly. As Louise says. Not socially, though.'

'Through business then?' Cressida pushed.

'I don't think that's any of... I mean, it has to be obviously.' Callum Irving seemed flustered.

'Cressy?' Dotty whispered, but Cressida ignored her. Manners be damned, there was a dead man on the train and connections needed to be made, before someone got away with murder.

'What did a manufacturer of cars and auto parts have to do with your business?' Cressida asked, her eyes wide with pretend naivety. 'Tea importing, isn't it? Or am I getting my Austins mixed up with my Assams?'

'Mr Warriner was—' Louise started, but her brother stopped her.

'Louise please, it's private business. Miss... sorry, I didn't catch your surname?'

'Fawcett. Cressida. The Hon,' Cressida filled him in.

'Well, Miss Fawcett, I'm afraid our connections with Warriner are private, family business. I hope you understand that.'

'Of course,' Cressida replied. She was about to press further, but Callum Irving started talking to his sister, directing her attention away from Cressida and her friends by pointing at something in the distance out of the window. Cressida, though a hothead, knew when she'd been given the cold shoulder.

Still, she'd learned something all right. The Irvings had a connection to Mr Warriner. Add that to the fact they had the opportunity and, by the sounds of things earlier, a motive. It certainly warranted telling Andrews about it, along with her findings about Mr Donaldson and his insistence that the previously unsuspected Clarence Derby might have a chip on his shoulder, too. Not to mention the note in one of Miss de Souza's shoes. Yes, she'd learned a few things all right, and gathered some clues, but Cressida couldn't help but think she was still no closer to working out who had killed Lewis Warriner.

The waiter returned, ready to take dinner orders, but was distracted as a glass of champagne on the Irvings' table toppled over, smashing and spilling.

'Damn,' Callum cursed as he stood up, dramatically wiping himself down with his napkin. The ministrations of his sister and her napkin seemed only to frustrate him more. After a moment longer, performing a polka in the aisle as Owen Edwards tried to squeeze past to get himself to a table behind them, Callum and Louise Irving left the dining car. Cressida heard him muttering something about changing a shirt and 'maybe changing trains at Edinburgh if we have to' as he led his sister out of the carriage.

Cressida swore under her breath again and Dotty raised an eyebrow.

'What was all that about, Cressy?' she asked when they were out of earshot. 'You were terribly rude to poor Louise and Callum.'

'Flushing them out.' Cressida leaned in. Alfred had a concerned look on his face as Cressida elucidated them. 'I recognised their voices, you see. I'd heard them talking about the murder—'

'What? When?' an exasperated Dotty asked.

'Oh, earlier. It was after I'd snuck in to see Mrs W. I heard their voices through one of the compartment doors so stopped to have a listen. Anyway, you can see why I had to work out how they knew Warriner.'

'Do you think they killed him?'

'I don't know. Louise definitely suspected her brother of it when I overheard them. Said he was only meant to "rough" Mr

W up a bit. And although he professed his innocence to her, having seen that display of bad temper, I'm not so sure I believe him. She obviously wondered if he'd be capable of it too, else she wouldn't have queried it with him.'

'But having something to *do* with Warriner and having a motive to kill him are two quite different things,' Alfred said sensibly. 'They seem well set up in India, with investments coming in and all that.'

'Investments...' pondered Cressida. 'I wonder if Warriner had been their Plan A?'

'What are you talking about, Cressy?' Dotty looked confused. 'And you still haven't told us about what you were doing to get such dirty hands before dinner. What have you been up to?'

Before Cressida could answer, the train fell once again into darkness as the tracks tunnelled through a lowland hill. Cressida shivered, and was about to give herself a stern talking-to about not getting the heebie-jeebies every time she found herself in the dark when she was brought up short by a now horribly familiar noise.

*Blam!* A gunshot rang out.

Then *blam!* Another shot. Again, from somewhere down the train.

Cressida froze, and heard others in the carriage gasp in shock and fear. Moments later, the tunnel ended and Cressida could finally see her friends and darling pup again. She looked at their wide eyes, their pale faces, and they at her. Only one thought was on all of their minds.

Had the murderer just struck again?

## 24

Cressida was half out of her chair when Alfred's hand clasped around her arm.

'Wait, Cressy,' he said, an urgency in his voice she hadn't heard before. 'Sit down for heaven's sake.'

'But those were gunshots, Alf, didn't you hear them? Just like last time.' Cressida looked incredulously at Alfred, then over to where Dotty was still sitting. 'Dotty, you did, didn't you?'

'Yes, I did,' Dotty said, a tremor in her voice. She pushed her glasses up her nose and leaned over to pick up Ruby and pull her onto her lap. 'And that's exactly why I'm staying put here and *not*, oddly enough, running in the direction of the person with a loaded gun.'

'You see,' Alfred said, relaxing his grip on Cressida's arm, but still holding on to her. 'Dot speaks sense. We all agreed to stick together, didn't we?'

Cressida bit the inside of her lip in frustration. Alfred was right, and Dotty was being exceptionally sensible. Even Ruby was panting in some form of agreement with the Chatterton siblings. *Traitor*, Cressida thought, narrowing her eyes at her little dog.

'Fine. I won't go and see what happened,' Cressida said as Alfred finally let go of her arm. She could feel the warmth where his hand had lingered. She knew he had her best interests at heart. 'Thank you, Alf. You're right. I shouldn't go charging off. It's just... I mean... aren't you both steaming with sheer inquisitiveness?'

'Yes, we are,' Dot replied. 'But not enough that I want to run straight into the barrel of a gun.' She picked up her glass of champagne and took a sip in a manner that suggested a certain stiffness of upper lip. Cressida could detect a shake to Dotty's hand, though, so merely nodded at her friend in understanding.

She then looked around the carriage. If her friends wouldn't let her investigate what had just happened down the passageway, she could at least see who was out of the frame, as either the victim or, indeed, the shooter.

Behind her, Cressida saw the Fernley-Hoggs, who were looking perplexed and pale around the gills, having only just moved through from the lounge car, no doubt. A porter bustled through from the other direction, but didn't stop to give any sort of report, instead barrelling straight through towards the engine. Cressida wondered if he was informing Donaldson and Sawyer, and, true enough, in a moment, the porter returned, followed by a grubby-looking Mr Sawyer, and, rather surprisingly, one of the chefs from the kitchen. It was hard to work out what was more of a shock to the tweed-clad Fernley-Hoggs; the noise of two gunshots or the sight of an oil-flecked train engineer appearing in the dining car.

Cressida was somewhat surprised to see Owen Edwards sitting alone at one of the tables for two, still sipping his aperitif and staring out of the window as the gently rolling hills of Perthshire glowed in the evening sunshine.

Cressida turned back in her seat and considered who *wasn't* there in the dining car with them. The Irvings, of course, who had just left; Miss de Souza, who hadn't been seen since Warriner's death; Mrs Warriner, who was still no doubt locked in her cabin; Lord Hartnell and his nanny; and Clarence Derby. Not to mention the porters and bar staff, and the tea lady, Margaret Drysdale, or her brother Hughie Donaldson.

'Chaps, something must have happened if the engineer was called,' Cressida said, still itching to go and investigate.

'Maybe those weren't gunshots after all?' suggested Dotty. 'Maybe it was a piston going off or a pipe exploding.'

Alfred shook his head at his sister. 'You might have passed Latin with flying colours, sis, but I'll wager you have very little working knowledge of a steam engine. Pistons "going off", I ask you!'

'Well, you know what I mean, Alf.' Dotty pulled Ruby closer to her.

'I'd love to agree, Dot, I really would.' Cressida took a softer tone with her friend. 'But I'm pretty sure those were gunshots. It sounded just like when Warriner was killed.'

'But who was... That's to say, I wonder who—' Alfred couldn't complete his sentence as before he could utter another word, the carriage door was opened and a flushed Sergeant Kirby appeared in the dining car. His eyes swiftly fell on the table of the three friends and he briskly covered the few steps from the door to their table. This time, Cressida did stand up, and this time, Alfred let her, standing up beside her too. Dotty stayed sitting down, with Ruby closely cuddled on her lap.

'Kirby, what is it? What's happened?' Cressida greeted him, gesturing for him to sit and join them, but he shook his head, then took a breath before speaking.

He was about to say something when a voice called over from the back of the carriage. 'I say, policeman chappy. What's happening, eh?' It was Mr Fernley-Hogg.

Kirby called over to him, asking him to be patient. 'Two

minutes, sir. Police business.' Then he turned back to Cressida, Dot and Alfred and in a lower voice said, 'It's the chief inspector, miss. He's been shot.'

'Andrews?' Cressida exclaimed. She felt Alfred's hand on her arm again, but this time she had no inclination to shake it off. Andrews shot... she braced herself for bad news. 'Good heavens. Is he badly injured?'

'Yes, miss, bad enough. He was hit in the shoulder.'

'That was one of the shots we heard,' Alfred deduced. 'And the other?'

'It's Mrs Warriner, Lord Delafield.'

'Mrs Warriner? But she was locked in her compartment, wasn't she?' Cressida asked.

'Yes, miss, and the chief was in with her, miss. Hence the assailant shooting them both.'

'While we were in that tunnel,' Cressida half whispered to herself.

'And is Mrs Warriner injured?' Dotty asked, the tremor back in her voice.

'I'm afraid so, miss, and seriously. Worse than the inspector. We'll need a doctor at Edinburgh.'

'So, that was the reason for the engineer being called in such a hurry,' Alfred pointed out.

'Yes, my lord,' Kirby agreed. 'He's the best person to get a message down the line. When we stop for coal, we'll need a doctor waiting on the platform. We can't stop for long, else the murderer – if it's not Mrs Warriner, that is – will have all the time in the world to escape.'

'It's looking less like Mrs Warriner is the murderer now, though, isn't it?' Dotty asked, but Kirby could give no official answer.

'Will she survive, Kirby?' Cressida asked. 'And Andrews?' Cressida had helped the detective solve cases before, but she was worried that, without him, the murderer would get away scot-free.

'He'd like to see you, miss,' was all Kirby could answer her with.

'Right, well, yes, of course,' Cressida said, straightening herself. 'Chaps, look after Ruby for me.'

'I should come too, Cressy.' Alfred looked at her, his eyes full of concern.

'Miss?' Kirby's voice, though close, seemed miles away.

Cressida touched Alfred's arm. 'No, stay with Dotty. I'll be back soon. I promise.'

And with that, Cressida followed the worried police sergeant to where his boss, darling DCI Andrews, had been injured in the line of duty.

## 25

Cressida followed Kirby at quickstep pace down the corridor of the train, her mind on nothing else except the plight of poor DCI Andrews. Shot in the line of duty! What would Mrs Andrews say? What would *her father* say? Andrews had been Colonel Fawcett's batman, a very special position, much like a butler or private secretary, in the last Boer War. Cressida even remembered a faded and torn photograph framed on the desk of her father's study of the colonel and his batman, on their way home from South Africa. Each was wounded and bandaged up, but obviously taking comfort in the company of the other, as they had each been responsible for saving the other's life in one way or another.

*Oh, how I've let Papa down*, she thought, as she realised the protection that Andrews usually afforded her should have gone both ways; she should have been looking out for the middle-aged detective on this deadly train, too.

'He's going to be all right though, did you say, Kirby?' Cressida asked for the umpteenth time as they neared the compartments at the rear of the train that had been assigned to her favourite detective and his sergeant.

'Yes, miss, he says he took worse in the war, miss. The one before last, of course.'

'Good. Well, not good. But I'm glad he'll be all right.'

'Here we are, miss, you can see for yourself.' Kirby stopped at the door of a compartment and knocked a sharp rat-a-tat-tat on the door. Cressida almost fell into him; the stop had been so sudden and the train motion so hard at times to counter.

'Come in!' the voice called from inside and Kirby pulled the door open.

Cressida slipped in and found what she could only describe as Andrews at his most deshabille. His tweed jacket was off, his shirt sleeve ripped off at the shoulder hem and a temporary sling kept his arm close to his chest. He looked both pale and yet also flushed around the cheeks, but Cressida was pleased to see that, despite only just having been shot, his first-aid requirements had stretched to a cup of tea, steaming beside him, as well as the bandage and sling.

'Andrews.' Cressida took the sight of him in.

'Miss Fawcett,' he replied, and she wondered if she detected a note of sheepishness in his voice. He picked up the cup of tea with his good arm and took a sip, wincing slightly at the effort.

'Thank heavens you're all right, Andrews. I thought I was the one who usually got myself into the soup, but here you are, being shot at. Do I need to lecture you now about staying out of mischief?' Cressida could sense Kirby shuffling awkwardly behind her, but kept her eyes on Andrews, who in turn chuckled, and then winced as he reached out for his cup of tea. 'Andrews, be still,' she muttered, passing the cup to the detective. 'I shall have to station Dotty here to look after you at this rate.'

'Oh, I'm sure Lady Dorothy has better things to do,' Andrews mumbled.

'Nonsense. Dotty would relish it. She's read so many books on just about everything, I think she'd be more than capable.

But...' Cressida paused. 'Will you both be safe? Maybe Kirby could stand guard?' She looked up at the young sergeant, who looked back at her blankly, having not received his orders yet.

Andrews took a sip from the steaming cup of tea and let Cressida put it down for him, then he said, 'I don't feel the need for an armed guard, but Mrs Warriner possibly does, and I feel Kirby should return to post there.'

'I'm sorry, sir, I should never have abandoned my position, sir.' Cressida could see now that the blank expression of the young sergeant, whom she'd also grown quite fond of over the last few months, had changed to one of devastation. 'I should resign, sir, really. Such a dereliction of my duty.'

'You weren't to know, Kirby,' Andrews reassured him, but Cressida could see the self-admonition on Kirby's brow. Something was going on that she hadn't been made aware of yet, that was for sure.

'Andrews, what's all this about? Why is Kirby giving himself the proverbial thirty lashes?'

Andrews exhaled and leaned back, cradling his arm.

'It was my fault, you see, Miss Fawcett,' Kirby said hurriedly, before Andrews could speak. 'I was supposed to be on duty guarding Mrs Warriner's door. Not for her safety though,' he said, looking down. 'But as she was the one arrested.'

'Kirby,' Andrews said kindly. 'How were you, or I, to know she would be targeted? Who would want to hurt the person who was already arrested for murder? And we still have the murder weapon here.' He winced again as he pointed to one of the brown paper evidence bags Cressida had grown familiar with over the last few investigations.

'Hang on a tick, you two. I'm confused.' Cressida raised a hand. 'So, someone, when Kirby wasn't looking, took a shot at Geraldine? And you too, Andrews?'

He nodded.

'But you have the gun...' She pointed at the evidence bag.

'So you were shot with a completely different gun to the one that killed Warriner?'

Andrews nodded again.

'And you were with Geraldine, in her compartment?'

'I had been called away, you see,' Kirby explained. 'One of those nice tea ladies came past and suggested I follow her to her trolley and get a cuppa for poor Mrs Warriner and myself, of course.'

'I see.' Cressida encouraged him to go on. 'You mean to say, you left your post and followed her?'

'Yes, miss, but she perambulated...' He shook his head. 'Well, she hurried off, so I just found the trolley next to one of the water closets in the next carriage over, towards the dining car. No one else was around, so I helped myself to a couple of cups and some of those biscuits.'

'Can't blame you for that, Kirby,' Cressida said, but then noticed as Kirby's face reddened. She cocked her head to one side. 'What then?'

'You see, miss, I hadn't secured Mrs Warriner's room. I'd popped my head in, see, to ask her how she liked her tea and she'd said milk and no sugar, and I'd closed the door and I... well, I forgot to turn the key. Or pocket it. She'd been so polite all the time we've had her under arrest, and what with this train going so fast and not stopping, it wasn't like she was about to escape.'

'Oh Kirby,' Cressida sighed. She looked at Andrews, who shrugged, then winced.

'Kirby, it's understandable,' Andrews said, once again reassuring the young constable. 'Anyway, it must have only been a moment after you left that I went in to see Mrs Warriner. How could either of us have known what was about to happen.'

'And what did happen?' Cressida asked, turning back to Andrews.

'That's simple.' Andrews looked at her. 'The murderer struck again.'

## 26

'While the train was in the tunnel,' Cressida stated, as Andrews readjusted himself on his bunk, resting his wounded arm on a stack of blankets and pillows.

'Yes. I'd just entered Mrs Warriner's compartment when we went into that tunnel. Then, next thing I knew, I heard the catch on the door open again and that was that.'

'You sound very pragmatic about it all, Andrews, but you could have been killed. The assailant wouldn't have known who they were shooting at.'

'Actually, now I think of it. They had a torch. I remember looking towards the door and having a light shone in my eyes. Then the two shots.'

'I suppose that means you couldn't make out a thing? Male or female, tall or short? That sort of thing?' Cressida pressed.

'You're the investigating officer now, are you?' Andrews said, raising an eyebrow.

'I might have to be, with you stuck in here with nothing more exciting than a hot cup of tea,' Cressida replied, thoughtfully picking up the delicate teacup and saucer and passing them to Andrews.

'Thank you. But no, in answer to your question, and to my own quite profound annoyance, I couldn't make out a thing in the dark.'

'Which means it could have been anyone... It was a tea lady who distracted you, Kirby, wasn't it? I wonder...'

'I was thinking that, what with the disappearing act the one who fetched me did.' Kirby scratched his head.

'So, the tea lady ran off in the direction of the trolley, as had you, Kirby. And, Andrews, you had just come from the other direction...' Cressida turned from Kirby to Andrews and back again. A familiar prickle crossed her shoulders. 'You do know what this means, don't you?'

Andrews nodded, slowly. Kirby's face went from flushed to pale, but he nodded too.

Cressida said then, what they were all thinking. 'The murderer was never Geraldine. Of course, it wasn't. She came aboard this train hoping to find out something to her advantage. Heck, she even thought her husband might be surprising her with a romantic overnight journey. No,' Cressida shook her head, 'this is a well-prepared ruse, designed by someone who so wanted Warriner dead, they've planned the whole thing. Plan Bs and all.' Cressida thought about it for a moment more before continuing. 'Geraldine was set up as a patsy. And, of course, there's an accomplice on board.'

'An accomplice?' Andrews questioned.

'There has to be. It was the accomplice, the tea lady, who ran off in one direction, distracting Kirby, while the murderer slipped into Geraldine's compartment just after you, Andrews. Whether or not they knew there was a handy tunnel coming up, I don't know. But they've planned so much already. Guns, two of them. At least. A disguise of sorts.' Cressida was thinking as she was speaking, listing off the things the miscreant would have had to have planned. She thought of Dotty and her timetable.

'Planning this all on an express train that means no one can get off.'

'Except in Edinburgh,' Kirby said.

'Yes, except in Edinburgh.' Cressida looked at the small clock by Andrews' bunk. 'Which we get to in about an hour's time.'

The prickle that had crossed Cressida's shoulders as she checked the time now shuddered down her spine.

'How are we going to manage it? Making sure no one leaves the train,' she asked pointedly. They'd not had time to discuss it yet: the stop at Edinburgh, for coal and now a doctor, too. 'The platforms will be well lit at least, that's the good thing about it being such a main station. And it won't be quite fully dark outside anyway. We should be able to see anyone get off.'

'We'll need trusted lookouts posted at each end of the train,' Kirby suggested.

'And hopefully the message will get through that we need a clear and quiet platform. But apart from us three, and Dotty and Alfred, who can we absolutely trust? Ruby is a wonderful pet and a superior hound, but I can't volunteer her, sadly.'

'I won't have you putting yourself in danger, Miss Fawcett,' Andrews all but growled, but Cressida put her hands on her hips and looked at him.

'Pot, kettle, I think, Andrews. Or horse and stable door. Bolted. Or whatever. But you know what I mean. Will Geraldine be all right until we reach Edinburgh?'

'The sous-chef is with her. Turns out he was a medic in the war, though saw too much to want to carry it on in civilian life. He's doing his best for her, but it'll be tight,' Andrews informed her.

'Doesn't bode well for dinner ever being served, but I'm glad there was someone on board with some trauma injury experience. I wondered why I saw him heading through the carriage earlier.

Oh, and I'm going to send Dotty here to look after you, Andrews, and I won't hear an argument. Alfred and I can take up post in the dining car and look up and down the platform from there and, Kirby, you can head down to the end luggage car perhaps? And maybe Sawyer or Donaldson could be called up and be trustworthy enough to help you – a lookout each side of the train.'

'No one else we can trust,' Andrews said. 'And they, after all, have the best alibis of anyone.'

'I'd be tempted to suggest Lord Hartnell, him being about nine years old and hopefully not yet up to planning complex and murderous schemes, but although I believe he may be the only other absolutely innocent person on this train, I think he'd struggle to get his finger out of his nose long enough to do any good spying for us.'

Andrews huffed out a sort of laugh. Then cleared his throat. 'Anything else to report, Miss Fawcett? I had planned to check up on your not-exactly-official investigations when I took this bullet.' He winced again as he resettled into a new position on his bunk.

'And you were right to, Andrews. I've gathered a few... well, would we call them clues? I don't know. Look here.' Cressida pulled out the luggage tag that had the name Smith on it, the piece of newspaper, and the threatening note about handbags. She pointed to the latter. 'This one I found in one of Miss de Souza's red suede shoes in the luggage car.'

'How do you know they were Miss de Souza's?' Andrews asked, looking at the note, holding it up to the light and turning it over once or twice.

Cressida cocked her head on one side and looked at him. 'Did you notice anyone else wearing such glamorous shoes as we boarded?'

Andrews took his attention off the note and looked at her. 'Well, no, I didn't, but then I don't tend to pay much notice to ladies' shoes.'

Cressida tutted. 'Well, if you did, you'd have realised that no one else on this train was wearing anything like them.'

'What does this mean? This handbag thing?' Andrews asked, passing the note over to Kirby for further examination.

'I don't know, Andrews, but it sounds a bit rummy. Oh, and speaking of rummy, I met Callum and Louise Irving. They're a brother and sister and were sitting next to us in the dining car. It all started out perfectly friendly, some link to India, I believe, and that's when I recognised their voices. I'd overheard them, you see, having a bit of a set-to in one of the empty compartments. Sadly, I didn't have one of Woolly's handy glasses around, but I could hear plain as day that they were discussing Warriner's death, with Louise asking her brother if he had gone further than the planned "roughing up" and had actually killed him!'

'Crikey,' Andrews replied, genuinely shocked at the revelation. 'So, you listened in, not knowing who was speaking, then recognised the voices when you sat next to them in the dining car or some such?'

'That's right. Dotty was discussing her love of mulligatawny soup and it all came from there. They're tea planters, you see, based in India – in the southern hills, I believe. Anyway, you can imagine that once I'd recognised those voices, I had to push to see how they might have known Warriner, what the connection could have been, and that's where it got really interesting.'

'Are you writing this down, Kirby?' Andrews asked, and Kirby, ever ready with his notebook and pencil, nodded.

'Sorry to disappoint, Kirby, but Callum put the kibosh on it all. "Private family business" and all that. Louise obviously didn't think it needed to be so hush-hush, but her brother all but fastened her lips up for her. That's what I thought was interesting. Why not just say, to the perfectly nice, and dare I say rather good-looking, strangers, that you knew the dead man and gossip like the rest of us? Why try to hide it all? It just makes you look more guilty.'

Andrews nodded thoughtfully and adjusted his arm, blanching as he did so.

'Gosh, you look in pain, Andrews. And pale. Let me get Dotty. I'm sure she can leave Alfred... Oh yes, that was the other thing that's been brewing in my mind.' Cressida raised a finger to her chin.

'What's that then?' Andrews asked.

'Brothers and sisters. There's what, twenty or so people on this train, and we have three sets of brothers and sisters. Isn't that a little strange? What are the odds? No doubt Dotty could tell me, but, you see, there's Dotty and Alfred of course, then the Irvings, who I think might actually be twins they're so similar, and then there's Mrs Drysdale and Mr Donaldson.'

'The driver?' Andrews looked over Cressida's shoulder to Kirby, making sure he was taking this down.

'Yes, and Mrs Drysdale is the nice tea lady. He hated Warriner, of course, but has the most perfect alibi. I wonder...'

'What?' Andrews urged Cressida on.

'Oh, I don't know. It'll come to me, I'm sure it will.'

'Well, let's hope it comes to you quickly, Miss Fawcett.' He looked up at Kirby again, who was carefully putting his notebook and pencil away. 'Kirby, for now I want you posted back outside Mrs Warriner's compartment, but when we get to Edinburgh, you'll get into position as Miss Fawcett described. We have an hour. Let's see what else we can find out before then.'

## 27

With an hour to spare before she, and she hoped a willing Alfred, kept watch over the platform at Edinburgh, Cressida decided it was time to look into this tea lady who had lured Kirby away from his post.

*An accomplice...* she hadn't even entertained that thought before speaking to Andrews. *Or two murderers even...* And almost two murders. Or three, if Andrews hadn't been so lucky.

Having potentially multiple murderers on board complicated things hugely. But Cressida couldn't help but think about the two most obvious suspects, since Mrs Warriner had essentially been cleared. The ones with the motive, the opportunity and perhaps the means... the Irving siblings. *Could Callum have killed Warriner, despite what he said to his sister, and then... But why kill Geraldine too?* Andrews, it could be assumed, was most likely collateral damage, but Geraldine had been targeted, as suggested by the fact that Kirby had been lured away. Lured away by the tea trolley.

Cressida hurried back down the carriages, past the bar and through the dining carriage – pausing to give Ruby a quick stroke as she sat perfectly contented in Dotty's arms – towards the lounge car. Dotty and Alfred had been full of questions, but Cressida hastened on; only stopping to forewarn Dotty that Kirby might be fetching her in a moment or two. Waving once more to the bewildered Fernley-Hoggs, Cressida passed by the other dining tables to the lounge car.

The sound of the kettle whistling, and the urn gurgling were almost as loud as the clattering of the rolling stock on the tracks and Cressida was relieved to see jolly Mrs Drysdale in charge of the contraptions, deftly lifting the heavy pot and pouring the hot steaming liquid out.

'How do, dearie,' she said without looking up. 'After another cup for that detective of yours? Though, at this time of evening, I wouldn't judge him if he wanted something stronger.'

'He's not mine, Mrs Drysdale.' Cressida laughed. 'But poor Chief Inspector Andrews. Shot in the shoulder.'

Mrs Drysdale shook her head. 'Terrible thing, dearie, terrible thing. Makes me worried to be out and working. Do you think it's safe for us?'

Cressida rocked back and forth as the train clattered on. 'Yes, I think we're safe. There seems to be something very rum going on regarding the Warriners, but while I can't be sure, I should imagine the rest of us are out of the soup. But speaking of Mrs Warriner, Kirby said a tea lady came and saw him and suggested he follow her to a trolley and fetch a cup of tea for poor Mrs Warriner. This was before the shooting, of course, so he did. But then the tea lady disappeared. But he found the trolley and was just helping himself when the train went through that tunnel and the shots rang out.'

'Dear oh dear,' tutted Mrs Drysdale. 'That's very unlike one of my girls. Well, I say girls, there's not so many of us now as the trains have got more frequent, so we're a bit stretched. I've got young Martha, though. I'll fetch her for you, but I don't think she'd be the one suggesting cups of tea for murderesses. It's not her way at all to find a job to do where there is none, more's the pity. Still, we're all clay, aren't we, waiting to be moulded.'

'Yes, I suppose so,' agreed Cressida, scratching her head and momentarily wondering what sort of clay she was made from. Fine bone china, she hoped, though she would settle for porcelain. 'And thank you, Mrs Drysdale. I'll wait here for Martha.'

'Righto, dearie. I'll be back in two shakes of a lamb's tail.'

At that, Mrs Drysdale wobbled off down the corridor and Cressida was left to her own devices. She was pleased for a moment or two to gather her thoughts. What was she going to say to young Martha? She couldn't well come straight out and ask if she'd been working with someone to distract the policeman. No, questioning people needed subtlety, and Cressida had to admit to herself, though she was loath to, that subtlety was at times not her forte.

She heard voices in the corridor and pulled herself away from the window, where pine forests with their tall, dark trees had given way to more heathers and lowland heaths. The sun was setting now in the west and the trees had been casting long shadows over the fields in front of them. She wondered again at the original shooter who hadn't thrown the gun away, where it would have been lost for good in those dense forests and wide rivers of the Highlands, but who had instead framed Geraldine and then... tried to kill her too? With another gun? She shook her head. It made no sense.

'Miss Fawcett!' Mrs Drysdale's voice interrupted her thoughts. 'Here's Martha for you. Go on, Martha.' Mrs Drysdale pushed her forward. 'She won't bite.'

'Thank you, Mrs Drysdale. And hello, Martha. Promise I won't. I just wanted to ask you a few questions about the cup of tea you might have suggested Sergeant Kirby fetch for—'

'That's just the thing, miss.' Martha interrupted, wringing her apron between her hands. 'I don't know what you're speaking of, miss. Mrs Drysdale just told me you had questions and I ain't done nothing, miss, except mind my own business.' She paused. 'It's true though, isn't it, miss, that someone is dead? *Is* someone dead, miss? And those shots, miss, just now. Were they the murderer again, miss?' The girl was as inquisitive as Cressida herself and she had to give her credit for it, while also trying to temper her enthusiasm and get an answer from her, not the other way around. Cressida frowned. Being subtle wasn't going to be easy.

'That's all for the police to know about, and I'm afraid us poor souls just have to wonder. But, Martha, Chief Inspector Andrews—'

'I heard he was killed, miss, is that right?' Martha looked both excited and terrified, but mostly excited.

'No, that's not right,' Cressida asserted, and realised as she said it how terribly, utterly sad she would be if Papa's old batman *had* actually been killed. She looked at Martha, who still had a glint in her eye, as if she'd just looked up from reading something terribly salacious in a Victorian penny dreadful. 'Detective Chief Inspector Andrews is quite well, Martha. Just a graze. But he has asked me most solemnly to help him.'

Martha furrowed her brow.

Cressida had tried this before, insisting she was working for Andrews, and mostly it worked. Not because those whom she wanted to question believed her – she had enough self-awareness to know that – but she did have a suspicion that, most of the time, people, and especially those in service, loved the opportunity to tell their theories and stories to someone like the Hon. Cressida Fawcett.

'There's a young sergeant here, named Kirby. He says a tea lady suggested he fetch a cup of tea for Mrs Warriner, who was under his guard at the time.'

'And is she dead, miss? Is she the one who was shot then?' Martha interrupted.

'No, Martha. She's... well, she's who we're interested in. But, more importantly, was it you who spoke to Kirby, Martha?'

Cressida watched as Martha's face changed from an expression of almost fevered delight to something near dejection. The look Dotty sometimes had when someone suggested that going outside and doing some exercise would be fun. Or her own, when the nice barman at Dukes Hotel declined to shake any more martinis. Martha's face showed the truth. That she had nothing to do with it, and she was disappointed with this fact.

'No, miss,' Martha all but whispered. 'It wasn't me that offered nothing like that. I've been polishing the cutlery and helping out in the galley and ain't been near the tea trolley until Mrs Drysdale there fetched me over to talk to you.'

'I see.' Cressida believed her. Her face told her all she needed to know. 'Thank you, Martha. That'll be all for now.'

Cressida accepted the nod goodbye from the young woman and herself nodded a thank you to Mrs Drysdale. She turned and looked out of the window.

Above all the little mysteries that surrounded the terrible events of Warriner's murder and the attack on Geraldine and Andrews, two things now struck her.

Who was the tea lady who came to fetch Kirby from the door?

And where was she now?

## 28

With her arms wrapped around her, and her brow furrowed due to the capital-T Thoughts she was having, Cressida almost didn't notice the newspaper in the rack at the end of the carriage. But a name in the headline caught her eye. She looked at it, then slipped it out of the rack and opened up the tabloid-sized paper and shook it until it was taut enough to read.

'Warriner pulls out of India...' Cressida murmured as she flicked through the paper to where the front column was continued inside. She glanced down the type, spotting the occasional now-familiar name and, despite not being terribly au fait with the business world, caught the gist of the article. Lewis Warriner had invested heavily in India but was getting cold feet.

*Very cold feet now*, Cressida thought, puffing out her cheeks and exhaling as she remembered the first, and hopefully only, death on this train.

She folded up the paper, pushing it under her arm as she walked with more purpose back towards the dining car and her friends.

'What ho, Cressy!'

Cressida looked up and then smiled as she saw Alfred in the passage just in front of her.

'What ho, Alfred,' she replied, pleased to see him. Then she paused. 'Alf, where's Dot? Have you left her on her own?'

'No fear. Dot is safe and well, and thanks to that young Kirby chap asking her terribly, terribly nicely, she's now tending to poor old Andrews. Quite a corker of a wound he's got there, by the sounds of things. Still, not so bad as Mrs Warriner. She isn't sounding good.'

'The sous-chef's with her,' Cressida replied as if that explained anything, but Alfred just looked confused.

'I'm not sure what you've heard, old thing, but I really don't think Mrs Warriner is at all in the mood, or health, for chicken ballotine and a couple of rum babas.'

'No, Alfred. The sous-chef, he's a medic too. Old war experience. Best person for it really, someone who saw ghastly bullet wounds in the trenches.'

'Ah, I see. That makes more sense. Though doesn't bode well for us ever getting supper.'

Cressida smiled at him, just a twitch from the corner of her mouth in the circumstances. 'That's what I said, Alf, to Andrews just now.'

'Great minds.' He raised an eyebrow.

'Or infantile ones.' Cressida smiled properly at him and couldn't help but notice how pleasant she found the little crinkles at the corners of his deep chestnut brown eyes.

'Cressy?' Alfred asked, and Cressida blinked back to attention. 'There you are, thought you'd gone off into a trance, old thing.'

'Sorry, I *was* a little distracted.' Cressida wondered why she'd never really thought about Alfred's eyes before, then reminded herself that she had recently suffered a knock to the head and really anything could come from a bout of concussion. 'Anyway, you said Dot was with Andrews?'

'Let me escort you there. And you can fill me in on whatever you've been doing. I'm sure whatever it is, it's been highly dangerous, irresponsible and probably outside of the law... and no doubt devilishly interesting. Lead on.'

With a gesture and a knowing smile, Alfred let Cressida lead the way down the passageway towards Andrews' sleeping compartment. As for Cressida, she let herself laugh. Alfred always seemed to know just what she needed to hear.

The sight that greeted them as they knocked and then entered the detective's cabin also caused the slightest smile to twitch at the corners of Cressida and Alfred's mouths.

'Oh, there you two are,' Dotty said, or at least tried to say, as the giant nursery pins in her mouth made it sound more like 'oh, err ooo ooh err'. She shook her head frustratedly, and Andrews tried to shrug but received a smack on his hand for his efforts.

Watching a middle-aged – one might even say, world-wearied – Scotland Yard detective be told off like a child in a nursery by a bespectacled young aristocrat was enough to elicit a giggle from Cressida and a brotherly smirk from Alfred. They couldn't help themselves as they watched Dotty fuss over Andrews, pinning a new sling in place in quite the most expert fashion. That Dotty had also brought Ruby with her, who was now sitting next to Andrews, her bug-like eyes looking adoringly at him, just made the scene even more comical.

'There,' Dotty said, a look of satisfaction on her face. 'That's better. Much more supportive. And you two can stop laughing.' She primly turned and faced her brother and best friend. 'And what have you got there, Cressy? Yesterday's paper?'

Cressida pulled it out from under her arm and checked the date. 'No, today's actually. But look at this.' She showed them the headline. 'Ties in rather well with the Irving siblings being added to my list of suspects. Plus, I just went and spoke to the only "tea lady" on the train, or at least the only one who wasn't Mrs Drysdale.'

'He would have known Mrs Drysdale,' Andrews said.

'Exactly. Mrs D introduced me to Martha. She was perhaps a little too interested in the goings-on, but I put that down to some sort of macabre fascination with it all—'

'Now, who does that remind you of?' Andrews asked, staring pointedly at Cressida.

Cressida gave him a withering look and carried on. 'Pish posh, Andrews. But, truly, I believed her when she said she hadn't been the one to call Kirby away from his post by Geraldine's door. She looked far too disappointed *not* to be involved.'

Andrews raised an eyebrow, but then nodded.

'You must keep your head still, Detective Andrews,' Dotty admonished him. Cressida wondered if she heard a slight growl come from the older man, but she let it pass without comment.

'Can I see the paper, Miss Fawcett?' Andrews asked, ignoring Dotty's admonitions and reaching out, wincing as he did so, for the newspaper.

'Of course. I must confess not to understand all the lingo of the press, but it looks to me as if Mr Warriner had staked a large chunk of cash in some India-based companies but was pulling out. Coincidence that we're on board now with two people who have a business in need of investment, who know Warriner... and who are based in India?'

Andrews held the paper with his good arm, flinching slightly as Dotty tied the knot of her makeshift sling tighter. 'I understand what you're saying, Miss Fawcett.' He read down a few more column inches and Cressida noticed his brow furrow as he did so. 'Hmm. Another coincidence,' he muttered, passing the newspaper back.

'What?' asked Cressida, taking it before Alfred, who'd also reached his hand out for the tabloid, could touch it.

'There's another very interesting story on that page. Not

about Warriner Industries, or Indian investment, but about someone else on this train with us,' Andrews answered.

'Who?' Alfred and Dotty chimed in sibling unison, but Cressida was busy scanning the page, trying to find the article to which Andrews was referring among the tightly printed columns. Her brow furrowed too as she clocked it.

'Ah,' she said, lowering the paper and meeting Andrews' gaze. 'Now, that is interesting.'

## 29

'Cressida Fawcett, you are a tease,' Dotty exclaimed. Then she glared at Andrews, who appeared to be both her patient and captive. 'And I thought better of you, DCI Andrews. What is it? What have you both spotted?'

'Sorry, Dot. There, read it yourself. Third column along, about halfway down,' Cressida said, passing the newspaper to her, as Alfred looked on, frustration etched across his face. Once again, he withdrew an arm back to his side, empty-handed.

Dotty took the paper. Ruby plopped to the ground and snuffled around, no doubt hoping that something from Andrews' tea tray might have made it to the floor. Dotty scanned the page and then, once she'd taken it in, read it again, this time out loud.

'Miss de Souza, resident songstress at the Firebird Club, a notorious hotspot for the likes of Al De Marco and Mickey "Pink Cheeks" Loretta, was brought in for questioning by the Glasgow police. Miss de Souza, 26, asserted her innocence in the case of the theft of three handbags, taken from the nightclub on the evenings of the 24, 27 and 29 July of this year. The case is with the Glasgow police force, pending a court date.' Dotty lowered the paper, 'Handbags!' she said triumphantly. 'Cressy, that note you found in the shoe...'

'Exactly,' Cressida said. 'Andrews, do you still have it?'

'Here.' Andrews pointed to one of the evidence bags and Alfred passed it over.

Cressida carefully pulled out the letter she'd found in Miss de Souza's red suede shoe.

'*The handbags are just the start of it*,' she read. '*You know what comes next unless you do what I ask.*'

'She was being blackmailed,' Andrews said, matter-of-factly. 'Blackmailed by whoever wrote that article.'

'Really?' Dotty asked, looking a little confused.

Andrews shifted uneasily next to her, trying to turn to face her, but winced with the effort. 'This is today's newspaper, isn't it?' he said, as a way of explaining his theory. 'And that letter must be recent, as it was scrunched up in a shoe Miss Fawcett says she saw Miss de Souza wearing as she boarded. Stands to reason that the letter was delivered to Miss de Souza today, on the train even, knowing that she would see that the blackmailer had carried out his or her threat and published the story about the handbag thefts in today's paper—'

'And a budding young starlet, one who wants to be in Hollywood, would not want stories like that written about her more, let's say, seedy background,' Cressida interrupted.

'Quite,' Andrews agreed.

Cressida leaned against the glossy veneer of the compartment's door while she turned over a few ideas in her mind. Alfred put a hand on her shoulder, which made her jump, but she quickly recovered herself.

'Sorry, old thing, didn't mean to alarm you.' Alfred pulled his arm away.

'No, Alfred, my fault. I was deep in thought. You see, that newspaper story about Miss de Souza, it's all very interesting.'

She paused for a second or two. 'Of course, that story doesn't just mention Miss de Souza, but Glasgow gangsters too.' She slipped her hand into her trouser pocket and pulled out the small piece of newspaper she'd stolen from Owen Edwards' folder. 'And this newspaper cutting refers to one of them too, if one can call them that.' She handed Andrews the cutting, who read it, his brow furrowed.

'Interesting. This links Warriner to them all right.' He sighed. 'And I might as well let you all know that the news on the police grapevine is that those criminals are doing a nice trade in buying up service revolvers from the Great War. There's plenty of old soldiers on hard times who'll accept a few bob, no questions asked, for a piece of kit that holds nothing but bad memories for them.'

'Especially if they're finding it hard to find work. From what Mr Donaldson the driver told me, Warriner wasn't making life any easier for veterans – he fired them with no second chances apparently.' Cressida pointed to the brown paper evidence bag. 'The gun that shot Warriner, is it an old service revolver?'

'Yes,' Andrews said. 'And the bullet that I took and I'm guessing the one currently lodged in Mrs Warriner's gut are most likely from one too.'

The four of them were silent for a moment or two, each one lost in their own thoughts.

It was Dotty who spoke first.

'Where did you get that clipping from, Cressy?'

'Owen Edwards. I bumped into him just after I'd over-heard Callum and Louise talking about roughing someone up. We'd just gone into that tunnel and it was dark and I must have been disorientated. I rather crashed into him while holding darling Rubes and he dropped this rather bulging manilla folder onto the floor. He had so many clippings and things crammed in that I managed to steal that one without him noticing.'

'Edwards? The young man keen on Miss de Souza?' Andrews asked.

'That's right. And he said the folder wasn't his, but that "one of the ladies" left it behind in the dining car. Well, I know it wasn't mine or Dotty's, and Mrs Warriner was barely in there. That nanny of Lord Hartnell had her hands full with, well, with Lord Hartnell, and I don't think the Fernley-Hoggs would be interested in newspaper clippings about Warriner—'

'Why not? Do we know anything about them?' Andrews asked, leaning forward. Dotty placed a hand on his shoulder and eased him back against his headboard.

'Yes we do.' She sighed. 'I had chapter and verse from Mrs Fernley-Hogg about every Munro and loch they visited while in the Highlands and all about their girl, who's had a baby, but the baby's a bit jaundiced, and how they can't get help these days and nursemaids aren't like how they used to be in her day... and all of that sort of thing.' Dotty exhaled and pushed her glasses back up the bridge of her nose. 'If there was any time left in Mrs Fernley-Hogg's schedule for cutting up newspaper articles on Mr Warriner, I'd be very surprised.'

'Good sleuthing, Dot,' Cressida said and would have winked at her friend, except, of course, that winking was deplorable. She resorted to flashing her friend a grin, which was caught by Andrews, who coughed an 'ahem'. He was not pleased with the fact that his two favourite aristocratic ladies were getting themselves mixed up in solving this heinous crime, despite now needing them to be his eyes and ears on the train while he rested. Cressida ignored his 'ahem' and continued. 'Ergo, my thoughts were that the only other ladies on board to whom he might have been referring are Miss de Souza and Miss Irving.'

'Makes sense perhaps that Miss de Souza might have a bit of information on Warriner,' Alfred supposed. 'Doing a bit of due diligence about the man who was promising her the world – if indeed he was.'

'Or it could be Louise Irving,' Dotty mused. 'Especially if her brother was going to "rough him up a bit" to try to shake down that investment we assume Warriner might have pledged.'

'Heck, they could even have been working together, Cressy.' Alfred removed his pipe from his pocket and jabbed it in the air with enthusiasm for his theory.

'But they don't know each other, that doesn't make sense,' Dotty disagreed.

'We don't know they don't know each other, Dot,' Alfred retorted, though he looked slightly deflated. 'They might have some connection we haven't discovered yet. Old chums from school, cousins.'

'There's been nothing to suggest that, Lord Delafield,' Andrews politely supported Dotty's assertion, which earned him a comforting pat on the shoulder.

'We can't jump to conclusions just because it suits us,' Dotty added as Alfred folded his arms in defeat.

'Or Mr Edwards could have been lying,' Cressida said quietly, thinking back to the scowl Owen had on his face when the daylight had poured back into the carriage. A scowl that had flittered across his face before he'd been able to compose himself.

A scowl of someone with something to hide?

## 30

There was a knock at the door, which made Cressida jump.

'Come in,' Andrews said, sounding more authoritative than he looked, what with his arm in a sling and his shirt torn to the shoulder. His face was looking paler too and Cressida eyed him with some concern before turning to see who wanted them.

'Just me, sir.' Kirby poked his head around the door. Even if he had wanted to, not much more of him could fit into the small compartment, not with four of them in there already, not to mention such a large-in-personality-if-not-in-stature dog, such as Ruby.

'I would ask you to come in,' Andrews smiled, while Cressida moved closer to the window, and, in so doing, bumped into Alfred. Over their awkward apologies to each other, Kirby said what he needed to.

'Just a time call, sir. Fifteen minutes until we stop at Edinburgh.'

'And Mrs Warriner?' the senior detective asked.

'Stable, sir. Chappie from the kitchen says it's bad, but the London hospitals have more specialism in this sort of wound, having been closer to the south coast in the war, sir. Field hospitals all up the Portsmouth Road, and in turn London itself. He thinks she'll fare better there than the general in Edinburgh.'

'Thank you, Sergeant,' Andrews said, and Kirby nodded. 'Lord Delafield, Miss Fawcett and Lady Dorothy here are all going to help you keep an eye out when we pull into the platform. We have to get that doctor on and the coal loaded as quickly as possible and make sure no one leaves.'

'Pip-pip to that, Andrews. We can take a corner each as it were. Two to the left, two to the right, or is it starboard and port on a train? I don't know?' Cressida looked to Dotty, who was often a fountain of information on such trivia.

Dotty didn't disappoint.

'I believe it's just boats and perhaps aircraft now,' she replied. 'We could try dexter and sinister instead?'

'Let's just stick to left and right, shall we?' Andrews cut in. 'But Miss Fawcett's right. If, Kirby and Lady Dorothy, you could head to the end of this carriage, or maybe even the end luggage van if possible and look out the windows either side of the train from there, and Miss Fawcett and Lord Delafield, you could look out of the windows in the dining car, then we should cover the length of the platform.'

'Aye, aye, Andrews.' Cressida saluted him and he rolled his eyes. She continued, though, 'Fifteen minutes then, was it? Marvellous. Time for me to go and find Mr Edwards and ask him about these newspaper cuttings of his.'

'Do be careful, Cressy,' Dotty said, her brow so furrowed that her glasses never stood a chance of staying up near the bridge of her nose. She pushed them back up as Cressida reassured her.

'Don't you worry, chum. I'll be as subtle as the perfect join in a good-quality wallpaper. The poor man won't notice a thing.'

Andrews coughed out an 'ahem'.

'Quite right, Andrews. Too much talk, not enough walk. I'm

off. I'll meet you all back here to liaise for our Edinburgh postings.'

With that, she gave them a little wave goodbye with the hand that wasn't under Ruby and slipped out of the compartment.

Cressida did fully intend on finding Mr Edwards. But when there was no answer when she knocked on his door, she decided he must be further along the train, in the lounge car or dining carriage. Everything about him, from his adulation of Miss de Souza earlier to that snarl she'd glanced when he'd dropped that folder of newspaper clippings, made Cressida feel as on edge as when she saw blue anaglypta paper under a green dado rail.

'Blue and green should never be seen, Ruby, we all know that.' A familiar shiver shot down her spine as she thought about the idiom. She whispered it to Ruby, 'Without a colour in between. Let's just hope that colour isn't blood red any time soon.'

Cressida had seen which compartment was his. *Mr Owen Edwards* had been written in neat script and slotted into the brass name-card holder on the door. She thought about the way Geraldine must have seen Lewis Warriner and Miss de Souza's names in the double compartment just before she confronted them in the dining car. She'd seen it herself; *Miss Phoebe de Souza*, she'd rolled the name around in her mind. *Every bit the Hollywood starlet.*

*Poor Geraldine.* Cressida thought about the perilously injured, and perhaps wrongly framed, woman in the cabin just next to her own. *To find out your husband is cheating, lose him altogether, be blamed for his murder... and then be shot.*

'It's really not her day, is it, Rubes,' Cressida murmured to her ever-attentive pup. She was just now passing the same cabin that Geraldine must have seen, the one in which Lewis and Phoebe had planned to spend the night.

Once more she was tempted to look inside, see the scene of the crime itself. Cressida rested her hand on the door handle and, to her surprise, it was unlocked. She stole herself to glance inside. Last time she'd tried, she'd been distracted hearing the Irvings arguing, but this time no one else was in the corridor – the opportunity was hers.

'For the sake of the investigation, Rubes, that's all,' she said, as much to reassure herself as her courageous pup.

She took a deep breath and opened the wood-veneered door.

The compartment had a double bed with the washbasin to one side, opposite the door in which she now stood in fact. The faintly metallic smell of blood caught in her nostrils and she raised the hand not holding Ruby to her face.

She looked towards the bed. The body was lying there, a sheet pulled up to cover his face. A grim splattering of dark red blood covered the glossy veneered panels around the bed and Cressida held Ruby tight as her inner wolf made her little legs paddle against the air and beat against Cressida's arms. 'No, Rubes, I can't have you sniffing around. What would Andrews say if Scotland Yard found as many paw prints as fingerprints in here?'

Ruby snuffled in displeasure but calmed down.

Cressida pulled her gaze away from the bed to where the basin and vanity unit were. Next to it was a pull-down luggage rack, for placing one's valise or day case so that it was a civilised height for opening and rummaging through. And a case there indeed was. Cressida took a step towards it, narrowing her eyes in concentration at what she thought she could see in it.

Wigs.

'How bizarre,' she muttered, moving closer to the case, her natural inquisitiveness taking over entirely as she forgot all sense of decorum or squeamishness at being in very close quarters to a murdered man. She leaned over the case, rocking slightly as the train thundered over a change in the tracks. She steadied herself and, with her non-pug-holding hand, pulled at some of the auburn hairs. A long-haired wig disentangled itself from the mess in the suitcase. 'Miss de Souza's, I assume,' Cressida murmured to herself.

'That's right.' The voice came from behind her. It was that same hard-to-identify, yet instantly recognisable, drawl of the wig owner herself. 'And what, pray, are you doing rooting through my valise?'

## 31

Cressida turned, Ruby still held in one arm. The auburn wig was still clenched in her other hand and Cressida felt her face blushing with shame. She was hot-headed, she knew that, but she also prided herself on her impeccable manners and riffling through someone else's private property definitely was not in one of Mr Debrett's useful guides to etiquette.

'I... I'm so terribly sorry...' Cressida stuttered, trying to find a viable excuse for why she was there. Not only going through Miss de Souza's case, but also in the compartment, with the dead body only inches from her. Ruby snorted and Cressida looked down at her, suddenly filled with inspiration. 'This pup, you see, she got loose, and the door was open and she scuttled in. She doesn't run, you see, she sort of toddles, so for her to *scuttle*, well, I had to take chase...'

Miss de Souza waved a hand to stop Cressida mid-flow. 'Fine, fine. But going through my case?'

'Ruby thought it was a rat,' Cressida said, as deadpan as possible.

Miss de Souza merely raised her eyebrows, which was the final cue for Cressida to drop the wig back into the carry case.

'I'm awfully sorry, honestly. Hugest apologies,' Cressida continued.

'I'll thank you to leave,' Miss de Souza glowered at her.

'Of course, yes.' Cressida stepped forward, but despite this compartment being bigger than most, there still wasn't much room for the two women to pass by each other. And Cressida, though intent on finding Owen Edwards and asking about his collection of newspaper clippings, really didn't want to waste this opportunity to speak to Miss de Souza alone. It was the first time she'd seen her since the murder of her lover. And, more than that, it was the first time she'd seen her since finding her beautiful red suede shoes in the luggage car.

*The shoes that held that blackmailing letter...*

Cressida paused as she hovered near the door where Miss de Souza was standing and glanced down at her feet. She was in plain black ballet pumps. 'My condolences. I know your relationship with Lewis Warriner wasn't exactly—'

Miss de Souza huffed, then with a raised eyebrow, answered, 'Legitimate?'

'Well, yes, I suppose that's one way of putting it,' Cressida agreed. 'Legitimate or not though, you obviously had a connection and, well, my condolences.'

Cressida studied Miss de Souza's face, looking for the reaction. What did she expect to find there? Sorrow? Satisfaction? Despite wondering about it earlier, Cressida couldn't really see what de Souza had to gain from murdering Warriner.

But the impassive look on de Souza's face added to Cressida's qualms about the young woman. She was, after all, being blackmailed about something, not to mention travelling with a wig in her valise. And with someone else's husband.

The silence between them was now becoming awkward and Cressida knew better than to think she was anything other than not wanted. But still, she had to know more about de Souza and her relationship with Warriner.

*And what she was doing with that wig...*

'I hear you're an actress?' she ventured, hoping it would break the ice. 'Is that what the wig's for?'

Miss de Souza raised an eyebrow. 'It's part of my trousseau, yes.'

'Right. Of course. Off to tread the boards on the London stage. Is that the plan?'

De Souza narrowed her eyes as she said, 'The plan, as you say, seems to be constantly changing.'

*Just like the Irving siblings*, thought Cressida to herself. *Miss de Souza sounds like she's on to her Plan B too...*

'You have fans, though, a real following. One on this train even. I'm sure you'll find success, whether it be in films or on the stage. That Owen Edwards chap seemed to think so.'

If possible, de Souza became even frostier towards Cressida. 'What about him?' she snapped.

'Nothing. Just that he seemed very excited about meeting you earlier. Asked for your autograph and all that.'

Cressida could sense de Souza's hackles lowering. But still, Cressida had noted the reaction. Something about that autograph hunter had riled her.

Cressida tried a different approach. 'It must be hard, fending off admirers and all that, especially when you're with someone.'

'What is this? The Spanish Inquisition?' de Souza hissed. 'I know you're working with the police. And I know they'd love nothing better than pinning Geraldine's attack on me.'

The reaction wasn't what Cressida was expecting, but she was glad to get something out of the young woman; something she could work with.

'Why do you think they'd want to incriminate you? Is there anything you can tell me about Mr Warriner's murder, or the attack on his wife? Anything at all that perhaps you might have forgotten to tell the police earlier?'

'I've told the police all they need to know.'

Cressida took a deep breath, then said something she knew would provoke a reaction. 'Au fait with them, I suppose, after having to answer questions about those stolen handbags?'

'How did you know about that?' Miss de Souza crossed her arms protectively across her chest.

'It's all over today's paper.' *And mentioned in a letter in your shoe...* Cressida kept that bit to herself for now.

De Souza screwed up her eyes, as if the thought of all of this was incredibly irksome; painful even. 'He promised...' she whispered. Her anger faded to resignation, and then to utter sadness.

'Who? Who promised what?' Cressida asked, but de Souza batted her question away with a flick of her hand.

Cressida changed tack again, determined to get some more information out of this woman before the train pulled into Edinburgh and she was needed as one of the lookouts.

'How did you meet Mr Warriner?' Cressida tried not to look over to where the body of that very man was lying.

'He came to the Firebird Club. I was dancing.' Miss de Souza looked down at her simple black ballet pumps and then to where Warriner was lying under the sheet, the glossy black of his own shoes showing. 'He seemed to have some business with the owner, Mickey Loretta.'

'Pink Cheeks?'

'Yes.' Miss de Souza looked at Cressida in a new way. 'You know him?'

'A little,' Cressida said, fingers crossed on the hand hidden under Ruby. Still, lie or not, Cressida's answer seemed to break through Miss de Souza's froideur.

'Then you'll know all about how a girl like me got into bed with a man like Warriner.' She gazed at the body on the bed. 'And why I would never have anything to do with the killing of him.'

## 32

'Lew came to the club, like I said.' The transatlantic twang had moved several thousand miles east and was starting to sound more Glaswegian. 'He spoke to the boss, he watched me dance. But he really watched, you know? Like he was interested and not just because of my—'

'Sequins,' Cressida interrupted, unsure of what Miss de Souza was about to say, but worrying that mentioning it in front of a dead body was somehow irreligious or unmannerly.

'Exactly. And afterwards he asked me to join his table. Said he would make me a star.'

'How? He was wealthy, but his expertise was in manufacturing car parts, investing in lowlifes like Mickey Loretta, or Al De Marco and his car showrooms, not, as far as I know, pressing the flesh in Hollywood.'

Miss de Souza rubbed a hand up her arm as if warding off goosebumps. 'He said he knew people down south. People who owed him a favour.'

'And he was willing to call in those favours to help you?' Cressida thought about poor Geraldine, heartbroken and betrayed by her husband. And now fighting for her life. Had getting rid of wife number two been one of these 'favours'? Was there really someone from Glasgow or London's underworld on the train with them all? As Cressida's brow furrowed in thought, de Souza answered.

'He said he was. He said all I needed was a hand up and then I'd be—'

*Grateful to him for a very long time*, was what Cressida was thinking, though she interrupted de Souza with: 'And that's why you were on your way to London together?'

'Yes,' de Souza replied, yet Cressida could sense there was more lurking behind that one-word answer. Like the back of an embroidery – one perfect stitch on the front could be extremely complex behind.

'But?' she prompted, hoping Miss de Souza would explain.

'But nothing. Not really.'

Cressida thought about it for a moment. 'Hard for a respectable industrialist to make a nightclub dancer a star, especially if she's mentioned in the tabloids with scandals attached to her name?'

De Souza blushed red. 'I really think you should leave now. This is so disrespectful to Lew, just lying there like that...'

'I'm sorry, but—'

'But nothing!' she snapped. 'Leave me alone! I'm tired of being told what to do. Tired of being pushed around!' She pushed Cressida out of the door. 'Tired of it, I say! I don't care what anyone thinks or writes about me anymore. I'm going to be in Hollywood movies, I have to be. I have to be.' She was in tears now and Cressida was perplexed at the change in emotion from anger to despair.

Up close, the blonde hair, which looked so perfectly bleached and waved when Cressida had first seen it, was greasy and dark roots were showing. The red painted nails on de Souza's hands were chipped, and the rings gaudy – no doubt paste rather than real diamonds. The only real piece of jewellery was a thin silver chain around her wrist, joined by a clasp from which were hanging two charm-sized silver letters. A 'P' and an 'S'. Warriner definitely wasn't her benefactor yet, and now her chance of a wealthier life was lying dead and lifeless on the bed next to her. Cressida felt a pang of pity for the showgirl.

'I'm sorry, Miss de Souza. Or can I call you Phoebe?' Cressida said, gently.

De Souza nodded, seemingly exhausted after her outburst. 'I just want to be alone. I'm tired. I'm so tired of doing everything for everyone else, and here I was, finally on my way to London, for myself. For screen tests and auditions and perhaps even parties with other actresses and important directors and now... I'm grafting again, aren't I? Still someone's pawn, still someone's piece,' she sniffled.

'What do you mean, Phoebe?' Cressida asked, desperately trying to work out to what the poor girl might be referring. She instinctively reached out and touched her arm, though Miss de Souza flinched it away.

The silver bracelet caught Cressida's eye again.

P and S. Phoebe de Souza... or perhaps Phoebe Smith?

Cressida pulled her arm back and slipped her free hand into her pocket. She pulled out the luggage tag and showed it to Phoebe. 'Is this yours? Are you actually Phoebe Smith?' she asked, as gently as possible.

Phoebe took it from her and just nodded.

'Why did you leave your shoes in the luggage car, your beautiful red suede shoes?'

Phoebe looked up at Cressida, tears swimming in her eyes. 'The note...' she whispered.

'I saw it,' Cressida admitted. 'Are you being blackmailed?'

Phoebe looked at her. Mascara smudged her cheek as a tear rolled down it. She looked as if she were about to sob. Cressida reached out for her again, but this time it was too much. Phoebe swatted her arm away and garnered some inner strength.

'Nothing. It's nothing.' She wiped her eyes and nose with her sleeve and pushed past Cressida. 'I've got to go. Leave me alone.'

At that, Cressida was left standing by the open door to the dead man's compartment, intrigued by this woman who had seemed so glamorous, so full of gumption; yet she was obviously put upon, tired and exhausted by it all too. And she was left wondering what had just happened.

# 33

Cressida, with Ruby still in her arms, was about to close the door when something else in the compartment caught her eye. There was a narrow gap between the end of the bed and the vanity unit, and in that gap Cressida had spotted something she recognised.

'Ruby, promise me you'll behave if I put you down.' She nuzzled into the soft fur of Ruby's ears as she put the young pup on the floor of the corridor. She crossed the short distance through the compartment as she carried on speaking to her pup. 'No investigating. I just want to get... Aha, yes. I thought so.'

Cressida pulled the manilla folder from out of the gap and held it in front of her. Aware of the fact that not only was time pressing on but also that she really shouldn't still be lurking in the compartment of the dead man – the crime scene, no less – Cressida thought it best to take the folder with her.

Then she remembered that the person she had been wanting to find, Owen Edwards, was the last person she'd seen with this folder and that he would be confused indeed if she met him brandishing the very same folder full of newspaper clippings at him.

'Tell you what, Rubes. Owen can wait until after we've got the doctor on board.' She glanced at her wristwatch. 'Which gives me about five minutes until I need to go and find Alfred.'

She checked that Ruby wasn't doing anything too terrible to the crime scene and then opened up the folder, using the vanity table as a desk. Carefully, she sorted through the clippings. Each one had been cut out from a different magazine or newspaper over the last decade or so. Some were just a couple of inches of tight column text and others were folded-over double-page spreads from glossy magazines. The largest of these came from a copy of *The Tatler*, a title she knew well and often appeared in herself.

Cressida unfolded the now-yellowing pages of the magazine article and noticed the date: 1901. There was a picture of a stylish woman, dressed in the fashion of the time. The lady reminded Cressida of her own mother – not now of course, but in photographs that had been taken at the turn of the century. That nipped-in waist and floor-length skirt, paired with a high ruffle-necked blouse and hair that haloed out around the head like a giant powder puff. This lady had a thick canvas driving coat on too and goggles dangling from one arm.

Cressida read the caption out loud. '"A Way With Wheels! The new Mrs Lewis Warriner, photographed with her motor-car, the Lickety-Split."'

Cressida looked at the longer text accompanying the photograph.

*Mrs Warriner has all faith that her new husband can take motoring to the next level. Having been widowed tragically and left with two small children, the whirlwind romance between Myra and Lewis Warriner is the stuff of dreams – for the automobile enthusiast at least! Mrs Warriner will be putting more than just her wifely support behind Mr Warriner as he embarks on the first of his manufacturing plants in Inverness.*

Cressida put the article down. *Interesting...* she thought as she picked up another clipping, this time from the less salubrious *Evening Post*. It read:

*The bitter divorce continues between Warriner vs Warriner, of Inverness. Recent claims in court, backed up by evidence first outed in this newspaper, show Mrs Warriner, 40, to have been adulterous in her marriage. Mrs Warriner denies all allegations against her and rebukes the assertions of her husband, wealthy industrialist Lewis Warriner, 45.*

Another similar one tracked the divorce further:

*An agreement today was reached at Inverness Magistrates Court in the case of Warriner vs Warriner. Mrs Warriner's representative said, 'My client has agreed a compromise with her former husband, relinquishing her personal shares in Warriner Industries in order to let him run the company unhindered, overages notwithstanding.'*

Again, Cressida carefully put the clipping back in the folder and then found the smallest piece of paper in the collection. A death notice, from an unknown broadsheet, that simply read: WARRINER, *Myra Anne. Passed away after a short illness, Glasgow, 5 December 1912. Thy vengeance will come.*

Cressida shivered as she read that last line. What was it that Andrews had told her the very first time they'd met? When she was desperate to find out who was ruining the happy lives of her dear friends the Chattertons... *'we seek justice, not vengeance'*...

She put the death notice down and turned to the letter she'd seen slip out when Owen had first dropped the folder. She hadn't known whose logo it was when she had spied it briefly earlier, but she'd seen it again since. It was the *Evening Post*, the tabloid she'd picked up from the newspaper rack at the end of the sleeper carriage. And the newspaper that had printed that piece about the Warriners' divorce. She read the letter to herself and sighed. Someone called Edward was being asked for a job interview with the head of news and editorial, and with salaries being discussed in the second paragraph, it looked like it was a done deal.

Cressida placed it back in the folder and then pulled out another piece of paper. Again, this one wasn't a newspaper or magazine cutting, but a page of handwriting. The edge down one side of the paper looked torn, as if it had been ripped from the binding of a notebook. Cressida squinted at the tightly formed words and hard-to-read cursive script. But she could make out well enough what it was, or at least what she thought it might be. Research notes, as if taken down during an interview or while looking in an archive. There was information about Mrs Warriner – the first Mrs Warriner that was: the date of her marriage, the date of her first husband's death, the amount of money she inherited from him. Then another paragraph listing various names. *Workers at Warriner Industries perhaps?* Cressida thought as she noticed Hugh Donaldson and Clarence Derby's names along with others that had been crossed through or struck out.

'How bizarre, Rubes,' Cressida said to her patient pup, who, to her credit, hadn't been tempted to form her own investigation of the crime scene with her nose or paws. 'Whoever this archive belongs to was fascinated by the first Mrs Warriner. But why that should turn up now, when we have a murdered Mr Warriner and his second wife not looking too rosy... I don't know.'

Glancing again at her wristwatch, Cressida swore under her

breath and carefully put all the clippings back into the folder. She tucked it under her arm and clicked her fingers at Ruby.

'Come on, Rubes. We have to get this to Andrews. There's something terribly, terribly sad going on here, I think. I just hope we can suss it all out before anyone else gets hurt. Or worse.'

## 34

Cressida left the compartment and headed back to Andrews' compartment to find Alfred. But other thoughts were buzzing through her mind.

Those clippings told a story, from the young bride, who came to a marriage with two young children and an enthusiasm for motorcars; to the bitter divorce about ten years later; to her death, with little fanfare, a mere two years after that. There were other articles in there too: 'Warriner Runs for Council' and 'Where There's Brakes, There's Brass'. The latter had been about how wealthy Warriner had become, due to the parts for motorcars he'd been manufacturing since his factories had opened in 1902. 'A British Success Story', another had read. And, of course, there was that letter inviting someone to work for the newspaper and that page torn out of a notebook that seemed to be piecing Myra Warriner's life together.

Cressida glanced down at Ruby, who was toddling along beside her and seemed much less fazed by the incidental jolts to the line or sway on the rails. Four legs, it seemed, being much sturdier than two, however spindly those four little legs were.

Cressida was just mulling over how the folder had got itself wedged down between the bed and the vanity unit, and in the deceased's compartment of all places, when a door opened and she almost bumped into the willowy, gaunt figure of Lord Hartnell's nanny.

'Oh, do excuse me,' Cressida said to the exasperated-looking woman.

'I've never known a boy like him. He won't sit still.' The nanny shook her head, and looked at Lord Hartnell, who was sitting cross-legged on one of the twin bunks in the room.

Cressida hadn't realised that the underaged lord was travelling in the compartment next door to her. She sighed. Was she to be in for a night of listening to him throwing an Indian rubber ball around? She peered in through the open door and noticed that the room he was sharing with his nanny was very much like the one Warriner was still currently lying dead in, but made up of two single beds, rather than one double. She also noticed that the pint-sized viscount had for once removed his finger from his nose and was now using his freed hand to pet Ruby, who had toddled into his room. She hoped she hid the grimace on her face as she thought of Lord Hartnell's mucky paws all over her own dear Ruby.

'That's not fair, Nanny,' Lord Hartnell called from his bed, his voice as haughty as a nine-year-old's could be. 'I sat still all through supper, and you weren't even there to see it. And I might have eaten that sausage if you'd left it on my plate.'

The nanny sighed. 'Well, yes, I suppose that should count. Though I was laying out your pyjamas, that you've now got cocoa all over. I'll have to get a cloth. And do leave Miss Fawcett's poor dog alone.'

'I think, surprisingly, she's quite enjoying it,' Cressida said, looking at Ruby disbelievingly. Cressida thought that she and Ruby had a certain understanding, a connection of the soul even; yet Cressida knew for certain that the last thing she'd want was Lord Hartnell's sticky fingers tickling her forehead.

She shook the thought from her mind. 'Anyway, come along, Rubes, let's leave Lord Hartnell and his nanny... I'm sorry, I don't know your name.'

The governess looked at Cressida and smiled. 'Ginny'll do, ma'am.' She bobbed a curtsy and gestured for Lord Hartnell to stay put while she hurried down the passage in search of a cloth.

'Ginny. How charming,' Cressida said to Ruby once she'd extracted her from the young lord's bedroom and held the door open for her that linked the two sleeper carriages. 'In my day, nannies had such severe names like Miss Whiplock or Madame Griselda. I think I might have made more headway with my watercolours if I'd had a Ginny.'

Ruby looked up at her mistress with her dark round eyes and blinked slowly.

'I knew you'd understand, Rubes. Come along, we have an Alfred to meet, and I can feel the train slowing.'

Alfred appeared just a moment later, and with the assurance that Dotty and Kirby were now stationed in the luggage car at the far end of the train, they swayed their way through the train, passing more sleeping compartments. Just before the grand platform of Edinburgh station came into sight, they reached the dining car.

Alfred squeezed himself in behind the very table where Warriner and Miss de Souza had dined only hours beforehand, before any of this had all happened, and was already leaning on the window catch, making sure it would open as the mighty train slowed to barely walking pace alongside the platform.

'That one looks like it has an easier catch.' He pointed over to the table the other side of the aisle from his and Cressida took her position.

'Just as I hoped, the platform is well lit. Do you think we'll see anything, Alfred?'

'Let's hope the driver doesn't release the steam bulb. If so, we'll be hard pressed to see the end of our own noses.' He frowned. 'We've got to try, though. Kirby escorted Dot down the train a few minutes ago. They should be in position by now.'

'Righto.' Cressida pulled the window down as the train slowed to a stop at Edinburgh station. A blast of a whistle greeted her and she instinctively ducked her head back in. She glanced over to Alfred, who had done the same, and he sheepishly grinned at her.

'Let's try that again, shall we?' he said, then stuck his head out of the window and Cressida saw him switch this way and that, checking the tracks in both directions.

She, however, was platform side and she peered out of the open window and mimicked Alfred, glancing in both directions before settling her gaze down the platform. The stationmaster had lowered his flag and the whistle had dropped from his mouth. What should have been a busy platform had been cleared by the stationmaster and porters, warned in advance by Sawyer that no one must alight or disembark, saving the doctor. And, of course, the coal, and water from a bowser for the steam.

Cressida couldn't see any of the coal or water being loaded on, but she could make out a man in tweeds standing next to the stationmaster, the familiar sight of a doctor's bag gripped in one hand, an overnight valise in the other. He was nodding to the stationmaster and then he took a few steps towards the train.

Cressida looked behind her again, checking that no one had slipped out of the glossy black door of the lounge carriage, or from the luggage van behind. There was nothing to see except a newspaper vendor, his A-board splashed with the headline on the evening press: *Mob Murder Hits High Places.*

A thunderous crash of coal being dropped into the tender just behind the engine caught her unawares and it was only as she looked again at the platform that a flash of reflected evening light caught her eye; a door had opened!

'By Jove! Alfred!' Cressida called for her friend to join her and he pulled his head back from his own post overlooking the tracks. He joined her in a matter of two or three steps, pushing the upholstered chairs away from the table. Cressida could feel his body pressed against hers and it caused her quite a few capital-F Feelings, which she dampened down in the face of the task at hand. 'Look, Alfred, that door is open. It's the next carriage down and it's not the one the doctor used to board only a moment ago.'

'Aha, I see.' Alfred stuck his head out above Cressida's and raised his hand to his brow to help him see further. 'No one's getting off, though. Looks like the stationmaster is about to close it...'

Cressida watched as the stationmaster slammed the door shut and turned around, oblivious to the small mushroom-coloured pug that was toddling along behind him.

'Oh no!' Cressida gasped, realising that it was her own precious pup that was in danger of being left behind. 'Oh Ruby!'

She clasped her hand to her mouth, then dropped it again as she shouted in desperation against the noise of the train engine as it prepared to move off.

'Ruby!'

## 35

Cressida shouted down the platform at the stationmaster. But he seemed unaware of the fact that Ruby, who had somehow got herself off the train, was now toddling over to one of the ironwork pillars on the other side of the platform and relieving herself up against it.

'How did she get out?' Alfred asked, but Cressida couldn't answer him. She was transfixed as the stationmaster raised his flag, still unaware of the precious pooch having a lovely sniff around the wooden bench near the newspaper vendor.

'He's raising his whistle, Alfred! Oh Mr Stationmaster, cooeeee!' Cressida called, waving her hand manically from the window.

Behind her, Alfred and his comforting presence had disappeared. Cressida felt terribly helpless as the stationmaster, who still hadn't noticed the mushroom-coloured treasure tootling up his platform, put the whistle in his mouth. Everything around her slowed, as he waved the green flag in his hand... and blew.

A cloud of steam barrelled down the platform, enveloping the train carriages and making the panic build in Cressida's chest even more.

'Ruby! Oh, Ruby!' she screamed again from the window, hanging out as far as she could as the huge engine behind her began its ponderous chuff-chuff, the metal of the drive shaft laboriously starting to pull the tonnage through the huge iron wheels. 'Ruby!' Cressida called again, as she saw the platform beneath her begin to roll away.

Then, as she thought all might be lost, she saw something that gave her hope. A flash of chestnut brown hair, a swoop as he scooped up the small dog from the platform, a quick turn and his pace quickened to match that of the train as it built up speed, a door flung open for him just as the train pulled away from the last of the platform.

Alfred had saved Ruby. Cressida wanted to weep as she took in the sight of the ever so dashing Lord Delafield, as he leaned triumphantly out of the door, Ruby safely tucked under one arm, and a rakish grin on his face.

'Alfred! Ruby!' Cressida rushed down the aisle between the dining tables, scattering cutlery in her haste, much to the tut-tutting of the Fernley-Hoggs, who had been finishing off their strawberry bavois at their table while all of this was going on. She pushed through the connecting doors of the dining car to the first *wagon-lit*, and almost crashed head-first into Alfred, Ruby held firmly in his arms.

'Whoa. Here she is!' Alfred said. 'Safe and sound.'

'Oh Ruby.' Cressida took her small dog from Alfred and pressed her soft, velvet-like fur up to her face. What would she have done if Ruby had been left behind on an unfamiliar station platform? What would Ruby have done? It all just didn't bear thinking about. 'How did you get out, Rubes?' she whispered into her dog's ear. Then she looked up at Alfred. 'How did she get out? She was right there next to me just moments before. I'm sure she was.'

Alfred gestured for them both to move back towards the

dining car. 'Come on, old thing. Much to discuss, but let's do it in comfort rather than hugger-mugger here in the corridor.'

'Walls, and doors, have ears too,' Cressida whispered, remembering her own skill in listening in on a private conversation.

Once they were seated in the dining car, with a stiff drink in front of them, Alfred brought up the question again.

'You're right, Ruby was next to you. But she wasn't there when I came to join you on your side of the carriage. Sorry, I should have said something at the time. But we were—'

'Watching that door being opened. The one that no one alighted or boarded from.' Cressida completed his sentence. She paused. 'Except Ruby did alight from it, don't you think? She must have done. No other doors were open at the time.'

'You mean to say she toddled off, leaving your side, which is most frightfully odd and unlike her, and decided to go through the connecting doors to the next carriage and then disembark. All by herself?'

'No. Not all by herself. She couldn't have done that, Alfred.' A thought occurred to Cressida and she paled as she articulated it. 'Someone must have lured her away.'

'When we were looking out of the windows?' Alfred reached into his pocket and pulled out his pipe, clamping it between his teeth as he thought. 'The door. That door you saw open.'

'The one she must have escaped from. Or been ejected from... oh poor Rubes, my darling dog. How could anyone have thrown you out of the train?' Cressida nuzzled her nose into the pup's soft fur again, much to a satisfied snort from Ruby herself.

'Yes, yes. But also opened to distract us perhaps,' Alfred said. 'I left my post on this side of the train when you called me over.'

'Oh. But for a very worthwhile reason, so it turns out,' Cressida said, rather sheepishly, realising that she had prioritised having her own pooch back more than their mission to make sure no murderer left the train while it was stationary. 'Thank you, Alfred, for your bravery and quick reaction. You are super.' She looked into his deep chestnut brown eyes, almost the same rich colour as his mahogany pipe. She held his gaze for half a moment, before he looked down to find some tobacco and 'ahemmed' a few times, followed by various mutterings of 'nothing of it', 'simplest thing in the world to do', 'anyone would' and that sort of thing.

Still, it occurred to Cressida that someone on this train had not only been so heartless as to kill a man, and possibly his wife and DCI Andrews too, in the coldest of bloods, but they were willing to do something else almost as terrible. They were willing to harm Ruby to get what they wanted, be that escape or distraction.

Cressida shivered. Murderers she could cope with; but anyone who was able to toss a small dog out of a soon-to-be-moving train was someone truly devoid of all feeling.

Someone truly evil.

## 36

A clattering at the door sounded the arrival of Dotty.

'There you two are,' she said, squeezing in behind Alfred and plumping herself down on one of the upholstered dining chairs. 'I feel like I'm running this train. The doctor's in with Mrs Warriner now. He's doing his best for her and agreed that she mustn't be moved until we get to London. The hospitals there will have more experience with gunshot wounds like hers. Though he did then also say that soon enough Glasgow infirmaries would have to be at the same level, due to the rise in illegal firearms in the city. Rather gives one the chills, doesn't it? Anyway, it meant I could then take the under chef, who was focused on Mrs Warriner's care, along to Andrews. And, I must say, he seems very nice. I did hear him remarking on what an excellent sling Andrews had on.' Dotty sat back and smiled in satisfaction at her brother and best friend, then clocked that they had very large, very stiff drinks in front of them, instead of their usual tipples, and narrowed her eyes. 'What is it? What's happened?'

Cressida took a deep breath, then filled in her friend, who

gasped and cried out in all the right places, as a best friend should.

'Which door was it?' Dotty asked, reaching over to stroke Ruby, who seemed utterly unaware of the drama she had just caused.

'The one at the far end of the first sleeping car,' Alfred told her.

'So, the one next to,' Dotty lowered her voice due to the company in the dining car, 'the Fernley-Hoggs' compartment?'

'Yes, but also not far from ours, or anyone's really.' Alfred shrugged. 'A quick pace down that corridor and you could cover the whole train in a matter of moments.' He stuck his pipe in his mouth, as if to say 'QED'.

'Alfred wonders if it was all a tactic to distract us,' Cressida said, and Alfred took his pipe out of his mouth and nodded.

'Did you or Kirby see anything out of your windows, Dot?' he asked, then clamped his pipe back between his teeth.

Cressida wondered if he felt bad about abandoning his post, but she was so very pleased that he had. Her heart would have broken if Ruby had been lost, or, worse, injured somehow as she was ejected from the train. That Alfred had sprinted out to rescue her was something so very wonderful indeed... She had to stop thinking of it, less the fizzing in her stomach quite over-come her just at a moment when Dotty was saying something interesting.

'We didn't get much of a view really. That steam really barrels down the top of the locomotive towards the tail-end of the train. And I was trackside and really couldn't see much from all the way down where I was. I had the bowser in the way and then the coal drop. Gosh, that made a noise as it went into the tender. Though I looked both ways a lot as Kirby and I couldn't get much further than the end of the sleepers, so we had to check behind us, as well as in front of us.'

'Us too. Just supposing, with Alfred distracted and you

turned the other way, Dot, someone could have jumped off the train,' Cressida pondered. 'Someone with a guilty conscience.'

Dotty sighed. 'Is it so very terrible that I rather hope the murderer *has* jumped off? I know we need to seek justice and all that, but I was rather worried about going to sleep with a killer on board.'

The three of them sat in silence for a little while.

'Justice not vengeance,' Cressida murmured, bringing the whisky to her lips.

'What's that, chum?' Dotty asked, and then followed it up with. 'I wonder if we will get any supper. It seems yonks since we had those cheesy gougères and you made all that fuss with the Irvings, Cressy. I never did get my mulligatawny soup.'

Alfred shook his head at his sister and turned to Cressida. 'What do you mean, justice and vengeance and all that?'

Cressida sighed and pulled the manilla folder from the side of her chair where she'd stashed it as she'd taken her post. She showed her friends the news articles, the death notice and the letter.

'And these were all being carried by Owen?' Alfred asked.

'Yes. Though he said they weren't his.'

'Tells us a bit more about the first Mrs Warriner, though, doesn't it?' Dotty said after a while, having rearranged some of the clippings so she could read them better.

Cressida nodded. They really did. And there was something in them, not just the sorry story about a wealthy woman who loved the exciting new world of the motor vehicle and helped her husband build his dream before being divorced and dying so sadly young. There was something else there, a thread she was trying to pull, something that nagged at her like the frayed edge of a silk cushion.

A reason for justice...

... A reason for vengeance.

## 37

The white-jacketed waiter, who was a paragon of professionalism bearing in mind what was going on around them, offered the three friends the dinner menus again and waited while they ordered.

'I know time is of the essence and all that, Cressy,' Dotty said a few minutes later, having swallowed down her first bite of chicken and apricot terrine, 'but, gosh, I was hungry.'

'No, absolutely right, Dot,' her brother agreed. 'Got to keep our energy up if we're to spend the night figuring this thing out rather than getting some decent kip. Sorry, they'd run out of your soup. Probably the sous-chef's department.'

'He's a sous-chef, not a soup chef, Alf.' Dotty sighed. 'But I see your point.'

Cressida smiled. Her friends were right, of course, and she'd taken the opportunity of not only ordering herself a decent course or two, but also a piece of fillet steak for Ruby, who deserved the best after her platform ordeal.

'We do need to go and talk to Andrews, though,' she reminded them once her plate was clean. 'And, Dot, might you be an angel and stay with him a little longer? See if you can find out any more information from those newspaper clippings. I know the doctor's on board now, but he'll have his work cut out with Geraldine, I should imagine. I can't bear the thought of dear Andrews being in pain and discomfort.'

'Of course, Cressy. Though I think dear Andrews is quite possibly my worst patient since I tried to play nurse to one of the farm cats when I was a girl.'

Cressida laughed at her friend. 'He's just frustrated, Dot, he doesn't mean it. And I know how he feels. There's just so much about all of this that makes no sense.'

'You mean Geraldine being framed, and then shot?' Alfred posed.

'Yes. And there being so many people on this train, save us, and perhaps the Fernley-Hoggs and little Lord Hartnell and his nanny, who have some sort of connection to Lewis Warriner.'

'I do agree with you that the Irvings do sound a little shifty, Cressy,' Dot said thoughtfully. 'I thought Louise was charming, but when you pressed her brother for information, he really did clam up.'

'And he obviously has a temper, or a wild streak, if even his own sister was worried enough to ask him if he'd killed Warriner.'

'Maybe he did?' Alfred suggested. 'We haven't seen them since the stop. Perhaps it was the two of them that absconded? One of those articles as much as says that Warriner was pulling his investments from Indian companies – I'd be livid if I were them and suddenly our investments were all pulled from under us like the proverbial carpet.'

'Their compartments aren't far from here, in the first sleeper carriage,' Cressida said, nodding and remembering seeing the name cards in the smart brass holders as she'd walked past. She noted to herself that it was neither of these compartments that they'd hidden themselves away in for their robust conversation about roughing someone up.

'Next to that Derby chap you said was Mr Warriner's private secretary,' Dotty added.

Cressida raised a finger. 'That's right, and it reminds me – Donaldson said Derby really didn't appreciate the fact that Geraldine, who had been a secretary in the typing pool under Derby when she first met Warriner, hadn't helped him once she had the ear of the boss.'

'Speak of the devil.' Alfred nodded over to where the instantly recognisable beak nose of Clarence Derby had appeared, along with the rest of him, in the bar area.

Cressida looked over to where he was leaning at the bar, then back to her friends. She pushed her whisky away.

'Chaps. You'll have to excuse me, but I have a sudden thirst for one of that charming barman's gin rickeys...'

Despite half-hearted protestations from Alfred and Dotty, Cressida laid her napkin on her chair as she got up, straightened herself out and approached the tired-looking man at the bar. That one person might have absconded from the train at Edinburgh was likely, that two had... well, that would have taken some doing given the brief window of time they'd been distracted. So, there might still be one of the suspected deadly duo of conspirators aboard. And Clarence Derby, accused by Donaldson of having a light-fingered approach to the company accounts, might be one of them.

'Hello there. Mr Derby, isn't it?' Cressida sidled up next to him, then ordered her cocktail from the barman. 'What an evening, eh?'

Clarence Derby looked at her and she met his gaze, noticing the dark rings under his eyes and the sallow colour of his skin. He looked exhausted. The heaviness of his crimes weighing on him, perhaps?

'I've not known one like it, Miss Fawcett,' the private secretary replied, then started to laugh at the lunacy of his own words. 'Not ever, not one like it at all.' He shook his head and chuckled some more, eventually wiping a tear from the corner of his eye with a scrunched-up handkerchief he found in his pocket.

Cressida wasn't quite sure she found it all so amusing, but smiled at him all the same, hoping to encourage some more out of him. 'I don't think any of us have, Mr Derby,' she said, wondering if he'd ever stop chuckling to himself, and quite what this outburst of frivolity meant. Was he happy that his employer was dead and Mrs Warriner was so badly injured she might follow suit next?

'Forgive me,' Clarence said, his giggles subsiding and the handkerchief, after one last wipe of the corner of his eyes, going back into his pocket. 'I don't know what came over me then. I don't really think it's funny that all this has happened, but it's all so... so...' He waved a hand in the air to show how extensive whatever it was that he was trying to say was. 'It's all so mad, isn't it?'

'Useful though, too, surely?' Cressida said, then sipped her drink, keeping her eyes firmly on his expression. As she suspected, it changed completely from the hysterical back to the haunted.

'Useful? What do you mean?' he asked, and Cressida noticed his grip on his tumbler of whisky tighten.

'Oh, just that now you're in charge, I suppose. Maybe not in title or inheritance, but you were the neck on which the head turned, I should imagine. I doubt much happened at Warriner Industries without you knowing about it, and I should imagine plenty happened that Warriner *didn't* know about.'

Clarence Derby stared at Cressida.

She pushed a little further. 'So useful, to have access to everything, the ledgers, the bank accounts, the bookkeeping, the—'

'Are you insinuating that I might have killed my employer because I was hiding something from him?' Derby raised his tumbler to his lips and Cressida noticed the shake of his hand as he took a sip.

'I heard that might be the case. Not necessarily the murdering bit, but the hiding something aspect of it all, yes.' Cressida kept her cocktail glass on the bar, hoping the vibrations of the train would mask any nervous shakes of her own.

'From whom? Geraldine?' He sounded wounded.

'It doesn't matter who, but I did hear that you'd been very upset that Geraldine hadn't helped you. Hadn't got you to the top of the tree, even though you felt she owed you, what with you having been senior to her when she caught Warriner's eye. And instead of achieving high office in the company, you decided to take what you wanted rather than wait for promotion.'

Cressida expected Derby to reply angrily, to admonish her and shout 'how dare you!' and all that sort of thing, but instead he just looked shocked, and, once again, terribly, terribly tired.

'Mr Derby?' she asked, going so far as to place a hand on his arm. 'Mr Derby, am I right? And are you all right?'

He nodded. 'Yes, Miss Fawcett, I'm all right, I'm just wearied by this whole affair. And yes, you're right.' He sighed. 'I did steal from Warriner. And I did despise Geraldine for never helping me. So, yes, in many ways I should be happy that he's dead, and she not far behind.'

'Did you plan all this, Mr Derby? Did you lure Geraldine on board in order to frame her and then kill Warriner?' Cressida withdrew her hand from his arm, remembering that Clarence Derby had been absent from the dining car, and therefore had no alibi, for when Warriner was murdered.

Had she just reached out and comforted a murderer?

## 38

'Have you ever loved someone and hated someone in equal measure?' Clarence Derby asked, to Cressida's surprise.

'No, Mr Derby, I haven't. Who do you love? And loathe?'

Derby looked into his glass, swirling the amber liquid around slowly, contemplatively.

'The purest ache, a waking dream, that is my love for Geraldine,' he said, the merest hint of a tune to his words.

'Oh Mr Derby, Clarence... you *love* Geraldine? I thought you hated the fact that she had risen so high above her station and not helped you along the way as you'd hoped. *Not* that you loved her.'

'And I thought once that she loved me too.' His eyes were still gazing at the glass in front of him. 'Before she caught Warriner's eye and threw me over. Stepping out we were. I impressed her, I think, being on the up back then. A clerk, yes, but one with potential. I had no formal training, but Warriner had taken me on in 1905 as a junior clerk and I'd put my time in and impressed management. Gerry joined us in 1908 straight from secretarial college, where she'd retrained after leaving her family's bakery business.' He paused. 'We used to chuckle about that. How she could get a loaf out of the oven before anyone else in that typing pool had even woken up. She was a hard worker, see, and it didn't take long for her to be noticed. Mr O'Malley, the private secretary at the time, brought her up to the main office and I remember celebrating with her that night. A bag of chips on the bench by the station.' Clarence sighed. 'I'd do anything to wind back the years and go back to that night. We both had nothing, and everything.'

'Then Warriner stepped in?' Cressida couldn't help but ask, intrigued by this desperately sad love story.

Derby nodded. 'I used to meet her for lunch every day at the sound of the factory whistle, swap a sandwich, chat and whatnot. Until one day she didn't show up and then nothing the next day, nor the next. I found her after that, and asked her outright what I'd done and where I stood, but she wouldn't tell me anything except that it wasn't my fault, but I mustn't blame her either. Then I saw her one day tucking her blouse back into her skirt. And when I saw him, Warriner, leaving the same empty boardroom a few minutes later...'

Cressida could see Derby's fist clenching and unclenching as he spoke, and the hand that gripped his tumbler of whisky was white around the knuckles. 'That must have been very hard for you, Mr Derby,' she said, and indeed her heart did go out to him, but she had to remember that he was still a suspect – and talking himself into a very good motive to kill Warriner, and maybe even Geraldine too.

'I accepted it. I had to. But then the requests from those journalists started coming.'

'What do you mean?'

'I was the undersecretary to Mr O'Malley, so I didn't have privy access to it all, but the divorce proceedings started against Mrs Warriner – the first Mrs Warriner, that is. The woman whose money had been the seed capital for the whole business. There would have been no Warriner Industries without the first

Mrs Warriner, but she had to go if Geraldine were to take her place. And Warriner was damned if he was going to give her a penny out of what he'd made. He's a cruel man.'

'So many businessmen are, I believe,' Cressida agreed with him. 'But what did journalists have to do with it?'

'Hmm?' Clarence looked up at her from his drink, then gulped down the rest of the liquor. 'Oh, yes, the *Evening Post*. Warriner started taking one of the young reporters out for fancy dinners – I saw the receipts on Mr O'Malley's desk. Then the next thing we knew, those pieces started appearing about Myra in the gossip column, who she'd been seen out with, "eyewitnesses say..." and all that. Stood up in court too when Warriner hit her with adultery. The nerve of it.'

'But you knew he'd been having an affair with Geraldine,' Cressida said. 'Could you not have said something?'

'I did. To Geraldine. She said to mind my own business. She said she'd done nothing wrong. Said she'd never let Warriner touch her, though I knew what I saw that day outside the boardroom.'

'For what it's worth, Mr Derby, I spoke to Geraldine earlier and she swore to me that nothing substantial had ever happened between her and Warriner before they were married.'

'She did?' He looked up at Cressida, then his face crumpled into a gargoylish grimace. Though there was no sound, and no tears, Cressida thought she could see the decade or so of pain etched into his features. How he'd loved Geraldine, then hated her for throwing him over. This was no simple case of a man on the make who despised his underling for doing better than him. This was a man who was heartbroken. But, Cressida thought to herself warily, still with a motive for murder.

'Mr Derby, please...' Cressida reached out to him again. 'Your compartment is only just along the way, isn't it? I feel like you've had a rather ghastly few hours, well, few years. Perhaps you should sleep it off.' She nodded at Alfred, who had appeared at Derby's shoulder. He helped the now sniffling man off his bar stool and hooked an arm under his shoulder in order to help him manage the few steps out of the bar and through the carriages to his own compartment.

As Derby was all but limping past Cressida, he suddenly stuck his arm out and gripped the top of hers in his hand. 'I didn't do it, Miss Fawcett. I wouldn't have hurt Geraldine, not for all the tea in China.'

'I believe you, Mr Derby,' Cressida whispered, relieved when his grip loosened on her arm and he left, compliantly, with the ever-gallant Alfred.

Then she whispered to herself as she turned back to the bar: 'I just don't yet know if perhaps you *did* kill Mr Warriner.'

## 39

Cressida was still sitting at the bar when Alfred returned. Dotty, with Ruby safely in one arm and the folder in the other, had joined her, and Cressida was telling Dotty all about Clarence Derby and his broken heart.

'That poor man,' Dotty said.

'Yes, it was really quite the tale,' agreed Cressida. 'How was he when you got him back to his bunk, Alf?'

'Almost catatonic. If you're looking for a cool, calm and cunning murderer with a killer instinct, then I'd say that poor chap ain't him.' Alfred clasped his ever-present, if unlit, pipe in his mouth.

'Hmm, that's what I'm starting to think too. Though he does have a humdinger of a motive to kill Warriner.'

'Except it's been fifteen years,' Dotty reminded Cressida. 'I doubt he'd wait until now to do something, especially if he has no notion of Geraldine returning his affections anymore.'

'He didn't seem to, no,' Cressida agreed. Then she slapped her hands down on her thighs and huffed out a breath. 'Right. There's not much can be gained by sitting around here. Dot, we really should get that manilla folder of clippings to Andrews?

Would you be an angel and check in on him? Alf,' Cressida paused and looked up at her friend, 'I wonder if you and I should start to have a sort of headcount – see if anyone has absconded?'

'Good idea, Cressy.' Alfred nodded, tipping his tobacco onto his plate and pocketing his pipe as he got up.

'Do be careful, you two.' Dotty looked at them, her eyes showing her concern. Cressida did wonder, though, if the little twitch at the corner of her mouth showed that Dotty was also rather pleased that her brother and her best friend had teamed up so naturally. Cressida simply had to ignore this, else she'd have no room left in her head for any other thoughts.

They none of them got too far, however. Ruby, who had insisted on walking, having obviously got bored now of being cosseted to the extreme after her platform high jinks, started snuffling and rootling around at the end of the first carriage.

'Chaps,' Cressida alerted her friends to what her pup was doing. 'Wait a sec. Look.' She pointed to where Ruby was scratching at the door to the water closet.

'I thought she took her opportunity on the platform at Edinburgh?' Alfred said, raising an eyebrow. 'At least to judge by that stationmaster's face as he blew the whistle...'

'I don't think she's pressing for a call of nature, Alf,' Cressida rebuked him, though she smiled too. 'I've seen her do this before. There's just the slightest hint of wolf still in her, I think, and see how she's doing that panting thing. I think that's her version of howling for her pack.'

'She really is the most darling little wolf,' Dotty said, adoringly.

'Isn't she?' Cressida looked at her small dog for a moment before clicking back into action. 'But, come on, let's see what she wants us to look at. Come on you.' Cressida bent down and gently moved Ruby out of the way as she opened the door to the water closet.

'Oh, dear me!' Dotty exclaimed, stepping backwards as a pool of water slopped onto the wooden floor of the carriage's corridor. 'I don't think that's meant to happen!'

'It's definitely not,' agreed Cressida, assessing whether the very bottoms of her trousers could be sacrificed in order to investigate what had made the lavatory itself overflow so much. She was about to give in and just hope that her woollens wouldn't shrink, or stink, once exposed to the sloshing wetness on the lavatory's floor when Alfred stepped in, his trousers already neatly tucked into his striped socks.

'Save yourselves, ladies, coming through!'

'Oh Alfred.' Dotty laughed at her brother, the sight of him in his homemade knickerbockers, his pipe still clamped in his mouth, obviously tickling her. 'But well done. What can you see?'

'Apart from water, water, everywhere... not much.' Alfred splashed further into the small cubicle. 'Ah, hold on a tick, ladies. There is something in here.'

'Spare us from the details, Alf,' Dotty baulked, raising the manilla folder in front of her face.'

'Sorry, Dot, but you will want to know about this. Cressy, there's something really interesting shoved down the pan.'

Cressida looked at Dotty, who was still protecting her sensibilities behind the folder, and raised her eyebrows. Then, holding the edge of the door, leaned in as far as she could to the water closet to see what Alfred was talking about. 'Go on then, what is it, Alf?'

Alfred, pipe still clamped in his molars, took off his jacket, passed it back to Cressida and then started to roll up his shirt sleeves. With only a moment's hesitation, he plunged his bare arm into the lavatory and started to pull. Whatever it was that was stuck down there causing the cistern to overflow gave some resistance. Then, suddenly, with a jolt, Alfred pulled it free and held the soaking-wet bundle of dark fabric aloft.

'Ta-dah!' he said triumphantly, then looked confused at the dripping mass of lightweight cotton he was holding. 'What do you think it is?'

'Shake it out, Alf, let's see,' Cressida asked, then added: 'You can look now, Dot. Nothing sordid, I promise.'

Dotty lowered the folder and looked on with rising interest as her brother shook out the fabric, then arranged it so that the shape of it made sense.

'It's a dress, I think,' Alfred came up with, holding it now at the shoulders and letting the black dress hang out as if on a hanger.

'Wasn't Geraldine wearing something like that?' Dotty asked. 'When she accused Warriner of cheating on her?'

'And still is, I should assume,' Cressida replied. 'At least she was when I last saw her and that was only a little while before she was shot. I don't think she's been in the mood to go flushing her clothing down the lavatory. Nor has she had the opportunity really. She's been locked in her compartment since Warriner's death.'

The three of them stared at the black dress, that now hung limply, soaking, from Alfred's hands. He gave it a twirl.

'Alf, wait there. Turn it back that way,' Cressida urged, suddenly inspired. 'There, yes. Do you see it? That bulging pocket. What's inside it?'

Alfred hoisted the dress over his arm and found the pocket. Cressida's heart was beating as he fought with the friction of the wet fabric. After a struggle, no doubt made worse by Alfred's rather gratifying unfamiliarity with female clothing, he produced the contents of the bulging pocket.

Cressida gasped. She knew what Alfred was holding. And it proved that they'd just found a very big, if rather wet, clue.

## 40

'What is it?' Alfred asked, seeing Cressida's reaction to the frilled piece of white fabric.

'It's a pinny. An apron. I thought I recognised that dress, and not just because Geraldine was all in black. I'd seen it somewhere else on the train... Of course, it all makes sense now.'

'Who is it, Cressy? Who wore it?' Dotty asked, looking as confused as her slightly damper brother.

'It's the same dress that the tea ladies wear. Don't you recognise it from the times we've met Mrs Drysdale? And I saw Martha wearing one too; she's the one I spoke to when we first learned Kirby had been lured away from guarding Geraldine's door.'

'Gosh,' Dotty exclaimed. 'And you said at the time you were sure Martha hadn't been the one to offer Kirby a tea as she looked too disappointed not to be involved. And this proves it, assuming she's still in uniform.'

'I'm sure I saw her when we were dining,' Cressida said, still looking at the soaking-wet dress. 'And sorry, Alfred, you might want to put that thing down now. Or at least get it to Andrews before you turn into a prune standing in all that water.'

'What does this mean though, Cressy?' Dotty asked, not needing to be told twice to start moving away from the overflowing lavatory.

'It means that someone on board this train disguised themselves as a tea lady to lure Kirby away and then discarded the costume as soon as they – or, I assume, she – could.'

'In the least convenient place,' remarked Alfred, stepping out of the closet and pushing the door closed behind him.

As Alfred shook the water from his brogues and unleashed his trousers from his socks, Cressida thought out loud.

'It all fits in with our theory about there being two people involved in Geraldine's attack. One who dashed off and slipped out of this uniform, hiding it as soon as they could. And, of course, the other who must have come from the opposite direction. That was the person with the gun.'

'As we reasoned before. Two bad'uns here on the train. Unless one has absconded,' Alfred clarified.

'Yes. And one of them is definitely a woman,' Cressida added, gesturing towards the sopping-wet dress. Then she paused and cocked her head to one side. Finding that dress somewhere where you wouldn't expect it rang a bell with her.

'You're looking very pensive, Cressy,' Dotty said after a while and Cressida looked up at her.

'I was thinking... finding something you don't expect to find somewhere you don't expect to see it. Well, it's like when I found Miss de Souza's shoes in the luggage car. Or Miss Smith as she really is. And, come to think of it, when I spoke to her just before we got to Edinburgh, she was wearing flat ballet pumps. I asked her why she wasn't in her lovely red shoes, but she didn't really give much of an answer. What if it was she who was dressed in this outfit? Those ballet pumps she was wearing – I've seen ones like it.'

'Where?' Dotty asked.

'Mrs Drysdale and Martha wear them. I thought it was odd

at the time that Phoebe was wearing them, seeing as how glamorous she is. But then she had just had a nasty shock and, as you say, it's difficult enough navigating these corridors in sensible flats. But don't you think perhaps that she donned that costume, hid her shoes—'

'Not down the lavatory like the dress, though? Why not hide them there too? Call the whole place "closed for maintenance" or something, pull the chain and down they go.'

'I'm not sure that a pair of shoes would ever flush down a U-bend, Dotty. Plus, I don't think she wanted to ruin them or get rid of them. They weren't part of the disguise, just a hindrance to her movements. I should imagine she hid them when she was changing, hoping to claim them back once the subterfuge was done. If I were her, and with not much to my name save a return ticket to London, I'd not want to waste a perfectly good pair of shoes.'

'We need to find her then,' Alfred said in a matter-of-fact sort of way. 'At the very least to check she hasn't absconded from the train when we stopped.'

'And quickly,' Cressida added. 'Time is ticking and we need an arrest by morning. I think Phoebe de Souza definitely has something to do with all of this. But if she's the bait who tempted Kirby away from his post... who's the predator that swooped in and shot Geraldine?'

'And worse than Geraldine,' Dotty added.

'Yes, worse than Geraldine,' Cressida agreed. 'Andrews.'

## 41

Cressida and Alfred watched as Dotty hurried along the corridor, rebounding off the glossy veneered walls as she went, like a chestnut-haired bowling ball ricocheting around its alley. Ruby, perhaps preferring the idea of a comfortable snooze in Andrews' compartment rather than a once-over of the whole train, decided to follow her. As soon as they were both out of sight, Cressida turned to Alfred.

'Right.' She forced herself to think once more of the case and how much they needed to work out before the train pulled into Euston. And not think about how utterly dashing Alfred was looking, with that intensity he had in his eyes as he looked back at her.

*Focus, Fawcett*, she chided herself and then spoke again.

'So, as far as headcount is concerned, we know Clarence Derby is still on the train.' She pointed back down to the first of the sleeper carriages. 'And the Fernley-Hoggs, of course, as they were still eating their strawberry bavois when we were having our tiffin.'

'Speaking of tiffin.' Alfred gestured for them to walk back down towards the first of the sleeper carriages, 'I remember seeing the Irvings' names on two of the compartments in this first carriage. You've thought they were dubious in their intentions towards the deceased from the off, haven't you? Might be the place for our headcount to start.'

'Good idea, Alf,' Cressida agreed, grateful that Alfred had such a sensible head on his shoulders at times such as these.

'Not just a handsome face, what?' Alfred waggled an eyebrow at her and Cressida once more found it exceptionally hard to focus on the task in hand. She let Alfred chat on as she tried to think about different things. '... Soaking-wet feet now, reminds me of the time we ended up at the botanical gardens with Spiffy Cartwright and you found that hose with the funny—'

'Nozzle. Yes.' Cressida shook her head. 'This is all terribly diverting, Alfred, but let's keep to the case in hand, shall we?'

'Righto, old thing.' Alfred nodded as they walked down the narrow corridor together in companionable silence.

Before long, they found themselves outside the compartment labelled Miss Irving. With a look and nod to one another, Cressida raised her fist and was about to knock when the door opened.

'Oh, hello—'

'Shhhh,' Louise interrupted Cressida, then gestured for them both to come in. She gently pulled the door to and cleared her valise off her bunk so that Cressida could sit down. Alfred stayed standing by the door as Cressida and Louise sat themselves down on the bed.

'Hello, Louise,' Cressida tried again.

'Hello. And sorry about that. I'm afraid I didn't want my brother knowing that we were talking.'

'How did you know we were outside?' Alfred asked, his voice low.

'I was keeping an eye out, hoping to catch you. Well, you

especially, Cressida. I... I was ashamed at how my brother acted towards you.'

Alfred coughed and Cressida took her cue.

'I think it's me who should apologise. I was terribly forthright. It's just finding out you both had some sort of connection to Warriner, well, I was intrigued.'

Louise Irving nodded. Cressida could see how she wrung her hands in her lap and found it hard to make eye contact. Was she scared of her brother? Perhaps she had good reason to think he might have murdered Warriner?

The article in the newspaper came back to her and, as gently as she could, she posed the question that had been on her mind since reading it.

'Louise, did Mr Warriner withdraw investment from your business out in India? I read in today's paper, you see, that he had withdrawn from several companies out there.'

Louise sighed and finally managed to look Cressida in the eye. 'Aye, that's right.'

'And it was a blow? Quite damaging for your business?'

'You could say that, yes. We were investing heavily in new land, not to mention bringing on more local tea pickers and clerical staff. And machinery to process the leaves, factories and packing warehouses.' She paused. 'Then, *poof*, all the money was withdrawn.'

'Just like that?'

'Just like that. Or at least that's how it felt. Over the course of a few weeks, we had to find the money to pay the suppliers we already had contracts for, for packaging and all that, and, of course, renege where we could on the deals to buy land and factory space. It was a very, very stressful time. Not just for me and Callum, but for our family back in India and, of course, our trusted senior staffers.'

'I can imagine. And so you came back to Scotland to find Warriner and ask him why?'

'Oh, well, we knew why. The official statement had come from his office. Economic depression or currency vagaries.' She shook her head. 'Callum deals with the business side, he understood it all more. I'm the one that had to go to the workers and explain why we couldn't pay them.'

'Gosh, I'm sorry. That must have been heartbreaking.'

'It was. But there you go. Money is as money does.'

As Louise said that, Cressida thought of what Clarence Derby had said earlier about following the money. There was much lost here, livelihoods at stake. Families at risk of losing everything. Perhaps this money was the root of it all?

'Excuse me for interrupting,' Alfred said, his voice low still, as he maintained his distance by the door. 'But if you knew Warriner's answer, why come all the way back to see him?'

Louise looked up at him, then back to Cressida. 'How did my brother put it? "Private family business".'

'Well, of course, I just wondered—' Alfred stammered, but Louise interrupted him.

'Sorry, no, I don't mean that now. I was just quoting him. Family business, you see. There's one thing worse than having your investment pulled from underneath you by some anonymous bank in London or whatnot.' Louise clenched her fists in her lap as she spoke, and turned to Cressida. 'That sort of skulduggery we could understand, if never agree with. But the reason we came back to Scotland, the reason we thought we might be able to prevail upon him and get the investment back is because—'

The train clattered over a particularly gnarly set of points and the whole carriage lurched from one side to the other. Once all three of them had caught themselves, Cressida turned back to Louise.

'Is because?'

'... Is because Lewis Warriner was our uncle.'

## 42

'Your uncle?' Cressida and Alfred said in unison, then apologised when Louise held a finger to her lips. 'Sorry,' Cressida whispered. 'But your uncle?'

'Well, he was. He was married to our aunt Myra.'

'Warriner's first wife,' Cressida filled in the blank.

'Yes, and our mother's sister. Aunt Myra was married to an officer in the army stationed in India. He was from a very wealthy family down Swansea way, I think, and they were happy – so we were told. She had her children at about the same time as Mother had us and, from what Mama tells us, it was all hunky-dory until Uncle Ned caught malaria and died very suddenly.'

'How terribly sad.' Cressida wanted to reach out and comfort Louise, but she also needed to find out more. If the Irvings were related to Warriner, perhaps they could be the ones to inherit everything on his death? *Especially if Geraldine were to die.*

'It was. Mama said she'd never seen Aunty Myra so upset. Her youngest was only small, barely a babe in arms, and I think she was very tired. She just wanted to go home, leave India and all the memories of Uncle Ned and their life there.' Louise shrugged. 'I can't blame her.'

'No, neither can I. Tell me, though, she and your mother weren't born in India then? They were Scottish?'

'Yes, Scottish sisters who both found husbands in India. Of course, our father is Scottish too, Irving, but his family have been in India for yonks. Mama and Aunty Myra were newly over at the end of the last century and I think it all just got a bit much for Aunty Myra, so she came back to Blighty.'

'Where she met Warriner,' Cressida pushed on, wanting to get as much information from Louise as possible before she either clammed up or they were interrupted. The thought of that page of handwritten notes all about Myra Warriner in the manilla folder crossed her mind. *Could Louise have compiled that folder?*

'Yes,' Louise said brightly, bringing Cressida out of her thoughts. Her tone suggested that perhaps the early years of Myra's second marriage had been a happier episode in her aunt's story. 'Aunty Myra's letters back to Mama were suddenly thrilling. She'd met this man who was happy to take her and the little ones on.' She paused and looked reflective. 'But, of course, she'd inherited a lot of money from Uncle Ned and I don't think his side were best pleased that it was all going into another man's pocket, but she was adamant that it was paving the way for a grand start for her children.'

'Ah, I see. So that's why she funded the beginnings of Warriner Industries?'

'Yes. For a while, she wrote about it being called Warriners' Industries, both of them named in it, once they were married of course. But then it just sort of became Warriner Industries and she never mentioned why.' Louise looked soulfully down at her lap again.

'And when they divorced?' Cressida asked, glancing up at Alfred, who had been stoically quiet since he'd last spoken, letting Cressida ask the questions. When she looked back at Louise, her face had gone from soulful to seething.

'*They* divorced?' she all but hissed. '*He* was the one doing the divorcing. Aunty Myra had no notion of it. Mama said that apparently out of the blue he told Aunty Myra that he wanted a divorce and that she would get nothing.'

'Why would he be so vindictive?' Cressida asked, wondering if perhaps this passion ignited in Louise could be the first glimmer that she was on to something.

'Why? Because if Aunty Myra left him, and took what was rightfully hers back out of the marriage, Warriner – singular – Industries wouldn't have survived. He had to cut her off and make sure the courts denied her any of what was hers on grounds of infidelity and adultery.'

'But she hadn't been, you don't think?' Cressida asked, cautious not to push the already upset Louise any further.

'Absolutely not! She was so in love with Uncle Lewis. You could see it in her letters. Mama always said she was the romantic one. I don't think it was anything against Uncle Ned, she'd loved him passionately too. I think she was just one of those women who falls wholly in love. And loyally too.' Louise looked down at her clenched fists in her lap, then back to Cressida and Alfred. 'And then when the divorce came along, she wrote to Mama and she said she was innocent of everything the newspapers were apparently dragging up about her. Why would she lie to her own sister?'

'I can't imagine. Go on, so what happened then?' Cressida leaned forward, keen to hear more, finally, about Warriner's first wife. The one for whom vengeance had been promised.

'The letters stopped arriving. They'd been getting harder to read and so many times Mama said she felt like she should get on the next boat home to go and help Aunty Myra. But then I came down with some fever and Papa was worried about the harvest. She never made it back to Scotland. Finally, Mama heard that Aunty Myra had died in a bedsit somewhere in Glasgow.' Louise shook her head. 'She had been a lady – a wealthy lady at that – with her own money and her own destiny to choose, and look what happened to her because of her lying, cheating husband.'

Cressida could feel herself blush. This was exactly the argument she had always put forward when she was asked, relentlessly, especially by her well-meaning mother, when she would marry. Why this now made her come over in a hot flush, she couldn't say, but it might be something to do with the tall, dark, handsome viscount standing by the door of the compartment. How could she even think of marrying when stories like this were evidence of the pitfalls of marriage? She screwed shut her eyes, willing the inner turmoil of her thoughts to shift to the back of her head, however much it still ached, while she concentrated on the end of Louise Irving's story.

'I'm so sorry for your aunt. That's not fair, not fair at all. I can see why you'd hate Warriner. And did you come all this way to confront him? In Inverness or here on this train?'

'Yes.' Louise's voice had lost some of its passion. Cressida could see she would have to be careful now not to overdo it with the questions, lest Louise tire of it all completely. 'Cal said it was our last chance at saving the business. We came back to Inverness to ask him why he had withdrawn his investment. The initial offer had come via his agent in India. The agent had described it as him building up a portfolio and all that. The agent didn't know we were related, but when the final paperwork came through, before we could sign it, it was kiboshed.'

'Just like that,' Cressida repeated Louise's words from earlier.

'Yes. Hence why we assumed it was because of our family name and the connections. Connections he couldn't stand to be reminded of. But he should have felt the opposite, he should have leapt at a chance to right his wrong of all those years ago.

Invest in his late, and former, wife's family. The locals near us would call it karmic. But no. He struck us off without so much as a second thought. We came back and made an appointment under a false name. Once we were in there, in front of him, well, it all became a bit heated. Callum was so angry, of course, and thumped his fist on Uncle Lew's desk, but to no avail. He said the whole Indian portfolio was closing as a bad lot and he didn't have anything more to say to us. Not even an apology for the way he'd treated Aunty Myra.'

Cressida leaned back, taking it all in. She looked up at Alfred, who looked a little pink high up in his cheeks, and wondered if he had felt moved by the story of Myra Warriner and her marriage. She stood up, sensing that Louise was tired. In some ways, they'd achieved what they'd set out to, she and Alfred, there was proof that Louise was still on the train, and unless it was all a ruse, then it seemed like Callum was too. But there was something still bugging her. *Follow the money…*

Cressida turned back to face Louise. 'Can I ask one more thing, Miss Irving?'

'Aye, what is it?'

'Your cousins. Myra's children from Uncle Ned. Where are they now?'

Louise shrugged. 'We've had no contact from them. Not since Uncle Ned's family took them in.' She yawned, exhaustion taking over suddenly. 'The extended family. Not rich like Uncle Ned had been. Still, Mama heard that the boy had done quite well, clever with words and things like that. And she mentioned once that Aunty Myra had done something rather cunning during the divorce. Made sure her children were named as successors should anything happen to Uncle Lewis or his next of kin. But I'm not even sure they'd know about that. We rather lost contact with Uncle Ned's family and, of course, we were thousands of miles away. India can be like a different world when you're there, you feel a lifetime away from London or Inverness or wherever.' Louise sighed. 'Will you excuse me now, though? I just thought you should know, and I don't know why Cal made such a song and dance about not telling you. I suppose he thought it made us look guilty. But the thing is, not telling you makes us look more so.'

'Yes, I'm afraid that's how I read the situation,' Cressida admitted.

'I must say it was a hell of a shock to come face to face, almost, with Geraldine. To see in the flesh the person who had been the reason for Uncle Lewis wanting to divorce Aunty Myra.'

'That must have been hard,' Cressida said, still hovering next to Alfred at the door.

'Yes. But then he got shot and... well...' Louise twitched the curtains closed against the dark sky outside.

'Justice, in a way, had been done,' Cressida prompted, remembering Andrews' sage words on the matter. She looked up as Louise turned back from the window.

'Yes.' For the first time, Cressida could detect a glimmer of a smile on her face. 'Or, as they say in India, karma.'

## 43

'Well, that was all in all rather interesting, don't you think?' Cressida asked as Alfred stifled a yawn in the corridor outside Louise Irving's compartment.

'Sorry,' he apologised. 'They must be catching. I saw Miss Irving yawn and...' He stretched his mouth out into another gaping yawn.

'I suppose it is getting late. But, come on, let's finish our headcount of the train and then we can see how Dot and Andrews are getting on with that folder full of newspaper clippings.'

'We forgot to ask Miss Irving if they were hers,' Alfred pointed out.

Cressida smiled ruefully at him. 'If by "we" you mean me, then, no, I didn't forget. But I figured that someone who had such a front-row seat via her own mother to the whole relationship and divorce and all that wouldn't need to gather information from the press. And, not to mention the fact that she's been in India most of her life, and those were very British, and sometimes quite local to Inverness, newspapers. So, no, I don't think the folder belongs to Miss Irving.'

'I say, top work, Cressy.' Alfred returned her smile, then whisked his pipe out of his pocket and clenched it between his molars. 'Where next?'

Cressida ran her fingers gently along the glossy surface of the veneered walls and doors of the sleeping compartments. 'Well, in this car, we have the Irvings, the Fernley-Hoggs, Mr Derby and, of course, Warriner himself. Miss de Souza's been moved to another compartment, quite understandably, so all accounted for.'

'Dead or alive,' Alfred agreed as they crossed through the clattering join between sleeping carriages, and as they walked along the next cramped corridor, Cressida recited off the names of the passengers. 'Well, that one is yours, then it's Dot, then poor Geraldine, and then yours truly, and then Lord Hartnell and his nanny.'

'Don't suppose we can hope that the vernal viscount is behind all of this and has absconded into the night, finger up nose and all.'

Cressida chuckled at Alfred. 'No. And, strangely, Ruby seems quite fond of him. Which I'm not sure how I feel about, but I saw him just before we stopped. And his nanny was definitely around too. Let's let them sleep, he'll need his energy for telling all his snotty-nosed friends about the murders he witnessed on the train he was on and whatnot. Gory details no doubt embellished and elaborated on with great relish.'

'I'm sure he'll grow up to be a fine young man,' Alfred noted, and then tapped on the last compartment of the carriage. 'This one's empty. Should have taken on passengers at Edinburgh, I'd wager.'

'Yes. So, on we go.' Cressida squeezed around past the water closet where they'd found the tea lady's disguise and then again to the next carriage.

The first compartment in the third, and last, sleeping carriage was supposedly empty, but Cressida knew Phoebe de

Souza was using it, now the one she had meant to share with Warriner was a crime scene. Cressida raised a finger to her lips as she turned around and Alfred almost fell into her.

'Oops,' he said, dropping his pipe. Cressida stayed still like a statue as Alfred bent down to pick it up, tutting to himself about chipping the bowl. 'Darn fine pipe that one was too.' He looked at it, then back at Cressida's pursed lips and mouthed a silent 'sorry'.

Cressida leaned her ear against the compartment's door and tried to listen. She could just knock and check that Phoebe was in there, but something told her that the interruption wouldn't be welcomed, and although she wanted to ask her about the disguise, she felt like there was more to the puzzle and Phoebe de Souza perhaps needed a moment or two longer to recover herself after their last conversation. One that had ended with Phoebe almost in tears, her dreams now well and truly set back, her life not what she expected it to be just a few hours ago when she had boarded the train in such style.

'Oh, it's you two.' A little chestnut head popped out from a door a few compartments along. 'Come on in, Andrews and I think we've found something.'

'Righto, Dot,' said Alfred, jamming his pipe back in his pocket. 'Come on, Cress. Let's see what DCI Andrews and Sergeant Dot have come up with.'

Once inside Andrews' compartment, with the door closed and one brother roundly elbowed in the ribs by his peeved sister, they settled themselves down and got to work.

'I've rung for coffees,' announced Dotty, who seemed very much in charge of her patient, even though they were all in his compartment.

'Good idea Dot,' Cressida agreed. 'I have a feeling we none of us will get much sleep tonight.'

Alfred checked his watch. 'Past midnight, if you can believe it.' He yawned again, as if the watch had reminded him how tired he was.

'You can get some sleep, Alf,' Dotty said, looking angelic until she followed it with, 'we ladies can help DCI Andrews. We're more than capable.'

'Come now, Lady Dorothy,' Andrews said, from his bunk. 'Four minds are better than three, however tired we all are.'

Cressida raised her eyebrows at him and his slight nod told her that he'd got the measure of the sibling spat in front of him. He looked pale though, and Cressida was worried.

'Andrews, how are you feeling? You must be tired. Your poor shoulder.'

Andrews looked at his newly dressed wound. 'I won't lie, it's no birthday party, but Lady Dorothy has been doing her best.'

Dotty glowed at the praise, then stifled a yawn.

'Way past our bedtimes, eh Dot?' Cressida looked at her and Dotty smiled.

'Oh, I don't know, Cressy. I'm sure you're up later many nights a week.'

'But those nights involve martinis and dancing. This one has been somewhat stranger. I've replaced tripping the light fantastic with tripping over clues.'

Andrews coughed, winced and then spoke. 'Speaking of clues, anything else to add to what you've found so far.'

Cressida perked up. 'Yes, the rather interesting revelation that Myra Warriner – Lewis Warriner's first wife – is in fact Callum and Louise Irving's aunt.'

'Making the now deceased Lewis Warriner their uncle?' Andrews asked, cocking his head on one side as he took in the information. 'That's very interesting.'

'Gosh, it is, yes.' Dotty looked wide-eyed behind her tortoiseshell spectacles.

'Add that to the tea lady's uniform we found, the blackmail letter—'

'The name tag saying Smith, not de Souza,' Alfred interrupted Cressida.

'Yes, and the letter Geraldine received. And, of course, that whole folder of newspaper clippings—'

'Speaking of which,' Dotty took her turn to interrupt. 'Did you notice this piece among them?' She pulled out one of the clippings.

'What is it?' Cressida asked, taking the piece from Dotty.

Andrews filled her in. 'A rather scathing piece about Warriner Industries, and Warriner himself. But it's what's *on* the piece that's the most interesting thing.'

Cressida looked at the newspaper cutting. It was several inches long, and looked as if it had been carefully cut from a broadsheet-style newspaper. *On the piece...* she thought to herself as she turned it over and then realised what Andrews meant.

'Another grease mark,' she said thoughtfully, looking at the clipping. 'Just like the mark on the letter that lured Geraldine aboard and the stuff I got on my hands after shaking Mr Donaldson's earlier this evening.' Cressida looked up at her friends.

'And look what the piece is about,' Dotty pointed to the text.

Cressida skim-read it as quickly as she could.

'It looks like it's about Warriner letting the war veterans go, and firing someone for stealing.'

'Exactly. The chap that Mr Donaldson and Mrs Drysdale told you about. You said Mr Donaldson in particular was very upset about it.'

'But Mr Donaldson has the most watertight alibi. He couldn't have killed Warriner or attacked Geraldine or you, Andrews. He's been in the engine all this time.'

'His sister hasn't, though?' Alfred reminded them. 'And guess who Dot has just summoned to bring us coffee?'

## 44

The knock at the door almost sent them all spinning, with Dotty nearly jumping out of her skin, Ruby making a dash for a hiding place behind Andrews and pieces of newspaper scattering to the floor.

'Coffees!' the friendly voice called from outside the door, and Alfred, who along with Andrews was either quick to recover himself or was making a good play of pretending not to have been taken unawares by Mrs Drysdale at the door, opened it up.

'Ah, Mrs Drysdale. Thank you.'

'Are you folks playing sardines in here?' She looked bemused. 'Usually our passengers are lights out by now, getting some kip before arriving in London. And you, Detective Andrews, you should be resting.'

Cressida took the first cup of steaming-hot coffee from the tutting Mrs Drysdale and passed it to Alfred, who in turn handed it to Andrews. As she passed another along the chain, Cressida thought she might as well take the opportunity of asking the tea lady a couple of questions.

'Can I ask something rather peculiar, Mrs Drysdale?'

'You can ask, lovey, but I might not know the answer.'

'Are the uniforms that you wear provided by the train company or do you have to purchase them yourself?'

'Well, that is a peculiar question, you're right, dearie.' Mrs Drysdale stopped pouring the coffee, much to Alfred's disappointment, as it was at his cup that she had paused. 'But easy enough to answer. Our uniforms are all provided by the company. Heaven knows, I wouldn't have a spare shilling to shell out on something like this.' She pinched out the decently thick cotton fabric of her black dress. Then she said something that struck Cressida as really Quite Interesting. 'Now, the funny thing is, I was talking to Lesley Muldoon, she works in the procurement office for the uniforms and whatnot, soaps and things too, you know, all the little pleasantries we have on board here. Coffee too,' she raised the pot. Alfred raised his eyebrows in expectation at that, but dashed them down again as once more the pot was lowered, unpoured, as Mrs Drysdale continued. 'Anyway, Lesley was saying that they'd had one or two things stolen from the store cupboard. Young Martha, who only started recent, like, had a struggle finding one to fit her as they were suddenly short.'

It was Cressida's turn to raise her eyebrows as she glanced over at Andrews and her friends.

Mrs Drysdale finished pouring Alfred's coffee and Cressida passed it to him. She ignored the funny feeling she had when one of her fingers accidentally touched his as she was desperately trying to stay focused on the terrible events of the last few hours... and listen to what Mrs Drysdale was chattering on about as she poured the final coffee. One that Cressida took from her, grateful that she could keep this one to herself.

'And I see you've got the newspapers out and all sorts of little stories. What are you all up to? I can find you some glue if you need to put anything back together.'

'Oh, no thank you, Mrs Drysdale,' Dotty chipped in, starting to gather up the clippings and hide the letter that was also in the folder. She slipped it under today's newspaper so as not to draw attention to it.

Mrs Drysdale shrugged and fussed around her coffee pot and cups a little more, before chatting away again. 'Funny seeing that *Evening Post* there too, reminds me that a journalist from that paper put a telephone call in to me, can you believe. I had to go to the kiosk on the street at a pre-arranged time as he said he wanted to interview me for the paper. But I've never seen anything in print, and I take the *Post* most days as my girl likes it for the puzzles at the back.'

'What did the journalist ask you about?' Cressida asked, not sure if Mrs Drysdale's answer would be of much relevance, but it intrigued her anyway.

'Oh, this and that. Bit of a personal interest story, he said. Terribly nice man he was, Mr Bowen or something.' She shook her head. 'Anyway, asked me all about poor Mr Drysdale and I told him what I told you earlier, that I'd said to myself that there was no place like the railways now, especially with my brother being on board.'

'He asked about your brother too?' Cressida was much more interested now. There was something about brothers and sisters and this case that sparked something in her mind.

'Aye, he did. I said Hughie had left Warriner Industries and come to work on the railways, much like how I was leaving service and coming aboard too. Brother and sister together, just like when we were bairns. Three times a week, up and down to London, regular as clockwork, Mondays, Wednesdays and Fridays.'

'But this story was never published?' Cressida asked. 'Did he say it would be?'

'Well, come to think of it, he never gave a date. Suggested he had some more work to do on it, but no, it hasn't been published and that was nigh on a fortnight ago that he spoke to me. I know that because the note came from the office and said a journalist would be phoning the kiosk at the end of my street on Friday midday just before my shift.'

'Well, let's hope you get your column inches, Mrs Drysdale,' Cressida said, smiling warmly at the older woman. 'And thank you for these coffees. I think we'll need them.'

'Just call when you need more, dearie, I'm not going anywhere.' Mrs Drysdale moved her tea trolley off down the corridor at that, leaving them in peace.

One collective exhale later, Cressida spoke up again.

'Well, I can put my shilling's worth in and say I don't think Mrs Drysdale is our killer. Though it is interesting that some journalist wanted to know all about her and her brother.'

'Her brother the train driver. He of the greasy fingers.' Dotty pointed to the mark on one of the newspaper clippings that was still showing through the folder, despite Dotty's best attempts at tidying it all away during Mrs Drysdale's visit.

'I can't help but think, what with Miss Irving's desperately sad tale about her Aunt Myra, and her being on board with her brother, and Mr Donaldson having a falling out with Warriner, and him being on board with his sister... and those two "bairns", as Mrs Drysdale would say, the Irvings' cousins...'

'But they're not on board. Alf and I are the only other brother and sister on board.'

'Or are you?' The voice was that of Andrews, who had been listening intently to all the friends had had to say. 'I need to talk to Kirby. I know we've all just had some coffee, but how about you three try to get some rest. Kirby and I need to collate these pieces of evidence, if that's what they are, and start putting our case together. Whether or not Mrs Warriner is guilty of killing her husband, and who on earth is responsible for attacking her—'

'And you, Andrews.'

'Yes, and me,' the injured detective, paler than ever in the face agreed. 'And it's my job, not yours, to work through the night to find out who that was.'

## 45

Kirby was poised and ready to go, it seemed, having had a cup of coffee from Mrs Drysdale too. He swapped places with the friends and saluted them as they headed off down the corridor towards their compartments.

'Don't you think we were rather rudimentarily excused.' Dotty seemed peeved. 'I thought I'd done a rather splendid job of Andrews' sling. And we found a mutual interest in historical churches. Passed the time quite amicably.'

'He did look tired, though,' Cressida suggested.

'I sure am,' Alfred added, stifling another yawn. 'Seems like hours since we woke up this morning somewhere in the Highlands.'

The three of them swayed down the carriage, Ruby clutched in Cressida's arms as she led the way. Then Cressida stopped in front of her compartment rather suddenly and she felt Dotty crash into the back of her and possibly Alfred into her.

'Oof, ow.'

'Gosh, sorry, sis.'

'Cressy, are you all right?'

Cressida steadied herself, managing to place a palm to the glossed wall without letting go of Ruby in the other hand. 'Sorry, chaps. Sudden thought.'

'We're all ears,' Dotty said, as Cressida opened the door to her compartment and gestured for them to go in.

'Just in case the corridor also has a pair of them, best come in here and shut the door.'

'And hope no one else went to school with Woolly,' said Dotty, sitting herself down on the bunk, which had been turned down and looked awfully inviting in a neat, dormitory-style way.

Dotty yawned, which set her brother off.

'I'll be quick. I think we're all as beat as Andrews suggested, but I was just thinking about something Mr Derby said,' Cressida explained, sitting down next to Dotty.

'That terribly sad story about being in love with Geraldine?' Dotty asked, pulling Ruby onto her own lap.

'No, not that. Something he said the first time I spoke to him. *Cherchez l'argent*. Follow the money.'

'Well, Warriner had plenty of it, by all accounts,' Dotty asserted. 'If those articles had any truth to them.'

'I'm sure they do, and I'm sure he did. But it's not just that. Solving this crime. Follow the money... if Geraldine was either behind bars, charged with his murder, or dead by either hanging or being murdered herself, then she couldn't inherit all Warriner's money. So, who does?'

'Did they have children?' Dotty asked.

'Geraldine didn't, no. She told me that she wondered if that was why Warriner had tired of her. And Myra did, of course, but not with Warriner.'

'The other brother and sister,' Dotty said. 'But didn't Louise suggest there was some skulduggery, the newspapers claiming the first Mrs Warriner was unfaithful. He divorced her and left her with nothing.'

'Left her with nothing,' Cressida thought out loud, trying desperately to remember what Louise Irving had said. 'But she made sure she provided for her children. Successors in some way. And what did one of those newspaper articles about the divorce say? It mentioned overages or something.'

'Overages?' Dotty asked, her face a mixture of utter exhaustion and bewilderment.

'Legal speak,' Alfred explained. 'A clawback of sorts. Mostly added to property deeds in case the land ever goes up in value. Odd thing to be attached to a divorce, or a business.'

'I think that's the issue. It probably is very odd as it was the only thing Myra could think of to do,' Cressida pointed out. 'Louise said she'd done something rather cunning that would see her children inherit in the case of Warriner's death. As long as there were no other heirs.'

'So, if Geraldine couldn't inherit the company, or at least Warriner's shares as his next of kin, and they don't have heirs either, then what?' Alfred asked.

'Then... if I've understood you both correctly, Myra's overage would be enacted. Her children would be the next of kin,' Dotty, who had caught up, despite how tired she was, completed the train of thought.

'*Cherchez l'argent*, you see,' Cressida stood up with a wobble. 'We have to find Mr Derby and ask him if he has any knowledge of any of this. He must know about the company rules and regulations and all of that sort of thing. He must know if there were heirs' or successors' names in the paperwork.'

'And then we see if they really are on this train.'

'Exactly,' Cressida shivered.

Alfred looked at his watch. 'Can we really go and knock the poor chap up now? It's almost one in the morning?'

'Alfred, it's precisely because it's almost one in the morning that we have to! We'll be pulling into Euston in a matter of hours and that's when the murderer, or murderers, can legitimately get off this train. And that's if someone hasn't absconded at Edinburgh who we haven't accounted for yet.'

Alfred nodded as Dotty blinked back sleep and gazed up at him through her spectacles. She then looked at Cressida and, with what appeared to be gargantuan effort, pushed her glasses up the bridge of her nose, from where they promptly fell back down to its tip when she yawned again.

Cressida smiled at her. 'Dot, stay here and get some rest. Alfred and I can go and find Mr Derby. And I promise I'll come straight back here and let you know what we find out.'

'If you're sure. I am...' She yawned again. 'Exceptionally tired.'

With Dotty, along with Ruby, content to stay in Cressida's compartment for a bit of shut-eye, Cressida and Alfred made their way back down the narrow corridor once again, to find Clarence Derby.

Cressida was tired too. She didn't mind Dotty having a rest, but she was pleased that Alfred was by her side as she carried on in her usual hot-headed way. Andrews had looked exhausted too, and she wondered if the summoning of Kirby was just to get all of them out of his hair for a little while.

*Hair...* she thought as she swayed along the narrow corridor. *There must be something to be gleaned from that wig I found.*

'Alfred?' she asked, still forming questions in her mind.

'Yes, old thing?'

'You don't think Myra Warriner's first husband could have been called Smith, do you? And Miss de Souza, or Phoebe Smith as she is, is one of their children? She had a wig in her valise and, well, I don't know, but it made me think of disguises.'

'The only disguise we've found out about so far is the tea lady's outfit,' Alfred said, quite sensibly.

Cressida nodded and went back to her thoughts.

And as she caught sight of Alfred out of the corner of her eye, his chestnut hair and his conker-brown eyes, she had to admit that perhaps some of her capital-T Thoughts might just have been about him too.

## 46

Before Cressida could develop her theory about Phoebe de Souza further, they found themselves outside the door with the nameplate: Mr Clarence Derby. However, two sharp knocks on his door, and no answer, later, Cressida turned to Alfred and shrugged.

'Asleep?' she wondered.

Alfred knocked again, harder. Still nothing.

'Let's try the bar, you never know.' Cressida sighed, worrying that their opportunity to quiz Mr Derby about the company paperwork might have passed them by.

'You never know, indeed. Come on, let's see if the old soak is still matching you gin rickey for gin rickey.'

Cressida rolled her eyes at Alfred, but inside she smiled.

It turned out that they'd both been correct as Cressida and Alfred found Clarence Derby slumped against the bar, his head resting in the crook of one elbow, the other arm resting on the bar, a cut-glass tumbler of whisky still gripped in his hand.

'He's not... is he?' Cressida lurched forward, but Alfred held her back.

A tired but otherwise still pristine-looking barman in his tightly fitting white jacket, a tea towel, as ever, over his arm, appeared from the far end of the dining carriage. 'Don't mind him,' he called, and then carried on in more normal tones as he got closer to where Cressida and Alfred were now able to see that Derby was alive, if not well. 'I think he helped himself to the whisky when we were doing the turn-down service. Said a few things about losing out on everything and then slumped face-first on the bar. Not the first time I've seen someone drink themselves silly. It's a rum old journey this one.'

'You can say that again,' Alfred agreed with him, while giving Derby a little shake. 'Shall we help him back to his compartment again. Let this poor chap close the bar.'

'That would be kind, sir. Let me help.'

Between Alfred and the barman, a near-comatose Clarence Derby was helped back to his compartment, with Cressida squeezing her way past them to get to the door so she could open it. The two men heaved Derby onto his bunk, and Alfred loosened his tie as the barman unlaced his brogues. Once Derby looked suitably comfortable, the barman nodded a goodnight to Cressida and Alfred and left them to it.

'I don't think we'll get much out of him like this,' Alfred mused, but Cressida, who wouldn't usually ignore him, was already looking around the compact compartment.

'We might not have to. Aha,' she said, pulling down the briefcase that she'd seen Derby board the train with.

'Not sure that's cricket,' Alfred said. 'Do you think you should really look through his private belongings when he's out for the count.'

'No, I probably shouldn't,' Cressida agreed. 'But then this is the most extenuating of circumstances I can possibly imagine.'

'You said that when Toppy Billingshurst caught you snaffling those balls from the Holland Park Tennis Club. Didn't you say it was for your mother's lumbago?'

'Tennis balls do really help with that, you know,' Cressida said sheepishly. 'But in this case, we really do have to have a look, don't we. There's a life at stake.'

Alfred nodded, and turned back to where Clarence was now gently snoring on the bunk. 'Better crack on with it, though, while beauty here is still sleeping.'

Cressida needed no further encouragement. The chance was slim that any important corporate paperwork would be carried about by the company secretary, but she riffled through the selection that was in Derby's briefcase anyway.

Various letters from clients and insurance forms made up the bulk of the papers, but Cressida stopped and took special notice at a few sheaths.

'Alfred, look at this,' she said, passing a letter over to him. 'It looks like a letter from Warriner to the *Evening Post*. Promising favours for a favour.'

'Could Warriner have been starting the smear campaign for wife number two?' Alfred asked, passing the letter back to Cressida.

'Divorce her, you mean? Leave her with nothing? Oh dear.' Cressida put the letter down. 'That rather suggests more of a motive on her part to shoot him.'

'Or, if Derby here was in fact in love with Geraldine, and despite the years since they were an item, still held a candle for her... well, he might be the one to have shot his boss.'

'Hmm. Good point.' Cressida stared at the letter again.

'It's a rascally thing to do too, this whole smearing campaign thing. Reprehensible, of course, but one understands his reasons for cutting off wife number one without a penny – he needed them all at the time. But he could afford to pay wife number two off a little, surely?'

'Perhaps it's just his modus operandi now. More money left

in the pot to spend on getting Phoebe de Souza to Hollywood. Or entice the pretty young thing to marry him. He might have wanted – and needed – heirs after all,' Cressida mused. She picked up the letter again. A carbon copy of it was slipped underneath it. 'Look, Alf, this is the sort of thing that secretaries keep once the original has been sent, but here's the original one signed by Warriner.'

'And not sent,' Alfred finished off her thought.

Cressida could sense its importance, so instead of sliding it carefully back into the briefcase, she folded it up and slipped it into her pocket.

'Let's pretend I found that on the floor, shall we?' she asked with a slight nod of the head.

'I never saw a thing,' answered Alfred, opening the compartment door and escorting Cressida out.

## 47

Cressida said goodnight to Alfred and watched as he opened his compartment door and slipped in, giving her a friendly wave just before the door closed. Her own door was just yards away and as she walked towards it, her mind was bursting with all sorts of possibilities. Sleep would be impossible, she feared, and as her hand rested on the handle of her door, she thought of how Dotty and Ruby were probably fast asleep on her bed and possibly even snoring away, getting some much-needed rest. What would be the point in disturbing them, moving poor Dot, only for her to lie awake anyway. Cressida pulled her hand back from the door and paused.

A shard of light caught her eye, coming as it was from under the door of the compartment next to hers. The rest of the corridor was dim, the train having been 'put to bed', as it were, by the staff on board. In contrast to this darkness, the light from the door next to hers was bright. She moved towards it and noticed why; it was ajar.

Cressida instinctively walked towards it. This was Lord Hartnell and his nanny's compartment – the brass-framed name label confirmed it. She was the first to admit that she knew next to nothing about the rearing of small children, save for the fact that nose-picking was frowned upon, as was wine for the under twelves... but she was sure that bedtime was usually long before whatever early hour it was now. She checked her wristwatch to confirm. Almost one-thirty in the morning – only six hours until they reached London.

Cressida was about to turn away when she heard a sniffle, or a sob perhaps, from the open door. It reminded her of how much interesting information she'd gleaned from the crying Geraldine when she'd heard similar sounds, so she ventured closer again and placed her hand on the door handle. She didn't know what she was expecting to see as she slowly opened the door. Perhaps the nanny in tears at something Lord Hartnell had done or said? Young boys could be horrible, Cressida knew this from her cousins, who had teased her mercilessly when they were younger. And Ginny hadn't struck Cressida as being all that experienced with the nannying game. Ginny, for a start, not Miss So-and-So.

Putting that young terror in his place and comforting the beleaguered nanny had perhaps been what Cressida had anticipated. But was not what she found...

As she pushed the door fully open, the sobs abruptly stopped.

'I... I'm not crying. I'm not,' Lord Hartnell said, his face screwed up in determination. He was standing in the middle of the compartment holding a very smartly dressed teddy bear in one hand; its pyjamas matched his own blue and white striped ones. Unlike the teddy bear, Lord Hartnell's were buttoned up wrong and had what looked like a cocoa stain on them. Cressida noticed this, as she did the twin beds in the compartment. One was undisturbed, its sheets pristine, the eiderdown unrumpled.

Cressida reached out a hand and placed it gingerly on Lord Hartnell's shoulder. 'It's Monty, isn't it?'

The small boy nodded, then wiped his pyjama sleeve over his eyes.

Cressida led him over to the bed that looked like it had been the scene of a steeplechase or perhaps some bedsheet version of a landslide, and was the one she'd seen him sitting on earlier. 'I think you're being awfully brave, Monty. Are you all alone? Where's your nanny?'

Lord Hartnell shrugged and then climbed into his bed. Though she had never seen a bed in quite such chaos, Cressida sat down next to him and tried to smooth the cocoa-stained tangle enough to pull the covers up over him, making sure his teddy bear's head was sticking out.

This was all highly irregular. Cressida had been sure she'd come in to find the nanny in tears and Lord Hartnell doing whatever it was to his bed that had got it into this state, but Ginny was nowhere to be seen.

Cressida smoothed down the edge of the eiderdown in what she hoped was a maternal and soothing way. 'When was the last time you saw her, Monty?' she asked.

'Not since Edinburgh.' He looked dejected. 'She said she was going to get a cloth, but she never came back. I had to get myself undressed and do up my jammies myself.'

As the small boy spoke, Cressida looked down to the floor to where a heap of clothing lay, as if Lord Hartnell had just propelled himself out of his shorts, shirt and socks and left them where they landed.

'You've been all alone since then? My, my. Well, in that case you really are the bravest boy I know.'

'Am I? Am I really?' The finger that was so often up his nose was now stuck in his mouth, the nail being chewed.

*This poor boy*, thought Cressida. *Abandoned by his parents for who knows what reason, and then abandoned by the nanny sent to chaperone him. Where could she be?*

Cressida made some more small talk about the train and the

exceptional handsomeness of Lord Hartnell's bear, who was called Bash'em apparently, but all the while, her mind was whirring. She'd seen Ginny on her way to fetch that cloth, exasperated at the fact that Monty had spilt his cocoa.

*That was just before the train had stopped at Edinburgh...*

## 48

Cressida stood up with a start, that thought now crowding all others out of her head. Despite the fact that Lord Hartnell had decided to tell her, in detail, about the sport of cricket, she could think of nothing else save the fact that Ginny hadn't been seen since Edinburgh.

'I wonder...' Cressida said out loud and Lord Hartnell, believing she had been listening to him and was interested in the mastery of the googly bowling of the English cricket captain, decided it was his cue to tell her more about the most recent match he'd played in. She let him chat on as she returned to her thoughts.

*Ginny hasn't been seen since Ruby was let out of the train. Not since Alfred got distracted by me telling him about the door I'd seen open and close. Not since we took our eyes off the plat-form and the tracks for a second or two...*

Lord Hartnell had reached the complex explanation of why professional cricket was better than village matches when another thought occurred to Cressida.

*Monty said she'd taken a sausage off his plate earlier. And Ruby would follow anyone carrying a sausage...*

Cressida sat back, taking it all in. Lord Hartnell was onto how the Fifth Test of the Ashes back in March had seen Tate take the Australians for 115 for five when she noticed something strange above the bed opposite. The one that was still pristine and unslept in, the one that would have been Ginny's. While Lord Hartnell carried on talking, she stepped across the narrow gap between the beds and focused on what she'd spotted.

The wooden veneer that covered so much of the train and especially in these well-appointed compartments was missing a panel right there above the bed. Cressida knelt on the bed and pressed her hands up against the glossy wood, feeling around the missing panel that was about the size of a tea tray. There was damage to one side of the veneer still in place, damage that looked like splintering. Cressida could imagine something like a crowbar... no, smaller, more like a nail file, being slipped in between the panels and levering the missing panel off. Where was it though? Cressida looked around her, and saw nothing out of the ordinary. Her eyes did alight on a leather valise, which was clasped shut and sitting on the end of the bed.

Cressida glanced back to Lord Hartnell, who was still reeling off English cricket captains from 1875 to the modern day, and she hoped this made him completely unaware of the fact that she was about to open the bag and delve inside.

Delve inside she did, and apart from some simple tunics and a few toiletries, she found nothing of much interest. Until a paper cut pulled her up short. Cressida muttered an oath and sucked her finger while scrabbling around for the culprit of the attack. She found it and pulled out the piece of paper. The hairs on her arms prickled as she recognised the same handwriting, even the same size notebook page as the one she'd found tucked into the manilla folder with all the newspaper articles. But this one didn't have any information about Myra Warriner on it.

All it had written on it was an instruction – *P get two of these then give to* G – and a few unfamiliar words; *Webley.* And *Miv.* Then the final word, a recognisable one, that gave it away.

*That's not Miv, it's Mark IV,* Cressida realised as she read the word next to it.

*Revolver.*

'Oh my,' Cressida said, then uncharacteristically leaned over and gave Lord Hartnell a peck on the forehead. He stopped talking about opening batsmen and gawped at her.

'Right, night night, Monty. "Pyjamas, pyjamas" as my father used to say.' She straightened the collar of his striped pyjamas. 'Lady Dorothy is in the next-door compartment, and I won't be far at all. You can knock on the wall and Dotty will hear you. In fact, I'll have someone come and check that you're all right in just a tick. But I need to make like a fielder in need of his tea and hop off toot sweet.'

Lord Hartnell blinked at her a couple of times before whispering 'Pyjamas, pyjamas' as he waved to Cressida.

As she quietly closed Lord Hartnell's door behind her, the realisation really and truly came to Cressida. Ginny, Lord Hartnell's nanny, had been missing since Edinburgh. She had been the one to distract them and risk losing Ruby on the platform while she made her escape. She had a note in her bag on which was the name of a gun.

*Perhaps she – heavens knows why – is the murderer?*

## 49

Cressida rushed down the train towards DCI Andrews' compartment. Ginny – the nanny who had been so quiet all journey – had been the one to escape during their vigil at Edinburgh! *But why?*

Steadying herself as she ran, Cressida felt the glossed veneer of the wood that lined the corridor beneath her fingers. She wondered how easily Ginny had prised it off the wall between their compartments. How easily she'd listened in to conversations Cressida had had?

She arrived, almost breathless from the exertion, at Andrews' door. A sharp rat-a-tat and, within moments, Kirby, helmet off, of course, and even jacket unbuttoned, opened it.

'Evening, miss.'

'Evening, Kirby. Though I fear we're long past evening. How's Andrews?'

'I'm fine, Miss Fawcett. For heaven's sakes, come in,' Andrews said, still positioned on his bed.

Cressida entered and Kirby closed the door behind her. Once again, the newspaper clippings, the letter from the editor, the still damp tea lady's uniform and Miss de Souza's red shoes and the blackmail letter that had been in them, not to mention the old service revolver which was used to shoot Warriner, were laid out on his bunk in front of him.

Kirby moved to one side and Cressida spied the letter sent to Geraldine and today's paper too. She also noticed how peaky Andrews was looking. His wound might not be fatal, but he was suffering, that much was clear. There wasn't much she could do about that, though. What she could do was help him solve this murder.

'I have something else to add to your hoard of clues. Don't ask me how I got this first one. Just thank the gods of broken hearts and strong liquor.' She withdrew the folded letter from her pocket and opened it up, passing it over to Andrews as she explained further. 'Derby had it in his briefcase, and it contains some valuable information. But I also recognised the name of the editor to whom it's addressed. It's the same as the one on the letter in the manilla folder, inviting that chap into his final interview for the paper.'

Cressida passed Andrews the letter and let him read it.

'How are you feeling, Andrews?' she asked, wary of distracting him.

'Hmm?' He looked up from the letter. 'Oh, fine. Fine.' His wince would suggest otherwise, but Cressida let him read on. Finally, he said, 'This sounds to me very much like Warriner was requesting a favour from this newspaper editor. Something he could well afford, I suppose. But for what?'

'Miss Irving – Warriner's niece, of course – did say that her aunt was hounded by press stories that claimed she had been unfaithful to Lewis. Hence why, when it came to the divorce, he was able to keep hold of all the money that was rightfully hers and keep the business. Cut her off with nothing.'

'And you think he's doing it again?' Andrews asked.

Cressida shrugged but picked up the letter regarding the job at the newspaper. She looked at it. 'This is dated quite a few years ago, 1920. Whoever this Edward person is, if we can assume he took up the role, would have been working as a journalist for five years now.'

'And the editor is the same?' Andrews pressed.

'Yes, by the looks of it. Mr Quince.' Cressida paused. 'It's the *Evening Post* too, isn't it? Kirby, will you pass me today's copy of it, please?'

'Yes, miss,' Kirby said, reaching over and passing the paper to Cressida.

She opened it up and had a look. 'Yes, look. The editor is Terrence Quince. Which means he's been in place for a while now. I wonder if he was editor when Myra was alive?'

'That'll be twenty-odd years ago,' Andrews worked out.

'A junior then perhaps. Keen for a story to get him a byline,' Cressida posed.

'And we think this Edward chap wanted to follow in Mr Quince's footsteps?' Andrews took the thought one step further.

Cressida shrugged again, but cast her eyes down the paper. She flicked through to the page where the report on the night-club thefts had caught their eyes earlier. Then she stopped and her jaw dropped.

'What is it, Miss Fawcett, you look like you've seen a ghost,' Andrews remarked, concerned at the look on Cressida's face.

'Not a ghost, Andrews. More of a ghost writer. You see here, the byline at the top of the article?' Cressida folded the paper and showed the detective. 'That article about Warriner Industries pulling out of India. See who the journalist is.'

'Byline Edward Owen.' Andrews looked up at her, recognition on his face.

Cressida nodded at him. 'Edward Owen. So, he did get the job... Could he be Mrs Drysdale's Mr Bowen perhaps? Did she mishear him, or was he deliberately not using his real name?' Cressida mused out loud. Her capital-T Thoughts were whirring, as threads connected.

And another possibility came to her.

'Or perhaps our very own Owen Edwards from right here on the train?'

'Owen Edwards, who was carrying that folder you found, including this letter. A letter offering someone called Edward, perhaps Edward Owen, a salaried position on the paper five years ago. Owen Edwards, who claimed not to know Miss de Souza except for her turn on the silver screen. Yet, if he's Edward Owen, has written about her thieving from nightclub guests...' Andrews was thinking as he spoke. 'And if he is perhaps the Mr Bowen that Mrs Drysdale said went to great lengths to interview her—'

'Finding out exactly when she and her brother would be aboard the train...' Cressida added.

Andrews nodded, slowly, painfully. 'Then—'

'Then what, sir?' Kirby asked, tentatively.

'Then what, Sergeant, was he doing getting on this train? Where not one, but two people he'd written not very flattering things about were also aboard. And why, assuming that is him, change his name?'

'That, Andrews,' Cressida said, 'is what I want to find out next.'

## 50

'You said you had something else for me?' Andrews said, and Cressida nodded and reached into her pocket.

'This,' she replied, handing him the piece of paper with the make of gun on it. 'I found it in Lord Hartnell's compartment. Though it's not his, of course. It's Ginny's.'

'The nanny?' Andrews asked.

'Yes. The nanny who I think might have absconded at Edinburgh. Little Lord Hartnell told me that she'd swiped a sausage from his dinner—'

'Sorry?' Andrews interrupted.

'To lure Ruby with, of course. Cause that diversion,' Cressida said, almost snappily, but Andrews took it on board.

'Continue,' he said, and Cressida did.

'I found Lord Hartnell all alone in their compartment. He said he hadn't seen his nanny since Edinburgh. He was upset, the poor lamb. Though made a remarkable recovery from his tears as soon as he thought he had a willing ear to bend all about bowling and batting and whatnot.'

'I'm sorry?' Andrews looked confused.

'It doesn't matter. What matters is that I found that note in her bag. "M-one-five Webley", what does that mean?' Cressida looked at Andrews. He was tired, his eyes drooped, and he looked pale as dishwater. But he looked up at her and confirmed what she feared.

'It means that the gun that shot me and Mrs Warriner, and the one that shot Mr Warriner, were likely both Webley Mark Fours. The old service revolver. Just like the ones being traded in Glasgow at the moment by the likes of Mickey Loretta.'

'Is it a Webley then that you found under Geraldine's mattress?'

'Yes. Just like this note says. And I'll bet anything it's a Webley that gave me this.' He winced as he shrugged his shoulder. 'And, as far as we know, that one's still on board too. I only hope this Ginny, if she did manage to disembark at Edinburgh, didn't take it with her. If so, it's lost to us as evidence.'

'Andrews...' Cressida had run out of ideas. There was too much swimming around her head.

'I don't know why I'm suggesting this,' the injured policeman said, 'but go and find this Owen or Edward chap. But take Kirby. And, for heaven's sake, be careful.'

Cressida, a fan of hot-headed action at the best of times, didn't need to be asked twice. And she and Kirby didn't need to go far. Owen Edwards' compartment was only two doors down from Andrews' own. She gave the door a sharp knock and listened intently. Over the clattering of the rails, it was hard to determine if the noise was from within the compartment or all around them.

Cressida turned to Kirby and shook her head. 'I don't think he's in there. Or maybe he's asleep?'

'Or maybe he got off the train too, at Edinburgh, miss? It was quite hard to see.'

'We didn't get around to checking on him, Alfred and I, when we were doing our headcount. We got distracted by Dotty...' Cressida sighed. 'But Owen was in the dining car with us when Andrews and poor Mrs Warriner were shot. He has an alibi, so would have had no reason to abscond.'

'Unless he was the one who shot Warriner?' Kirby asked.

'But the person who shot Warriner – assuming now it really *wasn't* Mrs Warriner – would have no reason to shoot *her*. She was being framed well enough.'

'Except you didn't believe it, not for long, miss,' Kirby reminded her.

Cressida thought back to the hole in Lord Hartnell's bedroom, above Ginny's bed.

'No, I didn't, did I?' Cressida bit her lip. The veneer... the letters... the names... overhearing and over-ages... Suddenly, a flash of inspiration came to her. 'Kirby, please keep trying Mr Edwards. Or Mr Owen. If he's there, ask him to come to the dining car. Don't say why, just police business or something. Something general. And could you see if Andrews can make the trip too? I think I might have pieced something together. I just need to check one more thing.'

'Righto, miss. Dining carriage as directly as I can, with Mr Edwards, or whatever his name is, and the chief, miss,' Kirby repeated it back to her and she nodded.

'And Donaldson and Mrs Drysdale perhaps too. Soon as you can, Kirby, soon as you can. We need to get a confession before we get to London.'

'Monty?' Cressida poked her head around the door of the young lord's compartment. Her soothing ministrations earlier had obviously worked, and as she turned the light on, she could see he was fast asleep in his bunk, Bash'em clenched under his arm, one thumb stuck in his mouth. He stirred as the light came on, but stayed asleep.

Cressida looked over to the place on the wall above the

other bunk, the unslept in one, and peered closer at the hole in the panelling.

'What are you doing, Miss Fawcett?' the young voice sounded, sleepily, from behind her.

'Oh, hello Monty. Told you I'd be close.'

'Is it morning? Are we in London yet?' Lord Hartnell asked, rubbing his eyes with his little fists. 'I can't wait to get to London. Nanny said we could go to the Natural History Museum and see the bones.'

'That's nice, Monty.' Cressida crossed over the compartment and sat herself down next to him. 'Can I ask you something, Monty?'

'Is it about sums?' he asked warily. 'As I'm not very good at sums.'

'No, it's not about sums,' Cressida replied, not the first time finding the mind of a young boy unfathomable in its workings. 'It's about gangsters.'

'Oh, that's more interesting.' Lord Hartnell sat up a bit further in his bed and flung Bash'em to the floor. Gangster talk was no place for a teddy bear.

'You said you thought that the man who was shot earlier this evening was tied up with Glasgow gangsters. How did you know that?'

Lord Hartnell screwed up his face in concentration and Cressida wondered if her question had, in the end, been as hard as sums. Eventually, he straightened out his face and said, 'Nanny must have told me. She was saying quite a few things about him. Not very nice things.'

'Oh really, such as?'

'I don't think she'd like me to repeat them. She said they were our secret,' he replied rather bashfully.

'Why don't we make them our secret? Like the one we had about that man being shot.' Cressida hoped Lord Hartnell would remember the pact they'd made earlier. It seemed he did, and his next few words cemented in her mind that she was definitely on the right track.

'All right then. She said that man was a no-good son of a gun and as soon as her brother was done with him, he'd be sorry.'

'She has a brother?'

'Oh yes.'

'Is he on this train too?'

Lord Hartnell shrugged. 'I don't know. But she was always talking to that funny man with the autograph book.'

'Was she now?' Cressida squeezed Lord Hartnell's shoulder. She had to admit that she'd warmed to the young viscount, more than she thought she might. 'Come on, you. There's a party in the dining car going on in a few minutes. I think you'll enjoy it.'

## 51

Cressida didn't think to knock on her own door, mind as full as it was, and quite startled Dotty as she turned on the light.

'Dot! Dot!' she said, still holding the perennially sticky hand of Lord Hartnell. 'Dot, wake up. I think I know what's been going on. It's all about the brothers and sisters. And all those newspaper clippings. And poor Mrs Warriner – the first Mrs Warriner, that is – who died all those years ago. And the current Mrs Warriner who hasn't got any heirs. And names all the wrong way round.'

'And my nanny being missing,' Lord Hartnell added rather excitedly.

Dotty blinked and reached out for her glasses, putting them on and then squinting up at Cressida, haloed by light. Ruby snorted, wakened by the light and the fact that Lord Hartnell's other, and probably equally sticky hand, was now stroking her head.

'Dot, bring Rubes will you. And knock up Alf on your way through. He'll want to hear all of this too. See you in the dining car in a few minutes.'

With that, Cressida and Lord Hartnell slipped out, leaving a bemused Dotty and confused-looking Ruby.

'She really is a wonder,' Dotty said to the small dog. 'But I do wish she'd have let me get some more kip.'

Cressida, a really very talkative Lord Hartnell in tow, roused the Irvings and Clarence Derby. The Irvings did not take kindly to the disruption, though Cressida saw through Louise's bluster and entrusted the young viscount to her care and asked her to take him through to the dining car while she spoke to Mr Derby.

Louise was treated straightaway to a lecture about fast bowling, much to her befuddlement.

Clarence was still fog-headed and took some time to rouse. Cressida shook him and flashed the light on and off and eventually he came to, rubbing his forehead and covering his eyes from the electric light.

'What on earth is this all about?' he said, sitting up in his bunk.

'I'd like you to come with me, Mr Derby,' Cressida said, as gently but as persuasively as possible. 'I believe I know who's behind these shootings.'

There was silence, as she waited for her words to sink through his sleep- and drink-induced daze.

'Mr Derby, I think you might want to hear what I have to say, but it can't be here. Join us in the dining car. Everyone will be there. We'll get justice for Geraldine, I promise.'

She squeezed his hand and then left him to freshen up. His journey had not been an easy one, and she knew the things he was about to hear would be hard. But she had to be sure justice was done; justice *not* vengeance.

.   .   .

When Cressida entered the dining car, the enormity of what she was about to do suddenly came over her. She was sure she had it right, as she pieced together all the clues. As far as physical clues went, she was pleased to see that Kirby had brought them all with him and had laid them out on one of the white-tablecloth-covered tables.

It worried her that a second gun had yet to be found. But perhaps, as Alfred had said all those hours ago, it would have been sensible to toss it from the speeding train. She hoped that it had been, for safety's sake, despite Andrews wanting it for evidence. Still, seeing the Webley revolver they had found sitting on the table with the newspaper clippings, the letters, the notebook pages, the beautiful red shoes and the uniform... well, it made her realise how deadly the revenge of the murderer – *murderers* – had become.

She looked around at the tired, pale and generally displeased faces. Even Dotty and Alfred yawned and looked tired. Lord Hartnell had laid his head down on his arms and looked like he'd gone back to sleep. Callum Irving, who had been so belligerent all journey, was made to look even more irritable by the dark circles under his eyes.

Cressida paused for a moment by the bar, shielded from the rest of the gathered passengers by the frosted-glass panel behind the last table, and tried to hold all the threads in her head together. There was one thing that didn't quite fit as neatly as she hoped.

'Myra's the link, of course... As are all these brothers and sisters. And the veneer, oh yes that was very clever and such a good way of thinking of it... And the newspaperman and his stories... It's just the name I haven't got...' Cressida leaned her elbows on the bar and pressed her fingers into her temples as she thought. She was tired and her bones ached, and in all honesty, the person whom she was trying to save from the noose could die at any moment. What did this all matter in the end?

*In the end.* Who else had died? Lewis Warriner, of course; and Geraldine was at death's door... then there was Myra Warriner... *Myra...*

Cressida pushed herself up. She scanned the faces in the dining car and settled on the one person who she realised could fit the last piece of information together for her. She wasn't ready for the whole dining car to see her yet, but she needed to grab someone's attention. Just then, Ruby tottered over from where Dotty was sitting and plopped herself down on Cressida's foot.

'Oh of course, Ruby. You darling dog. You can help me.' Cressida reached across the bar for one of the left-over cheese gougères.

Crouching down, she offered the snack to her ever-hungry dog, who looked excited and then toddled off after it as Cressida skimmed it down the aisle, landing it perfectly at the feet of Louise Irving. As Ruby followed, it took only a second or two for Miss Irving to notice the rasping tongue snuffling around her ankles and looked up in alarm from where she'd almost been nodding off again. Cressida caught her attention and subtly as possible waved at her and beckoned her over.

'Miss Fawcett?' Miss Irving said, when she joined her at the bar. 'What is it? And what are we all doing here?'

'I know who did it. Well, I'm almost sure. And *why*, most importantly. But I just need one more piece of information from you.'

Louise sighed. 'I've told you everything about Aunt Myra. Callum's very cross with me about it.'

'I know you did, and I'm ever so grateful. But you missed out one small detail.'

'What is it? What do you want to know?'

'Your Aunt Myra. You said she was married to your Uncle Ned before he died and she married Warriner. Tell me, what was Ned's surname?'

'Why, it's—'

The train clattered over a difficult set of points and Louise's words were hard to catch as she lost her balance and almost fell over. Cressida steadied her, and herself, and on repeating the name, Louise Irving had told Cressida all she needed to know.

The murderers were found.

## 52

'What's all this about?' Callum Irving raised his voice as his sister came back to sit by his side. 'What have you been saying to Louise? Louise, what have you been telling her?'

Louise quickly shook her head, silencing her brother, but his thunderous voice had roused the other tired people in the dining car.

Between them, Cressida and Kirby had gathered together the Irvings, Clarence Derby, Owen Edwards, who it seemed *had* been asleep in his compartment, Miss de Souza, who did nothing but eye her red suede shoes on the table, and Mrs Drysdale and her brother Mr Donaldson, who had left the train in the capable hands of Mr Sawyer. Martha, the young tea lady who had so wanted to be part of the excitement, hovered at the back, ostensibly helping Mrs Drysdale dish out steaming cups of coffee. DCI Andrews had placed himself at one of the tables and sat there gingerly cradling his injured arm. Ginny, Lord Hartnell's nanny, had been nowhere to be found, cementing Cressida's theory. She looked out of the window at the creeping dawn as she gathered her thoughts. The train was still steaming through the lush green fields of the northern Home Counties. She still had time.

Cressida drew her eyes off the view and back to the smart dining carriage, where the white tablecloths and glistening glassware had set the scene for the first dramatic incident of the trip. She took a deep breath and looked up at the glossed veneered ceiling. *Veneer... such a clever thing.* Hiding with a thin layer what ugly truth lay beneath.

She exhaled. 'Ladies and gentlemen. Lord Hartnell,' she nodded at the young boy, who smiled back at her, then went on with excavating his nose, 'there is a killer here in our midst.'

'I say,' Callum Irving interrupted. 'That's a bit dashed strong. Here? I thought you had her under lock and key?'

'What's this all about?' Owen Edwards asked, looking directly at Cressida.

'Veneer,' Cressida replied.

Owen threw his arms up in the air, puffed his cheeks out and looked about him. 'Well, it's clear she's gone mad, this one. Absolutely stark raving. What are we all doing here? And at such an ungodly hour.' He made to get up, but Andrews, paler than ever and ensconced in one of the dining chairs, nodded to Kirby, who gestured for him to sit down.

'Mr Edwards, please. Listen to Miss Fawcett,' Andrews said, then looked at her. 'She usually gets it right, even if it's not strictly procedural.'

'Thank you, Chief Inspector. And he's right,' she addressed the carriage, 'I don't do things by the book, but then neither do murderers. And what I *do* do is notice things. I love interior design, you see, so I understand when something looks wrong, a curtain for example is hanging badly, or if colours just don't go. And I've been thinking about this wonderful veneer in this train.'

'It's very smart,' Dotty added.

'Yes it is, Dot. And it tells a story – or at least it's helped me make sense of the story of this train journey.'

'You mean who shot…' Louise paused, 'Uncle Lewis?'

'Someone in this carriage, Miss Irving,' Cressida replied. 'But before we find out who, we need to go back quite a few years. In fact, right to the beginning of Warriner Industries. As I said to Dotty earlier this evening – which feels like a lifetime ago to me now – we have to approach this like a decorating scheme; add the layers rather than going in and just splashing paint everywhere.'

'Paint? Veneer? What are you driving at?' Callum Irving said, looking irked.

'I'll come to it, I promise. But first, Warriner Industries. Founded in 1901 by Lewis Warriner using money from his wife, Myra. Myra had been married to a wealthy man, who tragically died only a couple of years into their marriage. Distraught, and mother to two very young children, she left India, where they'd lived, and came back to her family in Scotland. Inverness to be exact, where she happened to meet Lewis. She had a passion for cars, as this article suggests.' She pointed to the magazine feature in question.

'Where's that from? That article?' Derby asked, looking up from his hunched position on one of the smaller tables, cradling his coffee cup between his hands.

'I found Owen Edwards over there carrying it. He claims it's not his, but I'm not so sure.'

Owen stared out of the window, ignoring Cressida.

She carried on. 'This article states that the new Mrs Warriner was supporting her husband in "more ways than one", which I take to mean she had put up quite a substantial amount of money in order to get Warriner Industries off the ground. But where did that money come from?'

'Her first husband,' Louise Irving said. 'I told you. Uncle Ned.'

'Correct. Uncle Ned who had passed away from malaria, leaving Myra a wealthy widow.'

Owen suddenly turned his head and glared at Cressida. 'So, it's these two then, is it? The niece and nephew? Revenging their aunt? Hoping to inherit the business?'

'They certainly had some beef with their uncle – if you could still call him that after the way he treated their aunt. I overheard them—'

'You what?' Callum snapped. 'How dare you eavesdrop on private conversations.'

'Shh, Callum,' Louise tried to calm him. 'Let her speak.'

Cressida smiled at her ally. 'I'm sorry, but yes I overheard you. You had obviously come aboard in order to finish what you'd started in the boardroom, which was to change Warriner's mind regarding his investment in your business. In the boardroom, he'd said no, but perhaps a bit of roughing up, away from his minions and lackeys, on a train where you were the tougher man, that might have changed his mind, yes?' Cressida looked at Callum, who at least had the good grace to look slightly sheepish.

'It wasn't fair. His reasoning wasn't solid,' Callum mumbled.

'And you stood to lose a lot of money. As Louise said to me, him dying had eased a few of your problems, as no doubt more reasonable people within the organisation could be drawn upon to invest. Hence, at the sound of that first shot, your problems were solved.'

'They did it?' Clarence Derby asked, his eyes still bloodshot red and rimmed with the pinkness of tears and tiredness. 'Did they shoot Geraldine too? On my life, if you were the ones to hurt her—' He started to get up, but Kirby, who was keeping an eye on everyone in the carriage, swiftly placed a hand on his shoulder and guided him back to sitting.

Cressida thanked Kirby, then carried on. 'No, they didn't

shoot Geraldine, or even their wicked uncle. But Miss Irving did tell me some very interesting things about her late aunt, things that go back twenty years,' Cressida paused. 'And they start to reveal the truth of what happened here tonight.'

## 53

'Two young children accompanied Myra Warriner back from India. Their mother married again quickly, and Lewis, for a year or so, was a father to them. Then, when Lewis and Myra divorced, we hear nothing more about the children. There's nothing in these newspaper clippings here, which have been gathered over the years.' Cressida pointed to the manilla folder. 'They keep track of Myra's life from her marriage, through to the divorce proceedings and finally the notice of her death.' Cressida pushed the clippings around until she found the small, innocuous piece of newspaper print and then picked it up, showing the rest of the carriage what she was talking about. 'Someone who cared about Myra collected these and curated them. Wrote notes in a notebook and tore out a page to keep it with them too. Then, also in this folder, was a letter. A letter from a Mr Quince, who's editor of the *Evening Post*, offering a chap called Edward a position.'

Cressida put the death notice down and gestured towards the letter from the newspaper.

'I know Quince. But who's Edward?' Clarence Derby

asked, more awake now, though still rubbing his temples from time to time.

'It's an important question, but almost as important is, who is Mr Quince?'

'The editor of the newspaper, dearie,' Mrs Drysdale said. 'See, I'm keeping up, Hughie.'

Mr Donaldson, who looked wholly unimpressed by the whole affair, shrugged at his sister. 'I dinna ken why we're all so bloody interested in who killed him. I take ma hat off to them, whoever did. Good riddance to the miserly fella.'

There were mumblings from Owen and Callum, but Cressida shushed them. 'He wasn't well liked, Mr Warriner, but that only made this whole thing harder. So many of you had motives to kill him. Take you, for example, Mr Donaldson.' Cressida looked at the driver, dressed in overalls, his face smutty from the coal, his hands blackened by dust and grease. 'You hated Mr Warriner and thought he was irresponsible in how he dealt with the poor veterans coming back from the war. And there's a rather suspicious greasy mark that could easily made by fingers like yours, on a letter sent to Mrs Warriner just a day before she boarded, when you would have been in Inverness between shifts.'

'Aye, but why kill him now when I've been out o'that company for years? And when, lassie, when would I ha' had the chance?'

'I know, Mr Donaldson. You couldn't have done it, you've never been out of the engine or luggage car. And I don't think your sister, Mrs Drysdale, has anything to do with it either... well, not quite, but I'll come to that.'

Mrs Drysdale looked both flustered and excited and Cressida could see young Martha's eyes light up at the mention that her mentor might have something to do with anything so grisly as a murder.

Cressida continued, 'Mr Derby, you had good reason to

hate, and therefore murder, Mr Warriner too. He took the woman you loved away from you, used you to do all sorts of underhand things that you hated. And potentially knew about you stealing from the coffers. I mean, if Mr Donaldson knew, I assume someone more involved in the business, like the owner himself, might have caught on. Perhaps that's what he had over you? How he kept you quiet, despite you knowing he was writing to the newspapers again?'

'I... I... I'm not a murderer, Miss Fawcett. I may be a thief, it's true, but I'm not a murderer.'

'I know, Mr Derby. You hated Lewis Warriner, but you loved Geraldine. You would never have framed her for his murder, or then shot her afterwards, which I don't mind saying greatly added to the head-scratchingness of this case. Why kill the person you've just set up to take the blame? No, Mr Derby, you hated Warriner, but the person who killed Warriner also wanted rid of Geraldine, and you wouldn't do that to a woman you've loved for decades, even if she didn't requite your love.'

'So who did kill him? And shoot his wife?' Callum Irving asked, then pointed to Phoebe. 'What about her? And what on earth is that small boy doing there?'

At this, Lord Hartnell sat up. 'I've lost my nanny. Is that something to do with all of this too?'

'Yes, Monty, it is. And I need to ask you a very simple, but very important question in a moment. No sums, I promise.'

'Pyjamas, pyjamas,' he said, knowingly.

'Exactly.' Cressida then addressed the adults in the room. 'Phoebe, you had a huge role to play in all of this, but you're not a murderer. You're a woman being put upon by the killer. Blackmailed in order to play your part, if that note we found in your discarded shoe is anything to go by. You so desperately wanted to be in films and leave the nightclub scene, so when Warriner came along and offered you his arm, you never thought about his wife or who might get hurt. You just wanted your dream of being in the movies and away from Mickey Loretta.'

'I hate to interrupt, Cressy,' Dotty said, looking as if she were mentally just keeping up with Cressida's chain of thought. 'But who could blackmail someone – and forgive me, Miss de Souza, for saying this – but who could blackmail someone who had already made her name in places like the Firebird. It's not blackmail if the person does what they do in public. And if that handbag story in the newspaper had a grain of truth to it, then Miss de Souza is also possibly a thief too, with a public record of her misdemeanour in the police station, newspaper article or not. Again, I mean no offence, Miss de Souza, but you can see what I'm driving at.'

'You're right, Dot,' Cressida said as her friend pushed her glasses up to the bridge of her nose. 'But there's always some-where where reputation matters. Especially if you're an aspiring actress, ready to take on the world. Ready, that is, as long as your reputation appears squeaky clean to the public eye and no one could read anything bad about you.'

'Oh I see,' Dotty said, holding Ruby tight to her, and pushing her glasses up her nose. 'The court of public opinion. And stories and pictures actually published, kept for posterity and archived and all that.'

'Exactly, Dot. American film producers wouldn't neces-sarily be checking Glasgow police records, but they do keep an eye on the newspapers.'

## 54

'Newspapers have played a rather important part in this investigation. Whether it's me reading one found on this train, or someone else keeping clippings from decades ago... the printed notice of Myra's death even. Newspapers are such a source of information. They were even used, all those years ago, as evidence in the divorce case when Lewis claimed Myra was having a string of affairs. The evidence? The stories in the *Evening Post*. Written by a certain Mr Quince.' Cressida picked up one of the clippings describing Myra being seen out in Inverness with a young man. 'Mr Derby, did you feed this information to the press?'

'No... not me... I was too junior then,' Clarence stuttered.

Cressida nodded thoughtfully. 'Someone else then. But Warriner had these stories put out there. I know this because, Mr Derby, you were carrying with you a letter, a letter you as his private secretary had passed over your desk to approve, no doubt, but you couldn't bring yourself to do that. It's a letter to Mr Quince, who is now editor of the whole paper, discussing favours. Warriner was about to do the same to Geraldine as he'd done to Myra. Disgrace her in the press so the divorce would be quick and financially painless to him.'

'So... he killed him? Derby here? You said he loved Geraldine,' Owen said, pointing an accusatory finger at Derby.

'I do love her,' Derby replied, more soberly than ever. 'My heart sank when I saw that letter cross my desk... Why would I frame her for murder?'

'Ah, and that brings us to another vital aspect of this case. The French would call it *cherchez l'argent* – follow the money. Who stands to benefit from Warriner's death? Certainly not Mr Derby.'

'And not me,' piped up Phoebe. All eyes turned to look at the washed-out showgirl, who now looked so different from the glamorous woman who had boarded the train all those hours earlier, her veneer of razzle-dazzle well and truly wiped off.

'No, not you, Miss de Souza,' Cressida agreed. 'Warriner was worth much more to you alive. But you did play a role in his death. You were being blackmailed; threatened with stories appearing about you in the press. Stories that could definitely damage your reputation and make your Hollywood dream fall apart. This one here, for example' – Cressida pointed to the paper she'd found on the train earlier in the evening – 'shows that your blackmailer wasn't afraid to carry through a threat. You were coerced into helping the murderers with their scheme, else more bad press would appear about you. "Handbags are just the start of it," the threatening note said. Once you'd seen that the author of that note meant business, you had to do what they said. But I don't think you knew what the consequences were.' Cressida said the last few words gently as Miss de Souza sobbed into a crinkled handkerchief. 'If you did, you might have weighed up the pros and cons and decided that a few bad stories weren't as detrimental to your career compared to losing your patron. Especially as it looked like he was starting divorce proceedings against his wife, I assume so he could make you the third Mrs Warriner. One who could give him an heir, perhaps.'

Cressida paused, collecting her thoughts, before carrying on.

'But the cunningness of the murderers was such that they played you in a way that once the shot was fired, you were implicated too – if the case fell apart against Geraldine, who would the prosecutors look to next?'

'That's what he said,' Phoebe murmured. 'Said I would have to help them kill Geraldine so that suspicion would fall on the Irvings.'

'Why would suspicion fall on Miss de Souza?' asked Louise, intrigued.

Cressida picked up the note she'd found in Ginny's valise. 'Because of this. "P get two and then give to G". I was more caught up in not really knowing what a Webley was, but once Andrews explained, it became clearer. I think Phoebe, under duress, was tasked to source the guns for the murderers. Guns amassed in the Firebird Club, in which she sang and danced; a club owned by Mickey "Pink Cheeks" Loretta, a notorious Glasgow gangster. That note we found in her shoe – "The handbags are just the start of it" – that's the warning that if she didn't keep complying, then she'd soon be outed as the procurer of the guns. Something someone in the press could easily do with a splashy headline and an exposé.'

Phoebe nodded, her face drawn and pale. 'They even asked for the note back and said my fingerprints were on it... and if I didn't comply, then a story sitting on his desk back at the news-paper office would be filed; a story all about me and the guns.'

Cressida met Phoebe's sad and tired eyes, nodded in under-standing, then continued. 'There's a murderer here, that's for sure, but there's also a journalist here. Someone who, five years or so ago, was recruited by the *Evening Post*, by Mr Quince himself. Someone who made sure, by securing an interview with Mrs Drysdale, that this train would have not only her on board, but her brother; a well-known hater of Mr Warriner, who could also fall under suspicion. A journalist who wrote a letter to Geraldine, urging her to board the train, covering it with a veneer of grease so that once again suspicion could be misdirected towards Mr Donaldson. A journalist who then mistakenly got some of that grease on his own collection of clippings. A journalist, who, after his mother lost everything because of vile stories written about her in the papers, decided to use his profession as the medium to get his revenge on the man he hated. A young boy whose extended family only remember as being "quite good with words". He became an investigative journalist. He tailed Warriner all the way to Glasgow. From there, he met Miss de Souza, finding out enough about her to blackmail her into going along with his plans. Blackmail her with stories about her thieving.'

'When I said yes, he promised he'd stop,' wept Phoebe into her handkerchief. 'But he printed them anyway, in that blasted paper.'

'He used you horribly, Phoebe. All because he was on the tail of his ex-stepfather.' Cressida stared at one man in particular.

'Who is it?' Louise asked. 'Our cousin?'

'Yes, your cousin. In fact, both your cousins were on the train, I think, but I'm pretty certain Ginny absconded at Edinburgh. But here's your cousin. Edward. The man who applied for the job at the *Evening Post*. The man who inverted his name for us here on this train, so easy to do when your surname is Owen. Your Uncle Ned gave him his name, all of it. Because your Uncle Ned was also an Edward Owen.'

At this, Owen shot up from his seat, but Kirby was quick to restrain him.

Cressida carried on, while she could. 'Owen, or Edward as I should call you, you made sure you had everyone on this train who needed to be here. You secured your patsy, Geraldine, by inviting her onboard, adding a little grease mark on the letter just in case the police worked out that Geraldine was being set up. She boarded, and to your delight, confronted her cheating husband in front of all of us. She couldn't have unwittingly played her role better, and had lined herself up to being prime suspect.'

'I even arrested her,' Andrews sighed.

'How could you not, Andrews?' Cressida reassured him. 'The gun had been planted in her room during the chaos after the shot. It was only her calm, and wholly believable, testimony that made us think twice.'

'Us?' Callum Irving asked. 'I very much doubt a senior police officer needed help from a mere socialite.'

Cressida raised her eyebrows at him, but otherwise let the barb ping off her.

'I happened to hear Geraldine's interview—'

'Good old Woolly,' muttered Dotty, rubbing Ruby's ears.

'And I think someone else, someone who didn't have the benefit of Minty O'Hare's Glass Receiver did some listening in on me, this time by removing the veneer above her bed, meaning she could hear better the conversations we were having. The conversations casting doubt on Geraldine's guilt. The conversations that put into motion the second attack on the train. That on Geraldine Warriner.'

'That's in my compartment,' Lord Hartnell said, removing his finger from his nose and looking as serious as a nine-year-old boy in his cocoa-stained pyjamas could. 'Ginny took it off the wall. Said it was rattling, which I suppose it would if one kept one's ear as close to it as she did.'

'You're right, Monty,' Cressida said, her praise bringing a little glow to the young boy's cheeks. 'And she told Phoebe what she heard. Now, it's time for the important question I need to ask you.'

Lord Hartnell straightened up, as if preparing for an oral examination at prep school.

Cressida let him settle, then continued. 'Monty, your nanny is called Ginny, isn't she? And I thought it was odd that she allowed you to call her that. But she couldn't let anyone hear you call her by her real name, her more formal name, as it were. So, Monty, do you know what her real name is?'

'Oh yes,' Monty said, and looked like a pupil expecting a top grade. 'Her name's Miss Owen.'

## 55

There were whispered, spoken and shouted exclamations.

Kirby kept a firm grip on Owen Edwards, or Edward Owen as he was now to be known.

Andrews, managing to stand, but still looking in great pain and incredibly pale despite the doctor's visit, shushed the passengers in the carriage, shouting 'Order! Order!' as if he were the judge in a courtroom.

'Please, everyone!' Cressida stood next to Andrews, her arm gently resting on his good shoulder. 'I can explain everything. I think.'

'Well, I'm all ears,' said Callum Irving, casting a suspicious look over to the man he now knew to be his first cousin.

'Is that really you, Edward?' Louise was more inquisitive. 'But what have you done?'

'What have I done?' sneered Edward. 'What have I done? What anyone else would.'

'It's true, it's him.' Phoebe pointed at him. 'He's the journalist who followed me and threatened me with all sorts of nasty stories. Said I had to play along or else.'

'But he claimed not to know you, not personally at least.

Nor you him, when he asked for an autograph at tea yesterday,'
Callum pointed out.

'All part of the veneer, if you will. He had to make it clear to
all of us that he had never met, and had never had any contact
with, the glamorous starlet Miss de Souza. She knew this was
part of her role on the train—'

'And that was all I thought it would be. He told me the
stories about me in the nightclub and being linked to those gang
members would get worse, but to stop them all I had to do was
pretend not to recognise him when he approached me on the
train. And get him those guns. But I swear I didn't know what
he was going to do, I promise. I promise—'

'I believe you,' Cressida said. 'Once Warriner was dead and
Geraldine wasn't necessarily the police's only suspect, is that
when he threatened you with the fact your prints were on the
guns and on that note?'

'Don't say a word, Phoebe,' Edward snarled at her.

But Phoebe de Souza wiped her eyes and gathered some
strength. 'With Lewis gone, I had no choice. If Edward printed
those stories...'

'Hence why you helped him and his sister, Lord Hartnell's
nanny, create the opportunity for killing Geraldine. And she
did almost die, as did an officer of the law, DCI Andrews here.'

Phoebe de Souza wept into her handkerchief again. Edward
just stared at Cressida as if willing her to carry on, if she dared.

She did.

'Phoebe was the tea lady. She had to take off her lovely red
shoes and stash them as she got changed in the luggage car.
Hiding that threatening note with them. Then, in a uniform
that Mrs Drysdale told us had been stolen from the storage
cupboard at Inverness station a little while ago, and one of her
own wigs, she lured Sergeant Kirby away from his post.'

'How did she know she'd need the uniform?' Derby asked,
looking much more awake now.

'She didn't. I should imagine Edward purloined it as he worked out various eventualities. It was all part of this veneer, you see. Making things look different to reality, covering his own ugly truth with a gloss. A greasy fingerprint here, a tea lady put under suspicion there... perhaps not enough to frame these people for good, but all good backup plans in case Geraldine wasn't suspected straight away.'

'It all got more tense when we knew we had police on board,' Phoebe said, through sniffles. 'I didn't know Edward would shoot him too. Edward,' she turned to the accused, 'how could you?'

'How could I?' Edward sat with his arms folded across his chest. 'How could I not?'

'Explain yourself, young man,' Andrews said, his voice sounding weaker by the minute. 'The courts go easier on a confession of guilt.'

'Explain myself? What's there to explain?' He stared at Cressida. 'This honourable annoyance has said it all.'

'You admit your guilt?' Andrews pressed.

'I don't feel guilty, if that's what you mean. Who would feel guilty about killing the man who had been the cause of his mother's death? Where's the guilt in righting a wrong?'

'Vengeance is wrong, Edward,' Cressida replied. 'You put that in the notice of her death, didn't you? But you can't seek vengeance.'

'Why not?' Edward spat at her. 'He was cruel. He used her, wooed her when she was most vulnerable, for her money. And as soon as he met that little redhead, he dropped Mother like a stone. And took all of it.'

'Terrence Quince helped with that. Why join him and become one of those gutter journalists now?' Andrews asked.

Edward sighed. 'I needed to know. I needed to know that they were false stories. And how could I ever find that out without becoming part of the *Evening Post* team. Mr Quince was still there. He was impressed by my early work and took me on. He had no idea who I was related to or why I was so interested in cases like Myra Warriner's. He thought I could be trained to be another grubby journalist, that's why I was always asking questions. And after a few years, I found out the truth. Over one of his lunches. It was all lies. All of it, printed about Mother. Lies that he'd benefitted from as well. Those favours didn't come cheap.'

'Your handwritten notes in the folder, that was you following leads?' Cressida asked, knowing the answer already.

'That's right. I couldn't take the older papers out of the archive, but I could take my notebook in.' He pulled out the autograph book from his pocket and placed it on the table, patting it gently with his hand. Now Cressida could see that between the smooth edges of the pages there were missing ones, and she would bet a month's allowance that those pages would match the ones she found in the folder and Ginny's luggage. But something else was bugging her and she posed the question to Edward.

'You were here in this carriage with us when Geraldine was shot. Meaning that attack was your sister?'

'Yes. She hated Warriner too, but particularly hated Geraldine. It was her idea to frame her. Have her hang for his murder, and then—'

'Then you'd inherit your money again,' Cressida interrupted. 'With no fingers pointed at either of you. *Cherchez l'argent*, you see. Who inherits? Louise told me that her aunt Myra had written something to her mother, something about naming her children as successors to Warriner and his next of kin. She'd wanted to save her investment in Warriner Industries for her children. Allowed him to cut her off without a penny in her lifetime, if her children were his successors.'

'The only thing that would hinder that overage was if he

had children of his own,' Clarence said. 'Legally speaking. He assumed he and Geraldine would have them, but—'

'But they didn't have any.' Cressida thought. 'She told me she thought he was tiring of her, and she mentioned some troubles between them. Even in the dining car when she first confronted him, he rather harshly said it had been years since she'd been "any use at all". She was becoming dispensable to him, I think.'

'And to this miscreant,' Clarence Derby said, seething through his tiredness. 'His sister, she's the one who shot Geraldine?'

'And was here on the train under false pretences too,' Cressida added. 'Tell me, Mr Owen, how did you manage that?'

Edward looked at Lord Hartnell, who had taken to eating sugar cubes again from the bowls on the table. 'Ginny's not a nanny by training, but she managed to get herself on board by replying to an advertisement this child's parents had placed in my paper. What luck! "Nanny wanted for accompanying minor to London on sleeper train". I never let it go to print of course, but they didn't know that. Easy enough then to make sure Ginny was the only applicant.'

'What scared her enough to make her jump off the train? Why leave you to take all the blame if you got caught?' Cressida asked.

The sound of a gun cocking took everyone's attention. Then a soft Scottish voice replied to Cressida.

'Because I never left, Miss Fawcett.'

Ginny Owen stood at the entrance to the dining car, her gun pointed directly at Cressida.

Alfred stood up, but Ginny brought up her second hand, and cupped around her trigger finger.

'Don't move. None of you move. Or I'll shoot every one of you.'

## 56

'Miss Owen,' croaked Andrews, and Cressida saw a bloom of red had appeared under his bandage. Whatever the doctor had done to patch him up wasn't enough. 'Where were you? We searched—'

'Be quiet,' snapped Ginny, moving the gun from person to person. 'Searched! Ha. Not the luggage car. I used a sausage to chuck that little dog off the train so you'd all think I'd leapt off too, but all I did was hide behind the vast amounts of luggage you toffs carry with you. Edward, stand up, get over here.'

'The hidey-hole Ruby found...' Cressida muttered under her breath. 'Of course...'

'Miss Owen,' Kirby spoke over Cressida's mumblings, starting to confront the gunwoman, but Ginny snarled at him.

'Stand aside, you useless lump. Let my brother through.'

Edward got up and pushed Kirby's hand off his shoulder. Cressida tried to think how she could stop this from happening. How had they failed to find Ginny in the luggage car? It had all been so chaotic, but she had been so close. So close to solving it and getting justice, but with Ginny holding that gun and Andrews as weak as a bad cup of tea, what could she do?

'Move.' Cressida felt the tip of the pistol against her shoulder, pushing her out of the way of the main aisle. She stumbled and righted herself against one of the chairs. A brief look in the direction of Dotty gave her an image she hated to see. Dotty's face, pale, shocked, pained even, at seeing her best friend on the wrong end of a gun. And Alfred... *Oh please don't try and be a hero*, Cressida prayed, striving not to look at him in case he suddenly got the urge to try to do anything.

*If anyone hurts him...* Cressida found herself in that moment realising quite how strong her feelings were for Alfred, and she clenched her eyes shut, desperately trying not to imagine what might happen next.

But a flash of inspiration came to Cressida. She had to pull herself together, if there was any chance to catch the dangerous duo. All she needed to do was distract Ginny before her brother got to her – together they would be stronger. But if she could dash that gun out of Ginny's hand, Kirby and Alfred could leap into action.

With Ginny beckoning her brother over, Cressida took the opportunity of her momentary lapse in concentration to click her tongue at Ruby. The little pug, ever a fan of her mistress, looked up straight away, and with one twitch of Cressida's eyebrow, she was off Dotty's lap and scampering across the aisle just as Edward was leaving his seat at his table. A well-timed jerk of the train as it trundled over uneven points in the line added to the chaos, and before he knew what was happening, Edward had tripped over Ruby. In his desperation to stay upright he reached out and grabbed his sister's arm, knocking the gun from her and sending it flying across the room.

Everyone present, from the shaking Mrs Drysdale who had buried her head in her brother's chest, to the Irvings, pale and shocked into saying nothing at all, watched as the gun flew through the air. Cressida had to take her eye off it, her priority of course being her darling dog, who seemed to have come through the tangle of limbs unscathed and hopped obediently into her mistress's arms.

As Cressida stood up, she saw where the gun had landed. Right in front of nine-year-old Lord Hartnell.

Before anyone could snatch it, the young viscount had picked it up and was looking at it with awe, as if he'd found a cigarette card of an English batsman he'd been waiting for.

'Give it here, boy,' Ginny shouted, righting herself and trying to push off Alfred, who had leapt into action as Cressida had hoped he would. Kirby had tackled Edward down again, but Ginny was persevering. 'Here, give it to me, boy. Give it to nanny...' Her voice was stern, though measured, despite grappling her way out of Alfred's clasp.

Lord Hartnell looked up at his former nanny. 'No,' he said, then pretended to shoot a rogue bandit out of the window.

'Boy!' Ginny shrieked this time. 'It's mine. Don't you have any manners, you useless thing?'

*Not a natural with children*, Cressida thought as she locked eyes with Lord Hartnell herself. *And I thought I was bad...*

'Pyjamas, pyjamas,' she whispered to the small boy, with a raise of an eyebrow and an outstretched hand, and Lord Hartnell smiled at her.

'Pyjamas, pyjamas,' he said and stopped shooting imaginary bandits and threw Cressida the gun.

'Thank you, Lord Hartnell,' she said more loudly, and then with a swiftness and confidence that she barely recognised in herself, turned the gun on Ginny. 'Andrews, I think the culprits are yours to arrest now.'

Keeping the gun trained on Ginny and Edward until Kirby had them safely in cuffs, she picked her way over the tangle of bodies on the floor of the dining carriage and stepped back towards the bar.

Taking a deep breath, one which was required to steady her nerves after all of that, she kissed Ruby on the head between her impossibly silky ears. Putting her on one of the bar stools, Cressida took herself round behind the beautiful glossy, veneered bar. One cocktail shaker, two shots of gin and three ice cubes later, she was shaking herself a much-needed very dry martini.

And as she saw the first smokestack, and row of terraced houses from the train window, she knew they were almost in London; almost home. She raised her glass to her friends in the dining car and took a well-deserved sip.

# EPILOGUE

Bernard, the barman on the Scotland Express had had a bit of a shock, waking up from his narrow bunk in the rear luggage car only to find three passengers at his bar drinking breakfast martinis, one pug on a bar stool, several other passengers looking shocked and shaken and an underage viscount sitting amid all the chaos chomping down on sugar cubes.

But it was Mr Fernley-Hogg, having passed the night soundly asleep next to Mrs Fernley-Hogg, who had the biggest shock. Taking one look at the melee in the dining carriage and declaring the whole thing 'gone to the dogs', he requested breakfast in their compartment.

It had been one of the more surreal scenes, etched into Cressida's memory of the journey on the train, seeing Mrs Drysdale step over smashed crockery and the sticking-out legs of the arrested felons, carrying two trays of perfectly presented bacon, sausages and eggs, with steaming coffee and a glass of orange juice through to them.

Cressida had relished her martini, but stuck to just the one. It was barely half past seven in the morning after all. But she had relished even more the fact that after everything that had happened, from shootings to flooded lavatories, abandoned lords and cunning ruses, she was now safely with her darling pup, her dear friend and, of course, Alfred. Andrews was being seen to by the doctor again, who had nabbed a bottle of vodka from behind the bar and used it to sterilise Andrews' wound.

'Lucky he's not a gin man,' Alfred had said, making Cressida laugh, just when she needed to.

It had taken no time at all for the police to be summoned to the platform at Euston as the train rolled in. Kirby, who was tired, but otherwise unhurt, had cuffed Edward and Ginny and led them off the train with the help of Donaldson, the driver. An ambulance had been called and, shortly afterwards, Geraldine Warriner had been taken off the train and rushed to the nearest hospital.

And now here they were, deposited on the platform of Euston station, their luggage being unloaded by efficient porters as the police led the accused brother and sister away, and a rather forlorn-looking Phoebe Smith, to meet their justice.

Cressida felt a small, sticky hand slip into hers as she stood on the platform next to her two valises, hatbox and handbag. She looked down at the small boy who was, in turn, staring up at her.

'I don't know where I'm supposed to meet Granny,' Monty said, matter-of-factly. 'So can I come with you?'

'Oh,' Cressida said. The last thing she wanted was to be responsible for a young boy, especially as her head thumped with pain, her eyes were dry with fatigue and each and every one of her bones ached with tiredness. But it wasn't Lord Hartnell's fault that his nanny had been a murderer and that he had no idea where to find his grandmother. Cressida crouched down, Ruby still held tight in her other arm, soundly asleep. 'Well, yes, of course, Monty. Why don't we ask Dotty to send a telegram to your grandmother and see what we can find to do with ourselves while we hear back.'

Dotty, who was standing surrounded by her luggage, looking ready to hit the hay for a day or two, had overheard and weakly nodded as Cressida stood up and shrugged at her. She called a porter over and gave him the instruction, having ascertained Lord Hartnell's grandmother's name and some form of address.

Cressida smiled at Monty and saw the look of absolute trust and expectation on his face. It felt very strange having someone so small look up to one, Cressida thought. She wasn't used to this; she was used to being fiercely independent, with no one relying on her except the precious pup that was currently gently snoring in her arm. She looked down at Monty again. *What did one do with a nine-year-old boy?*

Just as she was wracking her brains for ideas, she felt a gentle hand on her shoulder and she turned to see Alfred. He looked tired, bless him, the dark circles under his eyes no doubt mirroring her own. But he made no move to excuse himself, as he could so easily have done, especially after the night they'd both endured on the Scotland Express. She wouldn't have judged him for saying his goodbyes and then heading off to his club or to the Chattertons' London townhouse. Instead, with a smile to Cressida, he crouched down next to Monty.

'I say, old chap, what do you think about the Natural History Museum? Lots of old bones and stuffed bears in there. I think it'll be the perfect place for your grandmother to meet us. I'll even buy us all an ice from the kiosk by the gate. What do you say?'

Lord Hartnell's face lit up. 'Oh wizard! Yes please, Lord Delafield. That would be smashing. Will you come too, Miss Fawcett?'

Cressida nodded. 'Of course, Monty. There's just one problem.'

'What is it, Miss Fawcett?' Lord Hartnell looked worried.

'I think she means this...' Alfred, who had momentarily left their side, returned with the fluffy white Pomeranian in his arms. 'I think this little fellow might need to come with us too.'

Lord Hartnell beamed at Alfred and took the small dog into his arms. Like Ruby before him, the small dog took an instant liking to the small boy, which Cressida was begrudgingly impressed by.

And so, with a very tired Dotty tasked with seeing the luggage back to the Chattertons' townhouse, where she could crawl straight into a proper bed, Cressida and Alfred left the platform at Euston station.

As they waited for a cab, accompanied by one small boy and two small dogs, Alfred looked over to Cressida.

'Ready for the next adventure, Cressy?'

Cressida smiled at him and, despite her sore head and aching bones, simply replied, 'Always.'

# A LETTER FROM FLISS

Dear reader,

I want to say a huge thank you for choosing to read *Death on the Scotland Express*. If you did enjoy it, and want to keep up to date with all my latest releases, just sign up at the following link. Your email address will never be shared and you can unsubscribe at any time.

*www.bookouture.com/fliss-chester*

I really hope that you're enjoying reading about Cressida Fawcett and the mysteries she solves. If you love our amateur sleuth and her very precocious pup, I would be very grateful if you could write a review of *Death on the Scotland Express*. I'd love to hear what you think. Reviews from readers like you can make such a difference helping new readers discover my books for the first time.

I love hearing from my readers – perhaps you've got a tale about an overnight train trip in one of the world's luxury sleeper trains? You can get in touch through social media or my website.

Thanks,

Fliss Chester

# KEEP IN TOUCH WITH FLISS

www.flisschester.co.uk

 facebook.com/flisschester

x.com/socialwhirlgirl

# AUTHOR'S NOTE

I'd like to thank you, dear reader, for not only getting this far through the book, but for also (hopefully) forgiving me along the way. What for? Well, fans of the British railways and their rolling stock and engines in the 1920s will possibly have been tutting all the way through at the liberties I've taken with the design of the train and the journey it took from Inverness to Euston. Although I've tried as much as possible to keep the story historically accurate (for example, I'm now the proud owner of a four-inch-thick reprint of *Bradshaw's 1922 Guide to the Railways*), I've had to 'fudge' certain things to keep the story pacey and the descriptions of the train as deliciously tantalising as possible.

The Scotland Express is, of course, a fictional train; but sleeper services did run daily from the Highlands to London, and they did take around fifteen hours. The train stopped more often in the early part of the journey – Blair Atholl, Pitlochry and Perth, for example – but I couldn't have my murderers given a chance to escape in this story! Like Dotty, I pored over the pages of my *Bradshaw's*, trying to fathom what the timetables actually meant, and I take my hat off to the travellers in the Golden Age for being much more adept at reading them than me!

The Scotland Express is also much more luxurious than the trains probably were. I say probably, because in the limited time I had to research, I couldn't find much out about ordinary sleeper trains in the 1920s. All that's available are books and photographs, all celebrating the wonder of the Orient Express or the Blue Train. I don't want to diminish the glory of our own trains, but I doubt the run-of-the-mill sleeper train between Scotland and London was as luxurious as those glamorous ones or the train I've described... but then, that's the joy of fiction.

And who knows, perhaps Cressida and Dotty (and Ruby, of course) will get to go on the actual Orient Express one of these days...

# ACKNOWLEDGEMENTS

Thank you as always to the wonderful editorial team at my publisher, Bookouture. Natalie Edwards championed Cressida and her chums and I'm sure was responsible for getting this and the next two adventures commissioned – thank you, Natalie! Jade Craddock, the copy editor, and proofreader Anne O'Brien, have done amazing work as always, thank you both. And, of course, huge thanks to the art department for such a stand-out cover, and the publicity and marketing departments for making sure everyone hears about these books.

Thanks also to Emily Sweet, my literary agent at Aevitus, for all the behind-the-scenes work – and always being a great sounding board whenever I need you.

I'm lucky enough to have a wonderful group of criminally minded crime writers I'm so pleased to call friends. Our daily WhatsApps – and even better, good old chinwags at crime writing festivals and over lunches – make up a huge part of what I love about writing books. So pincers high to Heather, Jo, Kate, Lauren, Liz, Lou, Niki, Polly, Rachael, Susie, Victoria, Adam, Barry, Dom, Rob Who Is Bruce, Simon and Tim.

And finally, as always, thank you to my lovely family. Rupert, my husband, is probably verging on what could now be called 'long-suffering' – thank you, darling. And thank you to his cousin, Fiona, for sending me some fabulous pictures of the Belmond Pullman carriages she had the opportunity to go on.

This book is dedicated to my siblings – all six of them, be

they full, half or step! Andy, Penny, Freddie, Nico, Hannah and Adam – thank you for making up my large and fun family. And, so far, not murdering anyone...

# PUBLISHING TEAM

Turning a manuscript into a book requires the efforts of many people. The publishing team at Bookouture would like to acknowledge everyone who contributed to this publication.

**Audio**
Alba Proko
Sinead O'Connor
Melissa Tran

**Commercial**
Lauren Morrissette
Jil Thielen
Imogen Allport

**Data and analysis**
Mark Alder
Mohamed Bussuri

**Cover design**
Debbie Clement

**Editorial**
Natalie Edwards
Nadia Michael

Printed in Great Britain
by Amazon